COVENTRY
2091

THE COVENTRY CHRONICLES
BOOK 1

PETER KAZMAIER

COVENTRY 2091: THE COVENTRY CHRONICLES, BOOK 1
Copyright © 2021 by Peter Kazmaier

Scripture quotations are from The Holy Bible, English Standard Version® (ESV®), copyright 2001 by Crossway. Used by permission. All rights reserved.

This is a work of fiction. Names, drugs, medicines, medical procedures, characters, places and incidents either are the product of the author's imagination or are used fictitiously, and any resemblance to actual persons, living or dead, businesses, drugs, medicines, medical procedures, companies, events, or locales is entirely coincidental.

ISBN: 978-1-4866-2131-6
eBook ISBN: 978-1-4866-2132-3

Word Alive Press
119 De Baets Street Winnipeg, MB R2J 3R9
www.wordalivepress.ca

WORD ALIVE
—P R E S S—

Cataloguing in Publication information can be obtained from Library and Archives Canada.

For more information or to order additional copies, please contact:
Wolfsburg Imprints
2421 Council Ring Road
Mississauga, Ontario, Canada
L5L 1E5
http://www.wolfsburgimprints.com/

For online maps: http://www.wolfsburgimprints.com/maps/

To my friends in my youth group (1966-1976).
Your friendship, acceptance, and encouragement at a critical time in my life
has led to a lifetime bond as we continue to serve the Lord together.

CONTENTS

CHAPTER 1
THE CAUSEWAY TO IRON ISLE

JACOB KRAISER SHIVERED ON THE COLD METAL BENCH WATCHING THE snow blow in little cyclones outside the open front of the alcove that served as his waiting area. He needed to wipe his nose. The handcuffs, which fastened him to his seat, forced him to bend over as far as he could in order to use his handkerchief.

Straightening up, he tried to stretch out a cramp. The alcove reminded him of an empty truck-port with its three sides and roof. It even had a large garage door into the main building at the closed end.

Three guards, smoking cigarettes, huddled in a small group near a door on the far side. One of them swore. "It's so bloody cold!" he said to no one in particular. One of his fellow guards agreed, with a string of curses of his own.

"Why are they being sent here in the middle of bloody winter, anyway?" asked the third guard. "We don't get many Cretins for the penal colony anymore and those that do come, arrive in the summer. Don't they know how bad the roads are now?"

"Damned if I know why they're sendin' 'em here. These Cretins must have seriously pissed off one of our higher-level citizens to get a one-way ticket to Coventry in the middle of winter."

Jacob shook his head at these words, hoping to clear his muddled brain. *They're right. What was I thinking? Why did I defend her? Why didn't I let*

Connaught just have her? He has her now anyway. Here I am, five years an orphan, and going to prison on my twenty-second birthday.

The last four days were a blur in his mind. He had been rousted out of bed by the police just before he had been set to rise and go to his job at the Federal Technology Centre in Toronto. Two officers had watched him closely, allowing him only a few minutes to dress. One of the officers had given him a duffle bag and told him to fill it with necessities. When he had reacted too slowly, they handcuffed him and began stuffing his bag with his things.

Did they know then how this would turn out and that I would end up here? he wondered.

He had not been taken to court as he had expected—the sentencing had happened much too quickly for court—he had been taken to a tribunal.

He remembered the room. A large portrait of former Prime Minister Russell hung on the wall behind the raised bench. Written above the portrait in large gold letters were the words: *Dedicated to Peace, Order, and Good Government on Behalf of the People of Canada.* A single tribune in crimson robes had sat behind the bench.

Jacob had been disoriented from lack of sleep and the speed with which his life had changed. The charges had something to do with his conduct at work and minutiae in his austere private life. Each of the many charges referred again and again to "violations against peace, order, and good government." His state-appointed advocate had stood quietly at his side and said nothing in Jacob's defense. When Jacob had cleared his throat to ask what it all meant, his advocate pulled Jacob's handcuffed arm to turn him, shook his head gravely, and put a forefinger to his lips.

The tribune had looked briefly at Jacob, as if daring him to speak, and then asked the Crown Counsel to continue. After the charges had been read, the tribune requested witness affidavits to be read as well. The name of his boss, Clive Connaught, came up occasionally, and so did the name Cynthia Stapleton, the young woman he had tried to defend. The charges and written testimony made no sense to Jacob. It was as if they had been talking about someone else and he had been arrested by mistake.

"Guilty as charged," the tribune pronounced. "Sentenced to Coventry Penal Colony. Next case."

Numb with disbelief, his legs had buckled. Two guards half-marched, half-dragged him out into the cold and ushered him into an unmarked truck. He was the only prisoner. He had a seat, a bunk, and a small latrine in the sealed back. The truck had lurched into motion, throwing him against the wall and so began a long, bumpy, three-day journey. He knew from the few remarks the guards had made when they brought him his sparse meals, that they were travelling west and then north of Lake Superior. Jacob had never heard of the Coventry Penal Colony.

The sound of the alcove door opening interrupted Jacob's thoughts. Two guards shepherded a man and a woman—both in handcuffs—into the room. The guards directed the newcomers to sit on either side of Jacob and then handcuffed them to the bench.

Stamping out their cigarettes, the guards all retreated through the small door, leaving the prisoners alone.

On Jacob's left, the woman spoke with a quavering voice. "Hi, I'm Hanna. Do either of you know where we are?" She was bundled up in a parka so Jacob could only see her large brown eyes, moist with tears.

Her fear seemed to give Jacob courage. "Hi, I'm Jacob. I know we're outside a prison of some sort, north of Lake Superior."

The fellow that had entered with Hanna took off his glove and stuck out his hand only to realize his cuffs made a handshake impossible. "I'm Zeke Rempel. I'm pretty sure we're outside a place called the Coventry Penal Colony, on Iron Isle, Vulture Lake. The penal colony was established on an abandoned platinum group metals mine. I think that road ahead of us—" Here he waved out the alcove to a long, straight causeway that disappeared into the blizzard—"is the only access to the real facility."

"How do you know so much about this place, Zeke?" asked Hanna.

Zeke chuckled. His laugh jarred against the dread that crowded Jacob. "I come from a notorious family, I do. My uncle and grandfather were both sent here years ago. We never saw them again. We were never allowed to visit, but we did find out as much about this place as we could."

"Coventry Penal Colony," said Hanna. "Oh no! It's happened then! My friends at university warned me about this. I didn't believe them."

Before Jacob could ask any questions, the small door opened again and three more prisoners were brought in. Without a word, they were taken to a bench on the other side of the truck-port, four meters away.

"Oh my," Hanna muttered, her tone indicating danger rather than surprise.

The three newcomers were striking. All had their hoods down. Two were large, heavyset men with scowls on their faces. The third man was also tall but thin. His eyes were sharp, like an eagle searching for prey. The big men sat down leaving room for the third between them. The tall man gestured to one to move over and sat on the side closest to the alcove door. None of them spoke. The two bodyguards (no other word came to Jacob to describe them) kept their eyes moving as if watching for trouble. The eagle-eyed man examined Jacob and his two companions intently, as if interrogating them with his eyes.

Just then the large vehicle door at the back of the alcove opened and a van pulled into the truck-port in between the two benches. Three guards climbed out of the front passenger doors and opened the backdoors of the van. Two guards covered the prisoners with automatic weapons, while the third uncuffed Jacob, Hanna, and Zeke.

"Get in!" he growled and shoved them towards the van. They climbed in and sat on one bench bolted to the van's side. The other three prisoners followed them in and sat on the opposite bench. The two bodyguards continued to glare at them. One of the guards shoved a sealed envelope into Jacob's hands. "Don't open it. Give it to Hodgkins," he said before closing the doors and locking them in.

The van began to move. Looking out the far side window, Jacob noticed that a pair of heavily reinforced doors, previously blocking the entrance to the causeway, had swung open. The van proceeded down the snow-covered lane. Blowing snow limited visibility, but Jacob could see black, open water interrupted by patches of snow-covered ice. After a few minutes he saw the shore of an island ahead. Vulture Lake ought to have been covered with ice at these frigid temperatures, but apparently, a river entering this end of the lake provided enough flow to make the ice here treacherous. Open water showed that attempting to cross the lake here would be suicide. This was a perfect prison, especially in winter.

The long causeway came to an end and they rumbled across a drawbridge and entered a parking lot. Looking out the back window, Jacob saw a second heavy open gate, and had a better look at the drawbridge, which had been lowered from the far side.

They're not taking any chances.

The doors at the back of the van opened and the three guards carrying automatic weapons motioned the prisoners to climb out, then used their rifle barrels to shove Jacob, Hanna, and Zeke along. Jacob noticed the guards regarded the other three prisoners warily and did not molest them.

Beyond the parking lot stood a huge, dilapidated building that reminded Jacob of a factory. Heavy equipment covered in snow rested at the fringe of the lot, with tires and scoops protruding from the white mounds, looking like toys partially hidden inside huge pillows. Trailers from six, eighteen-wheel transport trucks were off to the right.

A man in an old, tattered parka came out of the building and shouted to get their attention. Watching the building warily, the guards pointed their automatic rifles at the prisoners and waved them toward the building entrance. The man in the parka didn't speak in the howling wind, but approached Jacob for the envelope and then waved for the six prisoners to follow. Then turning and leaning into the wind, he walked back toward the building.

Jacob glanced over his shoulder as he followed the others. The guards climbed back into the van, which made a rapid U-turn, and raced across the drawbridge. Jacob heard the drawbridge rumble as it lifted into the air leaving a large gulf of open water between the island and the causeway. The grinding of the gate shutting could be heard even over the wind. *I'm in prison!* Jacob thought, and felt himself panic at the clanging of the heavy gate. *What will become of me?*

CHAPTER 2
COVENTRY

The name for the Coventry Penal Colony comes from an English phrase "To send someone to Coventry," an idiom meaning to ostracize a person or group.

One explanation for the origin of this idiom is based upon The History of the Rebellion and Civil Wars in England, by Edward Hyde, 1st Earl of Clarendon. In this work, Clarendon recounts how during the English Civil War, Royalist troops who were captured in Birmingham were taken as prisoners to the Parliamentarian stronghold of Coventry. These prisoners were not received warmly by the locals, but were treated as if they did not exist.

Our penal colony is called Coventry, because in coming here, we were made to disappear. Prime Minister Russell's plan for the colony was brilliant in conception and ruthless in its execution. It could not have worked without the complicity of the media. When we were sent to Coventry after the passive resistance of 2051 by the Peace, Order, and Good Government (POGG) Tribunal, we effectively vanished. No one directly killed us, but we died in silence and away from the public eye. We could slavishly produce and exchange platinum group metals and rare-earth metals from the abandoned Coventry mine for food, yet we quietly starved in obscurity. Few journalists reported on our plight. Some who did soon joined our ranks.

From *A History of the Coventry Penal Colony* by Christian Mutembe

THE INSIDE OF THE MINING BUILDING LOOKED TO BE IN MUCH BETTER condition than the outside. The entrance hall was empty. The elderly man doffed his parka, shook off the snow, and beckoned the prisoners to follow him down well-worn but clean stairs to a small, self-serve cafeteria. There was fish chowder and a selection of sandwiches. Jacob was hungry and loaded up his tray.

Their host led them through the cafeteria. Jacob looked around. The cafeteria was almost empty. The few people at the tables did not seem unfriendly, but looked at the newcomers with mild curiosity.

Their host opened a door to a small side room with a heavy composite-wood table surrounded by plastic chairs. "Have a seat folks. My name is Simeon Hodgkins and I'm here to welcome you to Coventry. It's been quite a few years, but I came to Coventry just like you. When I came, I wasn't really sure what I had done to get here, nor did I know what to expect once I arrived. I'm here to answer those questions for you to make your transition to Coventry as easy as we can manage.

"First off, you need to know this is a prison that is truly run by the inmates. There are no guards on this side of the drawbridge. So how do they control us? It's very simple. Our power is supplied by conduits from the shore; much of our food arrives by truck. To keep the lights on and to have something to eat, we have to behave as exemplary prisoners and work this mine. Outside, in the parking lot, are six transport trailers. The vein of platinum and palladium ore near the surface is nearly depleted, but we still have some we can mine. However, mixed in with the platinum are small amounts of many rare-earth metals. We separate these; it's a painstaking process. We fill those transport trailers with platinum, palladium, and rare-earth ingots and buy our food and power from the Government of Canada.

"It's simple really. We work for our basic necessities. As long as we behave, we're left pretty much to ourselves. If we rebel or make a ruckus, they simply shut off our power and wait for us to deal with the internal problem. Without electricity, we'd be forced to deal with the rebels, and then have to beg the guards to please consider turning on the power again.

"Every two weeks, regular as clock work, the guards remotely open the gates and lower the drawbridge. An armed force enters to take control of our parking lot. After the proper inspections, six new transports arrive filled with food, medicines, and mining equipment. When the trailers have been exchanged, we're on our own again. You get the picture. We work to live. We make the mine profitable for the government because we're low maintenance and are unpaid labor. Since you're eating and living here now, you'll have to contribute."

He looked at a sheet. "Inmates are organized into companies. We work as a group and help each other. If we break the rules, we're often sanctioned as a group. You are now in F Company and you're under my command. I'll take you to the F Company common room and the adjoining dormitories. That'll be your new home. Any questions?"

Hanna raised her hand. "Miss Heidel?"

"Sir, how many companies are there?"

"There are twelve active companies now. We have the facilities for eighteen, but we've been receiving few inmates in recent years."

Hanna raised her hand again. Hodgkins nodded to her. "Sir, surely twelve companies aren't all the people you have here. Twelve companies could hardly justify a facility of this size."

"You are correct, Miss Heidel. These twelve companies are for inmates-in-training if you like. Once you have been properly trained and proven your reliability, you'll have an opportunity to join a guild, some other contributing group, or operate as a private contractor to earn your keep. A very few never make the grade. We keep them in the companies as veterans since they need the company structure to function effectively and often help the new recruits adjust.

"Don't ask me now about the extent of our prison population. You will learn that in due time."

Hodgkins rose to indicate that questions were at an end, and passed out identification badges with their names on them. He led them out of the cafeteria and turned right. The underground floor containing the cafeteria, was extensive, with locked doors labelled Company A to Company E at various places. In between the entrances to the group common rooms, there were doors identified as storage areas and work areas.

When they reached the F Company entrance, Simeon instructed each captive in turn to approach the door and say his name. Then Simeon spoke to register their voice print and the door opened.

Jacob was last to enter. Inside was a large, comfortable sitting room with rustic, homemade furniture. It was spacious enough to hold about two hundred people. "You men can head up to the men's dormitories once I register your voice print on the men's dormitory door," Simeon said, indicating the door on the left. "When you head up the stairs, you'll find that most of the rooms are already occupied. The empty rooms will have their doors open and won't have a voiceprint lock. Pick any empty room that you like."

"Miss Heidel," here he looked at Hanna, "you will find a room in the women's dormitories." He pointed to the right door. "Most of F Company is working, but you'll meet them later this afternoon at supper."

After their second set of voice prints had been logged in the dormitory entrance monitor, Jacob and Zeke climbed up to their rooms. Jacob noticed that the other three men, who he had learned were called Rousseau, Litch, and Dennison, were huddled in the corner having a private conversation.

Jacob and Zeke chose rooms next to one another as close to the stairwell as they could get. Jacob's room consisted of a bed, a night table, a dresser, and a wardrobe. There were no cupboards. In a bookshelf above the dresser he saw a Bible, a book called *Coventry Rules*, a book by Christian Mutembe entitled *A History of the Coventry Penal Colony*, and a couple of children's book series with worn fabric covers by George MacDonald and C. S. Lewis.

It took only a moment to store his meager belongings in the drawers and hang his thin coat in the wardrobe. Jacob glanced through *Coventry Rules*, put it back, and then took down the first MacDonald book entitled *The Princess and the Goblin* and began reading.

He had just finished the first two chapters when he heard a knock on his door. It was Zeke. "Oh, you're reading that," said Zeke. "If you'd been reading *Coventry Rules*, as I have, you'd know it's already supper time. After all we had a very late lunch. Why don't we go down and find Hanna? I'm hoping to see my Uncle Samuel and Grandpa Franz in the dining hall."

"Why not?" said Jacob, putting his book on his night table.

The common room was still empty. Hodgkins came out of a side door, which led to his office and his apartments. "I think the others have already gone down to the cafeteria."

Zeke led the way. They took a couple of wrong turns but eventually found the cafeteria and lined up. There were several hundred people there already. Most looked friendly but some decidedly not so.

When they had their trays loaded with food, they made their way to the cashier. Jacob saw everyone ahead of him paying for their meal. All of Jacob's money had been taken away from him after his very short trial. His heart fell at the prospect of returning all of his food.

He was about to speak to the cashier when she said, "I can see you're new here. This meal is free. You'll be paid when you work, and then you'll have some money to buy food."

Relieved, he thanked her.

He and Zeke walked up and down the table aisles with their trays looking for Zeke's relatives. The further they went the more crestfallen Zeke became. "Where are they?" he exclaimed.

Jacob said "This cafeteria looks far too small for all the companies to be eating here at the same time; maybe you'll see them tomorrow." But inwardly, he was more pessimistic. *They're probably dead.*

Finally, Zeke said, "Why don't we sit here and keep a lookout for Hanna."

They sat facing the food line and both began eating without speaking. The food tasted good after what Jacob had received during his transfer to Coventry.

"Doesn't it seem odd to you that this worn-out platinum mine can produce enough valuable metal to pay for our food and power and who knows what else?" asked Jacob.

"Maybe the prison guards and the penal system give us a break to keep us out of their hair."

"Maybe," said Jacob doubtfully. "But those guards on the other side of the causeway didn't seem like the love-to-give-you-a-break type."

"No," said Zeke, "they seemed more like the 'please give me a reason to shoot you and make my day' type."

Just then Hanna appeared in the line and both Jacob and Zeke waved. She eventually saw them and waved back. In a few minutes she came to join them. "This prison is nothing like I imagined it."

Jacob looked up and raised an eyebrow.

She looked at Jacob. "I mean it's true I've never been in prison before, but I would have expected bare walls and crummy mattresses. I have a clean room to myself. We get to eat and work for our food. No guards around to harass us. The prisoners are courteous—no sullenness or even hopelessness. I was expecting more trouble. Still, there's a part of me that's afraid my budding optimism will be dashed. Oh, I hope not!"

"I know what you mean, Hanna," said Jacob. "But there are more things about this place that are rather odd. Before I was arrested, I worked for the Ministry of Technology in the Federal Technology Centre in Toronto. We were supposed to be at the forefront of innovation in Canada. Yet we never had anything like this voice recognition software at our doors. How does a backwater prison get this kind of sophisticated technology?"

"Maybe it was left over from the mining company. I wouldn't be surprised if a private company was ahead of government in technology."

"I suppose," said Jacob. Inwardly, he thought it unlikely.

Hodgkins came by. "I'm glad you found your way to the cafeteria. We have a floor meeting in our common room in twenty minutes. I want to introduce you to the rest of our company."

They hurried through the rest of their meal without speaking. Returning to the common room, there were about two hundred people in F Company assembled there. After introductions, Jacob learned the group tackled jobs together. The previous week they had fished on the ice of Vulture Lake. This week they expected to be assigned a new task.

One of the senior members of their company, sitting at their table, explained the reason for this rotation. "We almost never work on the same task two weeks in a row. Over time we are taught all the basics of Coventry equipment maintenance, mining, and food production. If needed, we'll be qualified to fill any vacancy in an emergency. Tomorrow we're off to care for the greenhouses."

After the meeting, Zeke returned to the dorm while Jacob stayed in the common room talking to Hanna. Jacob's head was buzzing with all the names he had heard. "You know Jacob, the word *company* reminds me of an army. Do you think we have battalions, regiments, and brigades? I wonder what it all means."

"I don't know, Hanna, but I've seen no indication we're going to do more than work to survive and keep the place running. Do you think they're planning to break out?"

"No," said Hanna, "where would they go? They can't take over the whole country. Still we've only been here one day. I'm going to figure out what it is that makes this place so *unlike* a prison."

"Be careful. We're new here and we don't know what they'll do if they think we're trouble makers."

CHAPTER 3
TROUBLE WITH ROUSSEAU

The **POGG** Tribunal was established by Prime Minister Russell, by the cabinet, and by an emergency act of Parliament in 2050 to solve an existential problem facing the government. The peaceful protests that began as small, isolated incidents in late 2049 grew over time so that by 2050, it was reported that more than thirty thousand people were protesting at various locations across the country. The protests were of such a scale and so unrelenting that the courts were overwhelmed, facing years of court proceedings to process those who were repeatedly arrested. The temporary internment camps were overflowing, yet the protestors would not agree to desist if released, but instead immediately returned to the protest.

A tribune with both prosecutorial and judicial powers presided over Tribunal proceedings, which generally lasted only a few hours. On conviction, the protestor was invariably sentenced to the Coventry Penal Colony.

Although the protests were successfully silenced by 2052, the Tribunal remained operative, receiving a few dozen cases each year when the government or her representatives deemed the offense under consideration was in some way similar to the insurrection of 2051. As before, convicted offenders were sent to Coventry. The conviction rate was estimated to be almost one hundred percent.

From *A History of the Coventry Penal Colony* by Christian Mutembe

JACOB OPENED THE DOOR TO THE MEN'S DORMITORIES AND HEADED TO HIS room. He saw Rousseau, Litch, and Dennison coming down the stairs to the common area. Litch shoved Jacob into the wall growling, "Get out of our way."

What's eating them? thought Jacob.

He was troubled by Hanna's suspicions about Coventry being organized along military lines and possibly planning a breakout. He wanted to talk to Zeke about it. He knocked on Zeke's door.

"Come in."

Zeke was bent over the sink with a paper towel, dabbing at a cut over his eye. He was going to have a shiner. "What happened to you?" Jacob asked.

"Rousseau, Litch, and Dennison happened to me. I was coming up to my room while everyone was still downstairs. Those three goons were behind me and called my name. Rousseau said that he was heading up an informal prisoner group to make sure we were treated well and he wanted me in the group. I wouldn't commit. He didn't like that. I told him I didn't want any trouble. He said it was no trouble and then Litch and Dennison roughed me up until Rousseau said it was enough.

"Then he told me if I did as I was told, I'd be fine. If I didn't—well this beating was only a sample of what I would get."

"What are we going to do?" Jacob asked.

"What are '*we*' going to do? I'm new here. I don't want to begin my stay by kicking a complaint upstairs. I'll try to stay away from the three stooges, but I'm certainly not going to throw my lot in with them."

Jacob thought about this and came to a decision. "Let's stick together. Don't let them catch you alone again."

"Have you seen those guys? Will you really be able to help me, Jacob?"

"Maybe not, but it will make it a bit more of a fair fight. Besides, if you ever did complain, it would be your testimony against the three of theirs. At least I'll be able to corroborate your story."

The next morning the whole company had an early breakfast before heading to the greenhouses. Although Jacob could see that everyone looked at Zeke and his black eye in surprise, no one said anything.

Hanna was not like the rest. She pestered Zeke until he told her the story.

"You should tell Hodgkins," she said.

"You don't understand," said Zeke. "Men handle their own problems. Jacob and I have it figured out. I'll be okay."

"Men!" said Hanna. "Your black eye shows how well you're handling things. I still think you should go to Hodgkins."

Zeke didn't answer. Shaking her head, Hanna went back to eating her breakfast.

The twenty greenhouses were narrow glass structures about one hundred meters long and twenty-five meters wide. They formed a rectangle behind the main mine building with five greenhouses end-to-end and four side-by-side. Down the center of each greenhouse ran a canal that steamed in the cool air—clearly water from a geothermal source that warmed the structures—and kept the plants growing throughout the winter.

Hodgkin's company worked in two greenhouses that were growing root vegetables. The doors to the adjacent greenhouses were open. After weeding their assigned patches, Hanna, Zeke, and Jacob were told to water the vegetables. The pump was a two-man hand-operated reciprocating device with a seesaw handle. Alternately using their weight to force down the handle was hard work. After one-minute, Jacob was sweating profusely and he could hear Zeke taking deep, ragged breaths. Between gasps he said, "With all the high-tech equipment they have inside, they could have afforded an electric pump, couldn't they?"

Hanna, who was squirting the water over the plants, called out, "Can you guys put a little more oomph into it? I'm losing water pressure here. These poor turnips are crying out for a bit more water."

"Interfering female," muttered Zeke. "Maybe she should try using her scrawny frame to work this pump. She's so thin she could hang off the handle and it still wouldn't go down. Losing water pressure, my eye."

Zeke had his back to Hanna, but Jacob looked up at her. She was grinning from ear to ear.

"Heard that," said Hanna. "Oops. Sorry!" as a jet of warm water doused them both.

Zeke was red-faced, muttering a derogatory epithet. "She's teasing us," whispered Jacob. "She knows exactly how hard we're working. Lighten up, Zeke."

Zeke smiled sheepishly as he belatedly got her joke, but after that, the work went more easily. When they stopped for lunch, Hanna looked at Zeke's black eye. "The swelling seems to be going down, but you'll have the shiner for a while. So you told me Rousseau was trying to recruit you into a little group he's forming?

"Yes."

She pursed her lips. "I've seen the three stooges, as you called them, talking to others. Now they have five company members eating lunch with them." She rolled her eyes toward the other end of the greenhouse. "Don't turn around Zeke! The recruiting drive must be bearing fruit."

"Why are they doing this?" asked Jacob. "Are they just making a power play?"

Zeke had a mouthful of food and simply shrugged, as they heard Hodgkins call them back to work.

They continued working in the greenhouses all that week, until Thursday evening. Jacob enjoyed spending time with his new friends, and the work reminded him of happier times when he had helped his dad with the family garden before the tragic accident that had robbed him of his parents and siblings.

Thursday afternoon, Hodgkins came over and asked Jacob to help two of the more experienced members of their team as they serviced the water pumps. Jacob followed them to the far end of the greenhouse, where it abutted the back wall of the mining building.

Hodgkins opened a door at the end of the greenhouse, into a room with a large swimming-pool-sized reservoir. There was a door labelled "Emergency Exit" at the far end.

"This reservoir feeds all the greenhouse canals through underground channels."

The water must have been moving very slowly through the exit pipes since there was no visible current.

Hodgkins introduced Jacob to a group of men working in the reservoir area. Leonard Thompson, F Company's expert on heavy equipment, put his hands into the slot on a metal panel flush with the floor. He swung it open to reveal a ladder descending about thirty feet.

"Watch your step," he said, "it's a long drop to the bottom."

Jacob descended last. The ladder followed a vertical pipe about one meter in diameter. He could hear water whooshing through the pipe as it filled the reservoir pool.

At the bottom of the ladder, Jacob saw a tool rack with large wrenches, a pickup-truck-sized pump, and a valve system that fed water from the subterranean source to the greenhouses. There was an emergency exit in the other wall.

"Where does that lead?" he asked, pointing to the emergency door.

"That leads to Sub-Level 1, the cafeteria level," said Thompson. "The other side is always locked. If there's a fire up top or the pump has a catastrophic failure, we'll never make it up the ladder. It will open from this side—but we better have a good reason to use it."

Thompson shut the pump off and replaced one of the relief valves. He then turned the system on again and checked to ensure all the operational parameters were nominal.

"Let's head back up. You lead, Kraiser."

Jacob climbed back up.

After work on Thursday, Hodgkins called the six newcomers into his office. "Friday and Saturday are our study days. Sunday is our day off. Since you six are new here, you'll join relative newcomers in other companies to take the introductory courses. Here are your timetables and the classrooms. The first class begins at 0800 sharp. Any questions?" There were none.

Thursday night, when Jacob was expecting to spend some recreation time with Hanna and Zeke, he heard a knock on his door. He opened the door to Rousseau, Litch, and Dennison.

"I need to talk to you Kraiser," said Rousseau pushing his way in. Litch and Dennison followed. "Close the door!" said Rousseau.

Leaning against the open door, Jacob said, "What do you want Rousseau?"

Rousseau scowled, but said, "I'm organizing a little group in our company, to look after our own interests—you know, to make sure we're treated fairly and get our share from the likes of Hodgkins. Think of it as a union. I want you in our group."

"Is this what earned Zeke his shiner?"

"He told you about that, did he?"

"Yep."

"Stay away from him, Kraiser. He's toadying up to Hodgkins and the whole prison hierarchy. It won't end well. I wouldn't want you caught up in it."

"If you're done," said Jacob, gesturing toward the hall, "It's Thursday night and I have some friends to meet."

Litch looked questioningly at Rousseau, who gave a slight shake to his head. "Remember what I said." Rousseau walked out, followed by Litch and Dennison who each looked at Jacob as if they would love to tear him limb-from-limb.

After Jacob told Zeke about his own conversation with Rousseau, they renewed their determination to stick together.

Once, when Litch and Dennison caught Jacob coming down the stairs by himself, Litch stuck out his leg and Dennison shoved him headlong down the stairs. Someone opened the bottom door just as Jacob came tumbling out.

"Are you all right?" called Litch.

After that, Zeke or Jacob would knock on the wall that adjoined their two rooms before heading out. If someone knocked on their door, a wall knock would bring the other out at the same time. The stress of worrying about being caught alone began to wear on Jacob. He saw the same worry on Zeke's face.

Jacob also had another form of stress: his nightmares had come back. Shortly after the accident that had claimed the lives of his parents, Jacob started having nightmares that caused him to wake up crying out and in a sweat. After government services took him in hand and put him on a sedative cocktail, the nightmares had gone away. Now they were back. Even Zeke began asking about them, after a night when Jacob awoke screaming.

Still, their weeks began to take on a routine. There were six days of work with Sundays off. Four days were spent in practical learning: greenhouse farming, the basics of mining, and ore refining. Friday morning began with *The History of Coventry* class. They were also taught mathematics, chemistry, physics, and applied biology.

After one particularly grueling session of organic chemistry the three friends sat in the cafeteria eating lunch before their physics class.

Between bites, waving his sandwich, Jacob said, "I thought I had a pretty good government education, but it was nothing like this. It was all essays on how the power structure discriminated against this group and that group and meditation sessions on growing in empathy towards those less fortunate, and what a wicked person I was because I had enough to eat. That school work was easy to the point of being boring. I always achieved *excellent* or at least *exceeds expectation* if I figured out what spin the teacher wanted me to put on my essay. But this stuff we're learning now is different—I don't quite know how to describe it. There are right and wrong answers. It's so binary. You know the work or get zero. I can't fake my way through it anymore."

Hanna's eyes lit up. "Isn't it wonderful? It's as if both the student and the teacher are looking outside of themselves and seeing reality. It even extends to the books here. I used to go to the library back home all the time looking for answers. I never found any. The books in the back-home library were the same as the ones my teachers used. Endless essays empathizing with the vulnerable or hurting—who could argue with that? But no books that asked hard questions. None asked questions as if there was a truth to be searched for and cherished if found, even if it were unexpected or surprising."

She looked thoughtful. "My parents had a few good books that I cherished until they were confiscated at school for being too insensitive to the less fortunate. That puzzled me because in reading them, I think I became more attuned to real need. But here, there are wonderful books full of knowledge that I have never seen before. I could read every waking hour."

"I could tell," said Zeke, "that you're in love with the library. For me I like the work we do the other four days. Working with my hands and with machinery is much more in line with what I was used to at home. All this reading and problem solving makes me tired."

CHAPTER 4
OPENING OLD WOUNDS

JACOB RECEIVED A SUMMONS TO HODGKINS' OFFICE THURSDAY AFTER work. Hodgkins had another fellow with him; he had unruly hair and a sparse beard. He might have been Jacob's age, only the beard made him look older.

"This is Doctor Giesbrecht. I want you to talk to him. He's a counselor."

"I don't need a counselor," said Jacob. He could feel himself getting angry.

"Did I indicate this was a suggestion?" asked Hodgkins. He looked at Jacob for a moment, then said more gently, "You're frequently waking up from nightmares and your yells can be heard in half the dormitory. We're trying to help. I can't make you learn anything from Dr. Giesbrecht, but I can and will make you take the sessions."

Giesbrecht raised his hand. "Why not let me take it from here, Simeon."

"Alright, you can use my office today. Kraiser, don't let me hear that you're shirking these sessions."

"Yes, sir! You won't."

At least not if I can help it, thought Jacob.

Hodgkins gave Jacob a hard look then left his office, closing the door behind him.

Giesbrecht walked over to Hodgkins' chair, sat down, examined his cowboy boots and leaned back, putting his boots up on the corner of Hodgkins' desk.

"Are you a shrink?" asked Jacob.

Geisbrecht stroked his beard as he thought about Jacob's question. "I suppose I am," he said. "I don't think of myself that way. I'm really a listener. And, when appropriate, I might even give a bit of advice—take-it-or-leave-it advice."

"I'm not crazy," said Jacob.

"I think we're all a little bit crazy. But I don't expect you're crazy in the way that you mean."

Geisbrecht watched Jacob expectantly. When the silence had gone on for a time, he said, "Why don't you tell me a little bit about yourself?"

"There's not much to tell," said Jacob. "A couple of years after my parents and siblings were killed in a car crash, I found myself here—here at a place I hadn't even known existed."

Silence. "Go on."

"Doc, why do I feel so out of place here? My friends, Zeke and Hanna arrived at the same time I did but they seem so much more at home. Why is that?"

"Jacob, I can't speak to Zeke and Hanna's situation but let me say that the way you found yourself here in Coventry is a bit unusual. Most people who are shipped here are more like me. I grew up in a rural Mennonite community in southern Saskatchewan that, as a group, had been quietly helping Coventry survive. Because of that activity, I knew that I and my community were seen by our government as potential subversives and Cretins. I grew up helping relatives and friends trapped here in Coventry. So understanding a bit about the place, I lived most of my life knowing I might have the bad luck to be sent here myself.

"Others who find themselves here might not be Mennonites, but also were suspected of being subversive by the government because of their associations with some Christian community. Periodically, members of that community would disappear. Whispers would have told them these 'disappearing people' were sent to Coventry because they somehow stepped out of line. In any case, if someone from a community like that were sent here, it would not come as a complete surprise to them as it did to you."

"So how am I different from you?" asked Jacob.

"Jacob, your questions are leading me to talk far too much. I'm supposed to be listening, but I suppose if I get your questions out of the way, you'll feel more freedom to share.

"To begin with, you suffered significant emotional trauma when your whole family was killed in that automobile accident. Secondly, in our blessed government's idiocy, the fact that the accident caused your Victimization Index to skyrocket meant that they essentially took over your life, uprooted you from your home, and transplanted you into that concrete jungle, Toronto, undoubtedly believing they were showing you the greatest charity.

"You thought your nightmares were cured because of the medicinal cocktail they gave you, when they took you in hand. In fact, the symptoms were only masked. Now you're surprised and confused because they've come back. Finally, you were duped, lied to, manipulated, and eventually run over by someone's ambitions, and then sent here to keep you quiet and permanently out of the way. You find yourself in a place you never even suspected existed and you don't have the background to fit in."

"Doctor …"

"Please call me Rudy."

"Rudy, the two categories of people you described sound a lot like my friends Zeke and Hanna."

Geisbrecht smiled but said nothing.

"But if you already know everything about me, what's the point of talking?"

"Well," said Geisbrecht, "I need to get *you* to talk and I need to listen. Then, hopefully, you'll realize there are no easy solutions and no quick fixes. You'll further realize there will be many ups and downs, steps forward and relapses. Through that you'll need to keep going."

"So, what's next, doc?"

Giesbrecht smiled again. "Why don't you tell me about your nightmares?"

Jacob was deciding whether or not to cooperate. *Oh, what the heck. I may as well. Things can't get any worse with the nightmares, can they?*

"They started shortly after the accident. In the dream, I imagine myself in the car with my parents and siblings. I see the truck approaching from the side, but my father, who's talking to my mother, doesn't see it coming. I yell at him to pay attention but no one seems to hear me. It's as if I'm the ghost and I can shout but never be heard. That's when I wake up and realize I've been shouting in my sleep."

"Have your nightmares been continuous since they started?"

"No, when I went to Toronto, I was so busy learning and trying to fit in, they started to diminish, especially after the medical team put me on the standard cocktails they make up for everyone. You're right, the 'medicinal cocktail,' as you put it, seemed to help."

"When did they start to come back?"

"Shortly after I arrived here. When I had my tour of the greenhouses, it reminded me so much of farming back home that I started thinking about my parents and siblings again. That's when my nightmares started. What's going on, doc? Can you help me understand?"

Giesbrecht steepled his fingers. "Almost everyone in the cities is on some kind of pharma-cocktail personally designed for them to keep trauma at bay. We tend not to use them here for three reasons. First, they mask trauma symptoms and don't really fix the underlying problem. Second, they make you sluggish and stupid in the short term and we have data they do harm on the longer time scale. Third, even if we wanted to, we don't have many of those drugs here."

"So, you're saying they doped me up without my consent?"

"Try to think with the mind of a bureaucrat who views tax dollars as money they have earned. They don't need your permission, because in their mind they know better than you do what's good for you. After all, they're paying for your healthcare, as they see it, so they have a right to ensure the dollars *they* spend are used effectively."

"But I seem to remember they talked to me as if it was my choice. What would have happened if I'd decided I didn't want to take the meds?"

"From my experience with other inmates here," said Giesbrecht, "your handler would've tried to convince you to take the prescribed medication by predicting serious medical and psychological consequences if you continued to turn them down. If you continued to resist, you would likely have been labelled an uncooperative patient and denied even those services that you wanted."

Geisbrecht waited in case Jacob had more questions. Jacob was trying to process what he had just heard.

Geisbrecht went on. "You initially asked if they had doped you up without your consent. Essentially yes. Since you were already taking some meds yourself, you already had a patch on your arm for them. It's the easiest thing in the world for your handler to change the medications in the patch without your knowing. After all you can't read the barcode on the patch. The nanny state keeps its citizens in perpetual childhood and thinks nothing of doing things to you without your permission, simply because they think that making you useful and compliant is in the state's best interest. After all, they also believe that whatever's in the government's best interest is synonymous with everyone's best interest.

"Jacob, it's almost certain that everyone at your workplace was wearing a customized patch. The patch kept them from being troubled by their behavior, and depending on the particular cocktail they were being administered, could make them daring, ambitious, or even ruthless in their work. A lot of what you experienced, indeed, a lot of what eventually brought you here, was likely a byproduct of those patches."

Jacob rose out of his seat, shoved his hands into his pockets, and paced back and forth. He was so angry. He couldn't even hate Connaught anymore knowing that the man was also being strung along by a government-mandated treatment program.

What am I doing? Why am I being so irrational? Maybe Giesbrecht can help me.

Jacob sat down, straightened up, folded his hands in front of him, and asked, "Can you help me?"

"I can help you help yourself. First of all, time will make things functionally easier. You'll work through these things if you'll let yourself face up to them. You have to realize you've been deprived of two years in which you could've started to work through these thoughts. Now, in addition to coming to terms with the real trauma you've faced, you have to fight not to give in to despair after this relapse. Because of the time that's elapsed, it's natural for you to wonder if you'll face this forever."

"Will I? I mean, will I have these symptoms for the rest of my life?" asked Jacob swallowing hard.

"I don't know for sure," said Geisbrecht quietly. "I spend a lot of time reading the Gospels and they give me hope that we can be healed. I have a medical degree, but I consider myself a counselor. With regards to your question, at this point I don't know for sure if your nightmares will ever go away completely. Still, I believe facing them will help you cope and ultimately, I think God can help you get through this, even if the best medical opinion indicates otherwise."

Jacob was puzzled. *This God talk sounds crazy.*

Geisbrecht looked at Jacob for a moment and then said, "Here's what I want you to do. Start a journal. Write about the good times with your parents and siblings. By the way, do you believe you'll see them again?"

"I haven't really thought about it."

"Well think about it. If you really believe this absence is temporary—and I mean *really believe* because you are convinced that's the reality—then that conviction puts a whole different complexion on these questions. But don't fool yourself. Don't talk yourself into a conviction. Be scrupulously honest."

Giesbrecht looked at Jacob as he thought about the question. "No, I don't believe I'll see them again."

Giesbrecht sighed. "Well that makes things harder. Write down everything you remember about your parents and siblings, good times and bad. Especially, after you wake up after a nightmare, pull out your journal and write. If you were a Christ-follower, I'd tell you to pray. I'd also tell you to write about God's love and goodness. Maybe you'll be able to do that honestly in time, but right now you can't and I don't want you pretending and lying to yourself."

Giesbrecht gave Jacob a searching look. "Will you begin journaling?"

"Yes," said Jacob.

"Good, here's a book you can use as a journal and here's my office number. I'll see you in a week. I want you to bring your journal. I won't read it—it's for you. But I do want to make sure you've started. Next time I want you to tell me what you can share from your journaling. I answered your questions today, but next time I want to spend most of the time listening to what you've learned from your journaling."

CHAPTER 5
THE THREAD

JACOB RETURNED TO HIS ROOM AND LOOKED AT THE BLACK, SOFTCOVER book Giesbrecht had given him.

"Well," he said out loud, "what am I going to write about?"

He decided to make a start and wrote "Volume 1" on the inside blank page, followed by "DO NOT READ! THIS MEANS YOU! The private and confidential journal of Jacob Kraiser." He ended the inscription with the date.

Maybe I shouldn't have written that. Those statements are bound to pique any snoop's curiosity.

He thought about inventing a code and then decided he would have to find a way of hiding it.

There was a quiet knock on the door. It was Zeke.

"Come on in, Zeke," said Jacob after looking through the peephole.

Zeke came in, but didn't sit down. "Listen, Hanna and I heard that you were called away to Hodgkins. We were worried. Hanna made me come up here to get you. She wants us to meet in the common room."

"Why not?' said Jacob, "Maybe you two could help me write something in my journal. Right now, I can't think of anything to put down."

"Journal?" asked Zeke.

"Never mind, I'll explain when we get downstairs."

Hanna was sitting in an alcove along the far wall. She had brought three coffees from the cafeteria.

"Thanks Hanna," said Zeke and Jacob together. Sipping his coffee, Jacob recounted in detail his meeting with Hodgkins and Geisbrecht.

"So, the upshot is, I don't have the foggiest idea what to write. Any thoughts?"

Zeke looked blank and said, "Crikey, Jacob, I've got nothing."

Hanna gave Zeke a withering look and said gently, "I've been journaling a long time. It's hard to put down personal thoughts when you're not used to doing it. What I like to do is write about something that I've been reading."

"You would," said Zeke. That earned him another withering look.

"What are you reading, Jacob? I mean for fun, not compulsory reading for class."

"Well, I've been reading this children's book by George MacDonald. It's both weird and fascinating. It's about a young girl, Princess Irene. I guess I identify with her. She's nearly an orphan. Her mother is long dead and her father, the king, has sent her away from his palace for her own protection to live in a huge manor house, part house, part castle. She meets this mysterious old woman, during her wanderings to the deserted parts of the house. The old woman, whose name is also Irene, identifies herself as young Irene's great-great-great-grandmother. Young Irene is overjoyed to meet her. Later she eagerly tells her nurse about the discovery. Although Irene is scrupulously truthful, her nurse and the servants won't believe her and insist she's playing make-believe."

"I've read that book," said Hanna.

"My mom also used to read it to me," said Zeke.

"If everyone else has, how come I haven't heard of it before?" asked Jacob.

"Oh, you won't find it at school or in the public library," said Zeke. "It's one of the books that we'd carefully keep at home because we know we won't be able to buy it anymore. It's a book that's quietly been made to disappear. You can't really miss something if you don't know it exists."

"I don't know if your comment on 'not missing something you don't know about' is quite true, Zeke," said Jacob. "That's the funny thing. When I started reading *The Princess and the Goblin*, I realized I *had* been missing it. I think for a long time I had this vague feeling of something missing but I couldn't really put it into words. Anyway, when I started reading this book, somehow what I had been missing became a little clearer. Am I making any sense?"

Zeke looked bewildered.

Hanna clapped her hands. "Bravo! Now you're getting it. See how talking about the book has led you into thinking about important questions. You have something to write about."

Jacob hesitated as he tried to formulate a question. "There's something I was reading today that puzzles me. Irene's grandmother has just given Irene a gift. It's a fine spider's thread. The grandmother tied the thread to a ring, which she put on Irene's finger. The thread is so fine it can't be seen, but can be felt. The grandmother then put the magic ball of thread into her drawer so she could use the thread to help Irene.

"Her grandmother told Irene that if she ever found herself in danger, she should take the ring off and put it under her pillow. Then, she should lay her ring finger on the thread and follow it wherever it leads her."

"What does it mean?" asked Jacob.

"Hmm," said Hanna. "The thread's invisible. It's going to be the same problem all over again. Since the nurse and the servants can't see the thread, no one will believe Irene when she's following it."

"My mom would have said that it gave the princess a chance to exercise faith—you know, trust the grandmother and do something to show she trusts her." Zeke continued, "I never really understood that. If it had been me, I would've given the princess a cellphone and told her to ring me up if she was in trouble and I would've told her exactly what to do to solve her problem or I'd come to rescue her myself."

"I think my mother would've had the same idea as your mom, Zeke," said Hanna. "She would've told me to trust and obey."

When Jacob had returned to his room, he wrote down his thoughts on MacDonald's book and the comments his friends had made about it. He felt encouraged. He finished by writing "Trust and obey!" doubly underlined at the end of his description. And for the first time in many nights, he had a good sleep, without a nightmare.

CHAPTER 6
A TROUBLED PAST

THE HISTORY OF COVENTRY CLASS BECAME JACOB'S FAVORITE. THE VERY first day, the teacher, Edward Mutembe, walked in and introduced himself as the son of Christian Mutembe who had lived through the founding of Coventry and had written their textbook, *A History of the Coventry Penal Colony.* Thereafter, a portion of the textbook was assigned to the class for reading, and then Professor Mutembe would ask the class questions.

The small class met in a mid-sized lecture hall. Rousseau and his two bodyguards sat at the back. These classes proved a rich recruiting ground for Rousseau; over time more and more students sat in the back of the class. In contrast, Jacob, Hanna, Zeke—and others who resisted the Rousseau cabal— continued to sit at the front.

Edward Mutembe's penetrating brown eyes took in the scene as he leaned against his desk. His face was deep brown. He had closely cropped, tightly curled hair. He crossed his arms and addressed the students. "I gave you an assignment last week to look into the history of the drug, Cerebretocin-21. Who can tell me something about it?"

Hanna's hand shot up.

"Miss Heidel," said Mutembe.

"Cerebretocin-21, often called Cerebretocin for short ..." There was a titter from the back of the room. "... was a drug developed in Canada by 2041 to enable the culling of organs from human husks for the purpose of alleviating some of humanity's most serious diseases. By early 2048 it was ready for production and widespread adoption."

"That's almost word-for-word from the standard Canadian history book used in our universities," said Mutembe. "Are you able to elaborate how Cerebretocin-21 works?"

"The drug, when taken by the fetal carrier directly before or shortly after conception, ensures that the fetus never develops the higher cognitive brain functions. But since the lower brain functions remain intact, the fetus or husk continues to develop in the uterus so that when the pregnancy comes to term, the organs can then be harvested humanely for the benefit of newborns who have catastrophic organ malfunction. At that time there was also widespread hope that the brain-dead body could be kept alive and developing so that much later, adolescent or adult organs could also be harvested."

"Thank you, Miss Heidel. That's an excellent summary. So how did that relate to the founding of the Coventry Penal Colony?" Hanna's hand shot up again.

"I'm sure you know the answer, Miss Heidel. Perhaps I should encourage someone else to contribute. Mr. Rousseau, care to contribute an answer?"

"A bunch of religious fanatics, who were a bit soft in the head, decided to make a big deal about this and staged protests at all of the production, test sites, and warehouse sites of Cerebretocin."

"Very good Mr. Rousseau. People with strong religious convictions have protested various political and technological events before. Why was this protest different?" Mutembe looked around.

His eyes fixed on Jacob. "Mr. Kraiser, care to venture an educated guess as to why this protest was different?"

"I don't have the foggiest idea, Professor Mutembe."

"An honest answer is always to be appreciated, Mr. Kraiser. The difference had to do with the magnitude of the protest and the persistence of the protestors. At its height, there were about thirty-thousand active protestors at the Cerebretocin production and distribution sites. The government had reason to believe there were as many as two million sympathizers who were still too frightened or, perhaps, unsure to get involved. At the time there were about fifty-thousand prison spaces in the Canadian penal system and most of them were already filled. The prospect of processing thirty-thousand protestors through the courts and then finding enough spaces to confine them was simply not possible. Having that number expand to two million was frightening to the government."

Jacob's hand went up.

"A question, Mr. Kraiser?"

"May, I ask, Professor Mutembe, what was the population of Canada at that time?"

"Good question. The population was approximately forty-one million."

"But now our population is only twenty-nine million!"

"I know and that's a question for another day," said Mutembe. "Let me only add this. All the birthrates in so-called developed countries have been well below the replacement rate for some time. For a while the population did not decrease because increases in life expectancy kept the population numbers up.

"For example, in Canada our fertility rate is 1.5 children per woman that reaches childbearing age. It needs to be 2.1 for the population to be stable. It is inevitable that our population will decline. We'll discuss other significant factors at another time."

Mutembe scanned the classroom. "Now back to the original question. The second reason this protest was different from previous protests was the persistence of the protestors. At first the authorities tried arresting and releasing most of the protestors, while asking for harsh sentences for protest leaders. However, the released protestors immediately went back to the protest sites and continued to shut down the Cerebretocin facilities. Indeed, this constant return to the picket line led to growth in the number of protestors.

"From the point of view of the historian, we were fortunate that my father had access to a student summer assistant in the Prime Minister's office, who not only heard much of the conversation around the proposal that led to Coventry Penal Colony but also secretly recorded many of the conversations on his cell phone.

"Please read the full text of the transcripts of these discussions and submit an essay of not more than one thousand words on the salient points of the decision to found the Coventry Penal Colony, and to bootstrap the 2051 Tribunals, for next class. These spontaneous essays will make up twenty percent of your class grade."

"Hey Teach," said Dennison with a smirk on his face. "So, what happens if we fail this course? Do you stop feeding us?"

"To begin with, Mr. Dennison, you will address me as 'Professor.' To stop feeding rebellious freeloaders is an admirable suggestion. We would first try letting you repeat the course in the hope that the problem is simply that you're dimwitted. Failing that, we would consign you to the most menial jobs we have, since you refuse to learn what's required for the more challenging work. If all else fails, we likely would make your food contingent on your cooperation. This is a self-supporting prison, after all. Surely you won't want to go hungry?"

Mutembe looked around for more questions. "Dismissed."

CHAPTER 7
WHAT HAPPENED IN 2051

AT HANNA'S INSISTENCE, JACOB AND ZEKE WENT WITH HER TO THE LIBRARY, immediately after class.

"If we wait until next Thursday, we'll be fighting with the rest of the class for the transcripts," she said.

She checked out the source documents and they divided up the interview transcripts looking for the conversation leading up to the decision to found the Coventry Penal Colony.

"Here it is," whispered Jacob. Zeke and Hanna read the text over his shoulder.

TRANSCRIPT OF THE DECISION TO ARREST
CEREBRETOCIN-21 PROTESTORS

Secretly recorded using a cell phone by summer student, Hans Schneider, May 21, 2050. Transcribed to text by Hans Schneider and Christian Mutembe.

PM: What's happening with the protests, Dale?

SE: Sir, we're having the protestors arrested as quickly as we can, but there are now more than 30,000 of them. We've locked up about 2000 of the leaders, but the others refuse to promise to give up the protest and as soon as they're released, as far as we can tell, they return to the protest. There is also a real concern in my department that there may be as many as two million sympathizers, primarily in the rural communities, who are currently too frightened to become involved. If they do join, this'll likely be too large to contain without bringing in the army.

PM: 30,000 [expletive deleted]! These [expletive deleted] protests are growing and are way out of control. Dale, I want those [expletive deleted] country bumpkins and religious fanatics stopped. [Protracted pause] Here's what I want you to do. Find an abandoned military airfield. Have the armed forces tap into their emergency funding to set up a tent city for the prisoners. Arrest all of the fanatics and take them directly to the airfield until further notice.

SE: Respectfully, sir, isn't that against the law?

MJ: No, Dale, it's not against the law. This emergency entitles us to invoke the Revised Emergency Measures Act, which allows us, under these extreme circumstances, to hold people for an extended period of time without the usual legal proceedings.

PM: That's right Lyle. This gives us time to come up with a long-term plan. But a plan that I'm going to insist will provide a permanent solution. I'm not going to let those [expletive deleted] Luddites control our agenda. Our people want these organs and the future health prospects they promise. No one wants these fanatics to win.

[Silent pause in the recording]

PM: Look at the bright side. Think of this as an opportunity rather than a problem. You know this altercation provides us with the means to eliminate a long-standing political problem. If we play our cards right, this may remove a thorn in our backside that's been plaguing us for nearly a century.

SE: What do you mean, sir?

PM: Later. I have to think it through.

SE: What about the opposition parties and the media? Won't they be all over us if we invoke the Revised Emergency Measures Act?

PM: (Chuckling) The urban electorate will be strongly behind us. The three opposition parties know that and want these protests stopped as much as I do. We'll pass the specific enabling legislation tonight with minimum fuss. As for the media, as long as these protests are going on, people are glued to their monitors. Although I've had journalists privately telling me they want these protests stopped, they're a money-maker for the media right now. Still, if we let them go on for a while longer, the media will continue building a case for stronger and stronger countermeasures. Oh, the lot of them will be all over us as usual. They won't complain about the measures. They'll complain that I'm not acting quickly and decisively enough. When the time comes to act we'll do so reluctantly and regrettably in the best interest of Canada."

"Who are PM, MJ, and SE?" asked Hanna.

"They're defined here in the footnotes," said Jacob. "Prime Minister, Minister of Justice, and Special Envoy. I'm pretty sure the Prime Minister was Russell, but I don't know who MJ and SE were at the time. We'll have to look it up."

"We know how they locked people up initially, but we don't yet know how the Coventry Penal Colony and the 2051 Tribunal were established," said Zeke.

They continued searching the data and found an aerial photo of Vulture Lake in the Canadian Shield north of Lake Superior, and some information on the Iron Isle mine, a property acquired by the federal government after the company filed for bankruptcy protection.

Finally, Zeke found the correct transcript.

TRANSCRIPT OF THE DECISION TO FOUND THE COVENTRY PENAL COLONY

Secretly recorded using a cell phone by summer student, Hans Schneider, June 26, 2050. Transcribed to text by Hans Schneider and Christian Mutembe.

PM: I read your proposal, Dale. I think it's brilliant. Are you sure we won't have a full-scale insurrection on our hands?

SE: I don't think so, sir. The protests were never violent and many of the internees are religious pacifists predominantly from rural communities. The others seem to have theological convictions that make them avoid violence, except as a last resort. I think they'll go quietly.

PM: But if they get there and find they're starving?

SE: Ultimately, we don't care because we want to break their will to resist and to protest. We'll move them in during the spring of 2051 when conditions are not impossibly difficult. Iron Isle is almost 100 square miles in size—mostly rock, bush, and a small mountain of ore processing residue. I don't know the details, but apparently the mine and the ore residue contains some fairly valuable metals that are hard to isolate. With no labor costs, the inmates could provide that to us to pay for their upkeep. They also can use the abandoned housing. Assigning it will be their problem.

The company had built a nearby hydroelectric plant to service the significant power needs of the mining and ore-processing operation. We can use that as leverage. At first, we'll give them enough food and power to be comfortable. Maybe even enough to get them through the first winter. Then, down the road, we'll slowly cut back and make them work for what we give them and we'll have them under our heel. We'll cut back slowly enough that, if they work like maniacs they can just make it. They'll know we can cut them off at any time if they don't obey. In winter they'll be hundreds of miles from any road traveled by someone other than our specially selected security guards. There is no way out. There is no way for them to get their message out. They'll have to do what we want or starve. I think we'll break them and make them slink back to their farms and small towns, agreeing to spy on others in this movement, before Christmas 2052.

PM: What about the guards?

SE: Sir, we selected guards who'll have a special animosity towards the inmates of the Coventry Penal Colony and will show the inmates no sympathy. Some have been selected because they have a special animosity towards anyone religious. Others believe that the protests have denied them or members of their families a much-needed health benefit. We've also developed a training program to inspire them to regard their service as clearly for the common good, protecting the general population from these corrosive fanatics. Best of all, the guards will have little day-to-day contact with the inmates. They'll be imaginary enemies and the guards won't see the hardships firsthand if the fanatics decide to be less than cooperative.

PM: How soon will we be moving the detainees to Coventry?

SE: As soon as you give the word, sir. I'll need to set up a Tribunal, as we discussed, to circumvent the courts. We'll process them in batches.

PM: Excellent! You have "the word." Dale, this deserves a toast. We've fought through a challenge that threatened the core values of our democracy. I have an excellent brandy, I think you'll enjoy.

SE: Sir, we still have one problem.

PM: What's that, Dale?

SE: I think the optimum time to send them to Coventry is next spring. However, because of the numbers, we should begin processing them through the Tribunal now. What do we do until next spring?

[Long pause]

PM: Here's what you do, Dale. Begin processing them through the Tribunal as soon as you arrest them. Then release them on probation. Keep releasing them until next March. At that point all the Tribunal-processed protestors are immediately sent to Coventry when they are picked up at the protest site. We have a few months of lost time in which they can continue to shut Cerebretocin manufacturing and distribution down. That will only anger the public and the media further. When the protestors finally begin to disappear next spring, everyone will say "Good riddance."

There was stunned silence. "So how come," said Jacob, "while we're learning about the disadvantaged citizens of Canada in school, we never heard about these thirty-thousand protestors who just vanished? What about their families? Someone must've complained? How could they just disappear?"

"I think those are excellent questions we should ask as we write our essays," said Hanna.

CHAPTER 8
THE MANILA PACKAGE

THE NEXT WEEK, F COMPANY WAS ASSIGNED TO LOAD THE SIX TRANSPORT trailers parked in the lot on the Iron Isle side of the causeway with processed platinum and rare-earth ingots.

Working on a tight schedule, they retrieved the metal cargo from a warehouse on the main floor. F Company first loaded the loose ingots into stackable containers about a cubic meter in volume. Then they moved containers into the trailers using two old electric forklifts. Once inside, they maneuvered the loaded containers into position with the help of smaller loaders and stacked them. Finally, the containers were secured so that they didn't shift during transport. There was a great deal of manual labor involved, pushing and shoving the heavy containers into position. Everyone was sweating despite the cold, as they worked toward their noon deadline.

Finishing just before noon, most of the crew went inside for lunch. The less experienced, newer members were left to clean up in the warehouse. Litch, Dennison, and Rousseau promptly vanished so Jacob, Hanna, and Zeke were left to handle the remaining task.

Promptly at noon, the red warning light and siren at the end of the causeway activated. The gates on either side of the drawbridge swung open and the drawbridge lowered. An armored personnel carrier came across the bridge and discharged six heavily-armed guards. The guards set up a perimeter covering the front of the mining building. The heavy machine gun on top of the armored vehicle rotated ominously from side to side.

Jacob, Hanna, and Zeke stopped their sweeping to watch the proceedings through the open warehouse door.

"Why are we even here?" asked Zeke. "Those guys look like they'd shoot me if I hiccupped."

"I think we'll be okay if we stay inside. Let's just quietly sit near the door so we can see what they do without looking like we're up to something," said Jacob. The three friends did as he suggested and sat quietly on some boxes in the shadows.

The commander ordered two of the guards to enter the trailers and inspect the loads. Once finished, they latched the doors of each trailer. Within minutes, a convoy of six transport trucks pulled into the parking lot, circled around the loaded trailers and stopped. The tractors were decoupled and then reconnected to the loaded trailers. While the exchange was underway, Jacob felt Zeke's elbow poke him in the ribs. Zeke pointed to the officer in charge of the armed guards. He was carrying a manila package. Sauntering to the side of the building, the officer seemed to look for observers, and then moved to an alcove where he appeared to speak to someone hidden from their view. After a couple of minutes, the officer returned to his men without the manila package, remounted the armored vehicle, and then followed the straining tractor trailers back across the causeway. The heavy gates swung shut and the drawbridge raised.

"Let's go out for a better view," said Jacob. They left the storage area, went out into the yard, and crouched down beside the new trailers.

After a minute, Rousseau came out of the alcove, looked around and then went into the mining building. There was an obvious bulge on the front of his jacket. As soon as Rousseau had entered the main building, Jacob hurried to follow him. Checking the doors to see Rousseau's retreating form, Jacob quietly let himself in. Rousseau was not heading to the cafeteria, but went straight to the F Company common room. When the three friends entered, there was no sign of him, so Jacob and Zeke went up to their dorm. They heard Rousseau's door at the end of the hall close as they entered their dorm hall.

Jacob walked up to Rousseau's door and knocked. "Are you crackers, Jacob? What are you doing?" hissed Zeke, hurrying to his side.

It took a while but Rousseau eventually opened the door. He looked surprised to see Jacob and Zeke. "What do you want?"

"It's been a long day for us. Zeke and I are just heading down to the cafeteria. Lunch is almost over. Do you want us to bring anything back for you?"

Rousseau looked suspicious, moved to fill the doorway, as if to obstruct their view of his room and said, "No, that's alright. Err, thanks for asking." He slammed the door and Jacob heard the lock click.

Jacob and Zeke went to the common room, met Hanna, and made it to the cafeteria just before the lunch crowd returned to work. They sat at a corner table in the near empty lunchroom while Zeke and Jacob reiterated their brief conversation with Rousseau.

"Did you see the package in his room?" asked Hanna.

"Nope," said Zeke, "he deliberately blocked the doorway so we couldn't look into the room. Anyway, he didn't open the door right away, so he had time to hide it."

"Something's going on," said Jacob. "If Rousseau is a prisoner like the rest of us, why have secret meetings with the prison guards?"

"Maybe he's selling drugs," said Hanna.

"Maybe," said Jacob, "but the people here don't strike me as drug users. They even took the standard-issue drugs off us that are commonly issued to anyone who wants them outside."

"There's something fishy about Rousseau," said Zeke. "He strikes me more like military or intelligence than part of the underworld."

"I think I ought to talk to Simeon," said Jacob. "I'm sure that Rousseau's up to no good."

"But we don't have any evidence," said Hanna. "Won't he think you're just bad-mouthing a fellow prisoner?"

"When it gets back to Rousseau, I see another black eye, or worse, coming," added Zeke.

"I'll leave you guys out of it, but my gut tells me something is seriously wrong here," said Jacob. "I'm going to chance it and see Simeon."

Just then Captain Hodgkins gave the signal. It was time to return to the parking lot and begin unloading the newly-arrived transport trailers.

The trailers turned out to be filled with a combination of mining equipment components, medicines, and food. When they finally finished that assignment, most everyone left for afternoon coffee and sandwiches, but Jacob went to Simeon's office just off the common room and knocked on the door.

"Come in," said a tired voice.

Jacob entered and saw Captain Hodgkins sitting at his desk with his fingers steepled under his chin. He looked up. "Kraiser, come in, come in. How can I help?"

"Sir, I'm sorry to disturb you after our company's long day, but I saw something today that bothered me—enough to bring it to your attention. My friends told me not to speak before I have evidence, but my gut tells me it's important."

"Always listen to your gut, son. Now what's eating you?"

Jacob reiterated his observations from the loading of the ingots to knocking on Rousseau's door.

Hodgkins leaned back in his chair, stroking his chin. "So, you saw that did you? And it prompted you to report it to me? Good man."

"You knew about it sir?"

"Yes, I did. But since you reported it that tells me two things. Most likely you care enough about your comrades that you worry about bad things happening to us. But even more importantly, you're keeping your eyes open enough to spot potential threats. By the way, the fact that you and Rempel weren't cowed into joining Rousseau's toadies is also a major checkmark in your favor." Jacob opened and then closed his mouth in surprise.

"If you knew, why didn't you send Rousseau back?"

"Well, for one thing, we don't want the-powers-that-be to know the degree to which we're on to them. It's much better to have them think they've pulled the wool over our eyes. For another, if we send back agents as soon as we spot them, the only ones that remain are the ones we don't know about. It's much better for us this way. At least for a while. It's not better for you though since Rousseau is a bully."

Hodgkins leaned back in his chair. "Let me tell you something, son. You can tell this to Rempel and Heidel, but I'd rather that it doesn't go any further. Periodically, our warden and the government get cold feet about our operation here and try to reassert their authority. They usually begin, as they are now, by smuggling in a few undercover agents among the prisoners. Sometimes after they poke around for a while, it stops there.

"Sometimes, it gets more serious and they actually make a raid on Coventry. Then they take over the operation and search everything. They eventually realize this place is no threat to them. Indeed, it is much too difficult and expensive to manage like a regular prison. Finally they allow things to revert back to business-as-usual as they retreat back to the other side of the bridge and mostly leave us alone.

"With today's development, it looks to me as if this will at least be the second kind of incursion. We don't know when they'll attack, but in times past, occasionally, during the surprise incursion, some trigger-happy assault team member has gunned down innocent inmates that were slow retreating to the lower levels. We'd like to prevent that if at all possible. We have ways of knowing a short time before it happens that the raid is gearing up. When I warn you and tell you to go to the lower levels, don't hesitate or delay. Follow my instructions explicitly and take as many of our company along with you as will come. We try to keep our halls as empty as possible when the guards move in to prevent 'accidents.' Do you understand?"

"I think so, sir."

"One more thing: before we both go back to work, I also have a gut feeling. My gut tells me this incursion is going to be bad—really bad. So, steel yourself for a few surprises. Good bye, Kraiser. And thanks for your trust."

"Good bye, sir."

CHAPTER 9
YEARS OF TEARS

THE NEXT FRIDAY MORNING IN HISTORY CLASS THEIR ESSAYS ON THE founding of Coventry were returned. Hanna had received an A+, Jacob an A, and Zeke a B, even though Hanna had edited his rough draft.

"Any questions?" asked Mutembe.

Hanna's hand shot up. "Sir, having finished the essay, one thing puzzles me. I know from my university studies, there've been many social and technological developments that religious people objected to—dating back to at least the nineteen sixties. Most of their objections and protests led nowhere. I'm puzzled. Why did the Cerebretocin-21 drug provoke such an extraordinarily strong response from the government? Couldn't they have just waited it out?"

"Good question, Miss Heidel. However, we ought to ask another question first. Why did this protest involve many more people and continue for a much longer time than all previous protests? I can't answer that with certainty, although my father, putting on his sociology hat, tried very hard to find a definitive answer. He ended up with two hypotheses and couldn't decide which was the more probable.

"The first one might be called 'The-Straw-that-Broke-the-Camel's-Back' hypothesis. As you correctly observed, there were many 'social innovations' that were deemed to be catastrophic for the family, for children, and for society in general by people of faith. On each one they fought, lost, and from their point of view, saw the consequences of the 'innovation' further damage our society.

Finally, with the development and implementation of Cerebretocin-21, a tipping point was reached, and all that long-term, pent-up opposition coalesced into a determined multi-year protest movement, which for a protracted period of time hindered Cerebretocin-21 development and distribution, and ultimately led to the establishment of the Coventry Penal Colony. If I'm permitted a metaphor, this sequence is reminiscent of an army suffering defeat after defeat, yet regrouping to fight on new ground, closer to home. There comes a point, where retreat is no longer possible and the time has come for a 'last stand.' In this hypothesis, Cerebretocin-21 was 'the last stand.'"

"The second hypothesis that my father considered, categorized the Cerebretocin-21 protest as an extension of the protracted pro-life movement. I think a pro-life advocate in the nineteen eighties—if I can try to put myself into their heads for a moment—would look at a fetus, and observe that if that fetus were left alone and allowed to develop naturally, it would develop into a child with a life expectancy of some eighty-five years. But in the background there often was a young, frightened, pregnant girl, who in her great fear was taking this horrendous step of ending her pregnancy. In other words, there often were thought to be two victims. This, I think, in some way blunted the force of the protests.

"The Cerebretocin-21 development, differs from the abortion question, by eliminating the second victim. Instead you have a healthcare system that uses women to carry these human husks to term. The artificially inseminated women who were carrying these husks thought of it as a business or a job and considered themselves a kind of healthcare worker. In this hypothesis, the crucial difference from the protests of the nineteen eighties is the disappearance of the frightened young pregnant girl as the second victim.

"I don't know which hypothesis is true. Perhaps neither. The one thing we do know is that the magnitude of the protests left the government only two choices: capitulate on Cerebretocin-21 or eliminate the problem. The government, naturally enough, chose the latter. Good question."

Mutembe paced up and down in front of the class. Everyone was very quiet. Finally he turned and gestured with his hand. "There's one more thing that fed the government's fear about this protest. Since the early part of the twenty-first century, about eighty percent of our population resided in major metropolitan areas and only twenty percent on farms or in small towns. With our country's low birthrate and the slow decline of our population, towns were no longer growing into cities, and cities were no longer expanding to swallow bordering towns. So a political divide developed between rural and urban voters. The rural vote at twenty percent didn't matter. Politicians could curry and manipulate the thinking of the urban voter, but the rural voter became more and more independent and self-sufficient. Here's the key point: most of the protestors and their sympathizers came from the rural voting bloc. As voters, they could do virtually nothing to influence our government. But as protestors, they could cause great trouble. This, I think, was in the backs of the minds of all the politicians as they dealt with this unrest."

Hanna put up her hand again.

"Alright, Miss Heidel; one more question."

"Professor Mutembe, you haven't told us where you personally stand on this question."

"I suppose I owe you full disclosure. I think both hypotheses have merit and are likely contributing factors. If I had to choose, I would lean toward the second hypothesis. Speaking personally, it seems to me, the whole Cerebretocin-21 controversy was predicated on a very dangerous philosophical presupposition: if an agent were to destroy a fetus' higher cognitive functions in a painless manner, then that destruction is not a crime and does not matter, particularly if there is a perceived common good. Somehow, if something is perceived as painless and supposedly for the greater good, then it must be allowed. I think this opens the door for many injustices. Establishing Coventry and indirectly contributing to the deaths of thousands of people is simply the natural consequences of this philosophical system, in my estimation.

"Now, just to be clear, this is my personal assessment. Not everyone agrees with me. More importantly, you don't have to agree with me. If you choose to write from a different perspective, I will do my best to set my personal bias aside and grade you on the merits of your argument."

Mutembe looked around. "If there are no more questions, turn to the chapter entitled *Years of Tears*. What happened in this time period? Yes, Mr. Denton?"

"In the next ten years more than six thousand people died of starvation and disease, as the government gradually cut back on food and power."

"That's correct. Try as we might, using all the ingenuity at our disposal, we couldn't feed our population. It should've been much worse, but everyone shared their food and children were given priority. Essentially, all the adults starved together. They looked like scarecrows, if you've seen pictures from that era. The pictures, of course, were never shared with the public at large. All the suffering occurred here, out of the public eye."

Jacob put up his hand. Mutembe acknowledged him. "Professor, in the transcripts I read, it sounded as if the plan, as originally formulated by Russell, intended to allow prisoners to be released if they agreed to abandon the protests. Did that ever happen?"

"Yes, I remember that part of the discussion. Did it happen? I'm afraid the answer is 'yes and no.' Repeat offers were made to release inmates, but only if they agreed to spy on their family and friends. Any failure to comply meant an immediate return to Coventry. Hundreds took up the offer, and they initially caused great havoc in the external oppositional community. Most, inside and out, saw this spying as a great betrayal. Still, having these spies within the movement caused great fear and meant that, over time, no one who chose to leave Coventry, was trusted."

Zeke put up his hand. "Sir, I don't understand why things changed after ten years. We're not starving now. I don't get it."

"Mr. Rempel, that very question will be the subject of your next essay. I want you to research the period of time called 'The Years of Tears' from a different perspective, and focus on the impact of two people on their community: Josiah Kinsinger and Jonah Klemhofer. I'll be interested to hear your explanation as you answer your own question. You are dismissed to the library."

"Well," said Zeke as they walked to the library, "they obviously found a new energy source, didn't they? After all, look at those greenhouses warmed by the hot water streams and all the food they produce."

"Maybe they found a coal seam or geothermal source as they tried to work the mine," said Hanna.

"Some things still don't add up for me," said Jacob. "I see a few hundred, maybe a couple of thousand people at the mine if I count the workers coming to the cafeteria from the lower production levels we haven't even yet seen, but I don't see twenty or thirty thousand. Where are they all? Did most of them die? If they're here, I can't believe those large greenhouses and the food that arrives in the trucks is enough to feed even ten thousand, never mind twenty or thirty thousand."

CHAPTER 10
WHO WERE KINSINGER AND KLEMHOFER?

AS USUAL, HANNA HAD THEM ORGANIZED IN SHORT ORDER, SEARCHING various sources for all references to "Years of Tears," Kinsinger, and Klemhofer. A bank of personal computers of a type Jacob had never seen at the Ministry of Technology lined one wall, offering access to the library's electronic collection. Jacob had not used the machines before and the operating system was unfamiliar. But so many classmates were now searching for the same information in hardcopy that he knew he had to take the plunge and learn it. Once he started, he found it surprisingly intuitive. He soon located a list of references and copied the files to his personal account. Christian Mutembe, in the year he had died, had given a lecture on Kinsinger. So this seemed the place to start.

Jacob scanned the introduction. As he read, he could hear the voice of an octogenarian speaking about people and historical events he had known and witnessed.

I see the hand of God in Josiah Kinsinger's incarceration at Iron Isle. Josiah was a mining engineer with his own small company that specialized in recovering valuable minerals from mine tailings and ore processing residue. Fortuitously, or as I believe, providentially, before his incarceration at Coventry,

Kinsinger had worked on the problem of recovering trace rare-earth metals from the Iron Isle residues for three years, and had converged on what he thought was an economically viable means of production when he was caught up in the protests.

By 2054 when starvation was rampant, and the limited government supply of food and other essentials were woefully inadequate, the colony finally tunneled a shaft to the surface about forty miles from here. The external sympathizers set up a lumber camp there through a holding company, and secretly began shipping food and medicines to Coventry. Kinsinger convinced his friends in the charity to begin smuggling in some pieces of his processing equipment. By 2055 he delivered a kilogram of pure gadolinium to the guards, and asked to see the warden.

The warden locked Kinsinger up for a month in the guard facility, trying to get him to tell how he had managed to recover fifty thousand-dollars-worth of the metal. Kinsinger was stubborn and after a month came back to Coventry with a deal. We began shipping gadolinium and other rare-earths at the rate of a kilogram every month. As Kinsinger exchanged the metals for food, medicines, and above all production equipment, the yields increased until we were filling a transport truck with the metals. Platinum-Group metals were also being mined again and filled a second truck.

The first major crisis came in the fall of 2056. The rare-earth metal production had been so lucrative that the warden obtained the resources from the government to raid Coventry. They took over the compound, and searched for the production equipment. They tried to bribe various inmates to tell them how to find the equipment and promised even more if the inmates were to run the equipment for them. The raid had been anticipated and with miles and miles of tunnels, the equipment could not be found. By this point, everyone knew we faced starvation at the hands of the government if we gave up our secret technology, and no one was fool enough to cooperate.

After two months, they returned to the other side of the causeway and left us alone on the understanding that we would resume production. Two positive things came out of this. First, we had legitimate access to mining equipment as we expanded production. In the winter of 2056 we cut a single channel around Vulture Falls, the outlet from Vulture Lake, and built our very own hydroelectric plant with under-water cables to the Iron Isle.

Second, and more importantly, Kinsinger became fast friends with Jonah Klemhofer. Klemhofer had Ph.D. degrees in physics and inorganic chemistry. From our mining operation he had unprecedented access to rare-earth and transition metal salts and began developing an idea for fusion technology as a power source.

By 2058, he demonstrated a small fusion device that spot heated a hydrogen-deuterium mixture in a metal lattice to several million degrees. Because the heating was in a very small volume and only a few thousand hydrogen atoms were fused, the matrix is heated but not melted. The rest you know.

It was a privilege knowing these two men. But in closing, I want to acknowledge the words of Joseph to his brothers in Genesis chapter 45, when he ended up in Egypt after they sold him into slavery:

"I am your brother, Joseph, whom you sold into Egypt. And now do not be distressed or angry with yourselves because you sold me here, for God sent me before you to preserve life."

As an old man who has seen too many years and too much sorrow, I may be permitted to indulge in a little reminiscing and prophecy. I think Prime Minister Russell meant this exile to Coventry for our demise, our ultimate destruction, but especially to remove troublesome people like us from participating in the political process.

The presence of Kinsinger and Klemhofer here is one of those events that materialists regard as an amazing coincidence, but which I, as a Christian, regard as providence.

I think God has permitted us to be sent into exile to give us a new beginning and to rescue us from the rot and decay that I see everywhere around us. The Years of Tears imposed on us by our captors were terrible. Yet they proved our mettle and enabled us to make a new beginning.

As a young man I loved to read Isaac Asimov's *Foundation* trilogy. In it, psychohistorians founded an exiled colony to escape the rot and decay of the galactic empire as it slid into a dark age. Perhaps we can serve that role for our peoples.

In that light, Coventry has not only let us save ourselves, but also others. As a sociologist and historian, it is no coincidence that our rural communities in Canada are so different from the urban centers. Coventry has been able to influence and help many in our small towns and on our farms. Since the rural population has almost no influence on our elections and the government has little interest in catering to the rural vote, we have been given a free hand.

Think also of the Coventry communities we were able to found in central Africa and central Asia to accept refugees from the terrible consequences of Single Nuclear Exchanges in that part of the world.

Let us be grateful to Providence. Let us be thankful for the travails of our pioneers. Let us resolve to preserve our basic freedoms. Thank you very much. [Standing ovation]

When Hanna finished reading, her eyes were wide as saucers. "Do you think this is really true: they discovered a portable power source thirty-three years ago?"

"I don't know," said Jacob. "We supposedly still get power from the warden and the mainland in exchange for millions of dollars of rare-earths every month. Apparently, we also have an underground hydroelectric plant at Vulture Falls. Maybe the alternative power source is not that significant and the falls produce most of the power. After all, Mutembe left out some key information: how would you spot heat a tiny volume of the lattice to millions of degrees without melting the whole thing down?"

Zeke was smirking.

"Okay, wise-guy," said Jacob, "you know something we don't. Start talking."

"Well, to be honest, I don't know anything for sure," said Zeke. "Still my family and our friends were part of that charitable network that put up the money to buy the lumber company that secretly provided food and supplies for Coventry. There were a lot of whispered conversations and trips abroad by our family members and especially by friends in our community on the U.S. side. Although the adults were very closed-mouthed about things with the children, I'm pretty sure everything at Coventry is not what it seems. I just don't know what the reality is."

"Well, I think part of our Sundays are going to be taken up with detective work," said Hanna.

"As long as I'm not on latrine duty for the rest of my natural life here at Coventry because of your detective work," grumped Zeke.

"Aw, that would do your soul good, Zeke," said Hanna. "You need something to sober you up. Anyway, when have my ideas ever gone wrong?"

CHAPTER 11
A SURPRISE INTERVIEW

ON SATURDAY MORNING, JACOB WOKE FROM A RESTLESS NIGHT'S SLEEP TO a knock on his door. He suspected he had been shouting again, although he did not remember having his usual nightmare. He opened the door to Doctor Geisbrecht who was carrying two cups.

"Hello, Jacob. May I come in?"

Jacob did not speak but simply motioned Geisbrecht to the room's only chair, beside a reading lamp in the corner. Geisbrecht stopped by the chair and waited while Jacob removed a pile of clothes, then sat down watching the two cups to make sure he didn't spill.

Handing Jacob a cup, Geisbrecht said, "This is for you. The cafeteria staff, who know all and see all, told me what you like in your coffee."

Jacob took the coffee and sipped. It was perfect. Maybe Geisbrecht was right about the cafeteria staff.

"You didn't come to see me this week, Jacob."

"Sorry, about that. F Company was loading ingots this week into the trailers and I had a lot of assignments from my classes."

"That's what I figured. So, I thought I would drop in and see how you're doing."

"I'm fine, Doc."

"Have you started your journal?"

"Yes."

"Good, now tell me what happened when they brought you to Toronto after your family's accident."

"A grief counselor flew with me to Toronto right after the funeral, which she had arranged and handled. She had me on some kind of tranquilizer so I don't even remember that much about the memorial service. For example, I don't remember if I spoke. She did tell me that she had a professional colleague handling the sale of the farm. And also that given my increased Victimization Index, I had training and a good job waiting for me in Toronto. To take my mind off the tragedy."

"Go on."

"Everything in Toronto was ready for me. There was a small downtown apartment, and a six-week management training course that I attended. After that, I was put in charge of a small group of administrators, in the Ministry of Technology that funded trauma equity grants to people like me who had their Victimization Index bumped up because of personal trauma.

"At first I expected everyone to resent my being parachuted in to head up our group, when I'm sure many who were already there probably wanted my job. But everyone was very nice; they all stopped by my office and told me how sorry they were for my loss, that they cared for my well-being, and wanted me to succeed in my new position."

"Were they genuine?" asked Geisbrecht.

"I thought so at the time. Now, I'm not so sure. They seemed so sincere. No one back home would have said things like they did without meaning it. Now as I reflect back, I'm wondering if the combination of drugs, my naïveté, and the fact that they were accomplished liars completely fooled me."

"What happened next?"

"There was a pretty young woman in my group called Cynthia Stapleton. She was always friendly and upbeat. After a few months, one day she asked, in tears, to see me. She told me that my boss, Connaught, wanted to transfer her to his staff. She also told me, that he 'Creeped her out.' She was afraid of him and didn't want to transfer."

"So, you went to see Connaught?"

"Yes, I did. I asked Connaught if he intended to transfer Cynthia to his group. He said 'Yes' and told me he'd been too busy to tell me about the transfer. He asked if I intended to oppose him. I told him I thought we ought to wait—at least until Cynthia was reassured.

"Connaught said 'fine' but now, as I think about it, at that point things began to go wrong. Equipment began to go missing from my department and I heard it was rumored that I was taking it home to sell to the Cretins. I had to look up the word Cretins to realize they were using the word to refer to subversive religious fanatics. I didn't even know any Cretins.

"Things went from bad to worse and then I began receiving a series of speeding fines. Most were backdated to months earlier …"

"How did that work?" asked Geisbrecht.

"When I arrived in Toronto, I was loaned a government car. Apparently, this car had global positioning and a data recording systems built in. During the work term, these in-car systems logged and recorded every time I exceeded the speed limit. The fines I began receiving were for speeding tickets while I used the government car. The amounts became so alarming, I started using public transportation and gave my car back.

"Apparently, everybody with a government car has these fines hanging over their heads if they speed, but the fine-collectors use a lottery system to begin collecting. They told me I had the bad luck to have my name come up early.

"When I received the news about the fine, I got angry and stormed into Connaught's office. He pretended ignorance and looked at me as if I were crazy. I told him I wouldn't rest until I got to the bottom of this. I left and spoke to Cynthia and told her my predicament. She put her hand on my shoulder and told me I had been a good friend to her.

"The next thing I know, Cynthia had filed a harassment complaint against me and, I found out for the first time, she had made repeated complaints against me dating back six months. That is, since shortly after she came to see me asking for my help. Up until that point I naively thought the missing equipment, the traffic tickets, and the Stapleton complaint were nothing more than an office squabble. Then the police came to my apartment, woke me out of my sleep and I found myself bewildered and numb standing before a tribune. After making all kinds outrageous and untrue claims against my family, about them and me being subversive Cretins undermining peace, order, and good government, I was sentenced and shipped off to Coventry. All within an afternoon. It all made my head spin."

Geisbrecht spoke softly to himself, "They all lie in wait for blood, and each hunts the other with a net."

"What did you say?" asked Jacob.

"Oh, your story, Jacob, reminded me of what I was reading this morning from the biblical prophet Micah. It's in chapter seven, verse two. You should look it up some time."

Giesbrecht continued. "In Coventry, we depend, in part, on intelligence for survival. We have contacts, certainly in the Justice Department, but even in the Ministry of Technology. I asked for some of our sources to make discreet inquiries.

"In a general sense, there's a huge cultural gap now between the cities and the rural areas. One hundred years ago, the gap would have been there but not nearly so pronounced. In the cities, there's a veneer of civility and fair play that cover a ruthless, almost Darwinian struggle for supremacy that's the hidden motivator behind social interactions. Specifically, in your case, here's what I have been able to find out: You were taken advantage of almost from the beginning. Everyone has to be outwardly in favor of rewarding people with High Victimization Indices. But when they can, people work to subvert the system. Coventry has a number of contacts and sympathizers that keep tabs on the Ministry of Technology. You'll be interested to know that Cynthia Stapleton is now Executive Assistant to Connaught. They work intimately together. She played you off against Connaught right from the beginning and converted a simple internal job transfer into a significant promotion. Since they both know what the other has done as part of this deal, they have enough dirt on each other to destroy the other's career if either one was determined to do so. So, for now, they cooperate under an uneasy truce.

"So, you see Jacob, your only fault, if there was one, was your inability to see the truth about your situation. I think you can only clearly see others when you clearly see yourself."

"So, I'm even more of an idiot than I realized."

"No, I wouldn't say that. Being naive is not the same as being an idiot. It means you're asleep to the truth. That's quite different from being stupid. We're all stupid when we're *impervious* to the truth."

"Regardless, it still landed me here and left me with these nightmares. So, what should I do, Doc?"

"I'm hoping you'll come to see your incarceration here as a blessing over time. Perhaps even see your transfer here as a rescue by God … err, a rescue by the God you don't believe in. For now, keep journaling. Try to be thankful you escaped from that sociological cesspool, the Ministry of Technology. View your banishment to Coventry as a severe mercy that allows you to have a new start."

CHAPTER 12
THE LAZY RIVER

AFTER SUPPER, ZEKE AND HANNA MET WITH JACOB IN THE COMMON AREA. Almost everyone was out somewhere.

"I saw you had a visitor today," said Zeke.

Jacob nodded.

"Did he come to see you about the nightmares?" asked Zeke.

"The nightmares Jacob has because of his family tragedy?" asked Hanna.

"That's right" said Jacob. "Geisbrecht is a shrink who's trying to help me. Remember he has me writing in a diary."

"Has it helped?" asked Hanna.

"Too early to say. Funny thing though: I never told Geisbrecht, but the writing brought back memories I'd forgotten. About my grandfather who died well before the car accident.

"There used to be a small, meandering river near our home. My grandfather and I used to fish there. I remember once, when I was maybe eleven or twelve, he reminisced: 'Jacob,' he said, 'when I was your age, my friends and I would take the inner tubes from the tires on our farm equipment ...'

"I remember asking him what an inner tube was.

"He looked a bit sad and explained that in his day, many big tires had a rubber tube inside the tire for inflation. The boys would take those and float on them.

"He told me that when he was about my age, on hot summer days, his older brother sometimes drove him and his friends to that very spot where we were fishing, dropped them off so they could float down river for a couple of miles, then pick them up at the other end and drive them back upriver to do it all over again.

"Then he looked at me and asked if I understood what he was saying. I said that I did, although I was only half listening.

"Then he told me he remembered closing his eyes while lying back on the inner tube, listening to the birds, and smelling freshly cut hay. It seemed to him that when his eyes were closed that he wasn't moving. But when he opened them again, everything was completely different, because of course, he'd drifted on. The scenery'd changed. Standing still was an illusion because he'd closed his eyes.

"He kept asking whether I was really listening to him. I remember wanting to change the subject, but something stopped me, so I just smiled.

"Then he said, 'I'm an old man and life is like that for me. If I close my eyes, I can pretend that life is still the same and not changing. But if I open them, I see that things are changing a lot, and not in a good way. A part of me says that I'm just getting old and making the same complaints all old people make.'

"He looked at me again. I smiled again and then he went back to fishing."

"So that's it?" said Zeke. "That's what you've remembered? What does it mean, do you think?"

Jacob thought for a minute. "That's what I'm trying to figure out."

"My mom was from Sri Lanka," said Hanna. "When I was growing up, she told me that as an outsider, and one of the few immigrants let into Canada at the time, she'd seen many changes. Much as your grandfather had, especially in the city where she later lived. She felt much more at home in the small rural town where she met my dad."

"Maybe," said Hanna, "your grandfather, like my mom, was seeing the changes that brought us to our current situation. That led to the creation of Coventry."

"Maybe, you're right, Hanna. Like the lazy river, when my grandfather closed his eyes, things were changing so slowly, he didn't realize there was change happening at all. But if he looked around, because of his age, he saw things becoming worse and worse."

"Only, no one believed him?" asked Zeke.

"That's right," said Jacob. "Everyone wrote him off thinking he only thought that way because he loved the old days and hated change."

"So," he added, "I feel at home in Coventry because I'm truly coming home. This is the place and these are the people I've been yearning to meet all my life even if I didn't know it."

"You're right, man!" said Zeke. "You are so lucky to have a friend like me." He looked at Hanna scrunching her eyebrows together. "And Hanna too, of course," he added hastily.

Jacob started to laugh. Soon all three of them were laughing. Jacob's side hurt, but he couldn't stop.

CHAPTER 18
THE MYSTERY OF IRON ISLE

"SINCE IT'S SUNDAY MORNING AND EVERYONE'S ON BREAK, WE'RE GOING to do some detective work to find out the secrets of this place," said Hanna.

"Okay," said Zeke, "as long as we don't end up on perpetual dishwashing duty because we poked our noses where they don't belong."

Jacob watched Hanna's face. It showed growing incredulity. "Zeke, you must have some curiosity about this place's secrets. It only makes sense to learn more about where we've landed."

Zeke's eyebrows shot up. Heading off a retort from Zeke, Jacob asked, "So Hanna, where should we start our detective work?"

"Well, we've been in the greenhouses, the heavy equipment repair shop out back, and in the packaging and small equipment repair shop in Level 1. We've never been down to the smelting area on Level 2. I think I remember someone saying that some of the shallower mining tunnels also head off from there."

They walked down the stairs to Level 1 and then found the door to Level 2. It was locked. Hanna went up to the voice recognition microphone and said, "Hanna Heidel."

A pleasant woman's voice answered back, "Miss Heidel, I'm afraid you are not authorized to enter Level 2. Perhaps, Captain Hodgkins has sent you to Level 2 on an errand. Would you like me to get his explicit permission?"

"No, thank you," said Hanna. She waved to the others to accompany her. When they were well away from the microphone, she said, "Well, the mystery deepens. What are they hiding in the smelting area that they don't want us to see?"

"So, what's next?" asked Jacob. He had to admit the locked door had piqued his interest.

"I think we should take a hike to the end of Iron Isle and try to find the cables coming from the hidden hydroelectric generating station they built around Vulture Falls.

"It's a relatively warm day and I figure it's about ten miles to the point on the island closest to Vulture Falls. Since we're in good condition, with sunshine and no wind, we should be able to snowshoe to the end of the island in less than four hours. If we leave now, we should get back before curfew."

They went back to their dorm rooms to get their rucksacks. Jacob packed his binoculars. The three friends checked out three pairs of snowshoes from the gym on the main floor and then left by the main front gate. No one asked where they were going. Walking around the main building, they found a well-plowed road—from the heavy equipment and storage garage at the back of the complex—that headed in the general direction they were going.

After about a mile, they saw the huge hill off to their right and a branch of the plowed road going in that direction. Hodgkins had told them that originally a processing plant had been built above ground, and that the small artificial mountain was the residue from its metal production. When Coventry was first established, the colony's inhabitants had used the original factory. However, because of the risk of incursion, they had gradually moved the operations underground and repurposed the old factory materials. All that remained was a large building foundation next to the mountain.

At Hanna's insistence, they continued straight on. Soon, the road ended at a large clearing. When Jacob saw where they were, it made him stop short. There were row upon row of wooden crosses with names on them. There were thousands of crosses, like in the photos of military cemeteries he had seen. Snowshoe tracks showed where visitors had come to visit graves. Even now, in the distance, Jacob could see a handful of people visiting what he assumed were graves of loved ones.

"You know, I've got to come back here and look for my grandpa and uncle," said Zeke, his voice choking. Hanna put a hand on his arm.

"It would take forever to search all these crosses," said Jacob. "I bet we could search the list of names in the library, and if they're here, we could find their location."

"Yeah, you're right. I guess we'd better keep going. Seeing all these crosses is shocking. It brings home what they mean by the 'Years of Tears.'"

Jacob looked at the sun and pointed in the direction they ought to head. The road had ended and they walked through a light coniferous forest with huge but widely spaced trees. Rocks scoured of snow, protruded, reminding Jacob of almonds in white chocolate. The snowshoeing was much more difficult than before.

Three hours later, the trees ahead ended, and they looked at a snow-covered Vulture Lake. They hadn't quite reached the point closest to Vulture Falls so they walked on the ice just off shore toward the promontory at the end of the island.

Jacob, who was leading, suddenly veered toward the shore and waved to the others to take cover. Pulling out his binoculars, he studied the end of the island.

"What is it?" asked Hanna.

"I saw two men on the ice," said Jacob. "They were out about fifty meters from shore with their backs to us."

Jacob handed his binoculars to Hanna. Zeke pulled out his own pair.

Jacob continued. "It looks as if a lot of ice has piled around the promontory and they're studying the ice formation."

"I'd guess," said Zeke, "that they're worried the ice pile-up might damage the cables from the hydro plant. I don't see any cables coming out of the water. It makes sense. If the powers-that-be at Coventry want to keep the power plant secret from the guards, the appearance of cables would be a dead giveaway. The power cables must enter the island rock under water."

"Let's watch where they go," whispered Hanna.

"They're dressed in white and blend in well with the snow," said Jacob. "I only saw them because one of them has red hair. We can't really hide very well in our regular issue clothes. We'd better stay put."

"They're walking back now. We'll see their tracks and know where they went," said Zeke, still watching through his binoculars."

After ten minutes, the three walked through the bush toward the promontory. Seeing the tracks the men had made, they followed them into the woods. The tracks ended at what looked like a large grey rock. From the pattern in the snow, it had clearly been lifted.

"They're working pretty hard to keep things secret, if they disguise doors as rocks. We may as well head back," said Hanna.

"They're going to know someone's been here," said Zeke. "We can't disguise our tracks. We'll have to hope it snows again before anyone else comes out this door."

Finding their way home was easy. They only had to follow their own tracks. Even after the sun went down, there was enough moonlight on the white snow to find their way. Jacob found it eerie and quiet. They heard the distant howl of a wolf. The shadows were stark, and the rocks and fallen trees made Jacob think of large, dangerous animals, until his nerves were taut. Finally, they reached the graveyard and the road, and Jacob's heart felt lighter since they were almost home. Hanna had kept looking back over her shoulder ever since they'd heard the wolf howl. When she saw the greenhouses, she laughed in relief.

Back in the common room, they saw Captain Hodgkins reading a book. Everyone else seemed to have gone to bed already.

He looked up and smiled. "I heard you tried to have a look at the smelting and separation operation. Things are pretty quiet down there on a Sunday although we never idle the furnaces. If you'd let Martha ask, I would've been happy to give you permission."

"Martha?" asked Jacob.

"Martha's the name of the computer voice that handles all of our verbal interactions with our networked computer processors."

"An artificial intelligence program?" asked Hanna.

"You might call her that, but I don't think she has any real intelligence. At the end of the day, she simply does what's been programmed into her, or should I say, 'it.' Still, the programmers work pretty hard to fool you into thinking she's intelligent and that there's a person at the other end of the communication unit."

Hodgkins waited a few seconds, but when no one said anything else, he went back to reading his book. Jacob had the distinct impression the Captain knew about their trip to the end of the island, and was hoping they would volunteer information about it.

CHAPTER 14
A BAD TIME TO BE LOST

THREE MORE WEEKS PASSED, WITH F COMPANY TAKING ON DIFFERENT jobs each week. One week they were ice fishing, cutting holes into the frozen surface of Vulture Lake away from the treacherous area around the causeway. Another week they were clearing brush on the northeast side of Iron Isle for some additional greenhouses and indoor fish ponds. In the third week they were taken to the smelting operation on Level 2. Here they observed furnaces, converters, and froth flotation cells, all in operation. Engineers explained most of the devices, but the information came so quickly that Jacob could not really think through it well enough to understand what was going on with these processes.

They also saw that there were a number of doors that indicated entrances to the mine shafts; these were protected by Martha.

On the Sunday beginning the fourth week, Hanna insisted they head out on another expedition. It was a bright, sunny day, the ice was beginning to break up, and the open water extended further around Iron Isle than it had a month ago. Hanna's idea was to explore the huge hill made up of tailings and processing residue from the earliest days of the mining on Iron Isle, which everyone called "The Mountain." She thought there might be outside entrances to the mine shafts that weren't protected by Martha. Since gangue was still being moved to the tailings hill, the road was well maintained, but it had no traffic on a Sunday. The tailings hill was a broad, high mound on the east side of Iron Isle, not far from the mining building. On the outside, there was a switchback road up the west face to the flat top that had been used at one point by trucks dumping tailings down the east side of the hill. The hike to the top was strenuous, but once they reached it, they had a spectacular view of the whole of Iron Isle.

"What's going on over there?" Zeke pointed to the guard compound on the other side of the causeway.

Jacob shaded his eyes to look. "I wish I'd brought my binoculars. It looks like there are many vehicles there. I think I even see several helicopters."

As if in confirmation, they heard a helicopter arrive, flying into the compound just above the tree tops.

One section of the tailings hill had been chewed away. "I think this is where they're collecting the old tailings for processing to separate the rare-earths," said Zeke.

They had seen several entrances into the hill from the switchback road. Hanna seemed fixated on exploring under the hill, unconcerned about the unusual activity at the guard compound.

Jacob looked at her. Chewing her lip, she said, "Now that we've explored the outside, I want to see if we can find an access tunnel to the mine that bypasses Martha. I think our best bet is to go back down and use the lowest entrance shaft to get into the mine."

With determination in her step, Hanna headed down the switchback to the base of the hill. A short distance away, a road led to a ramp that descended into the mine. As they made their way down the ramp, it quickly grew dark.

"Well, that's it," said Zeke. "We can't go on since they switched the lights off."

Hanna pulled a flashlight from her pack, as if she had expected this. She switched it on, and led the way down the ramp. Jacob saw that she threw Zeke a look that said "Men!" as she walked down the mine ramp with a determined step.

"I expect she thinks you're not showing enough enthusiasm for our exploration," whispered Jacob.

"Well, it's Sunday, ain't it? I could be home relaxing instead of being out here earning a lifetime of latrine duty."

Zeke looked up and continued. "Let's catch up and stick together. I don't want to lose Hanna and have her fall into some hole." They hurried after her.

Hanna followed the road down a gentle slope. It had shafts branching off at regular intervals. She continued down. Finally, the road ended in a cavern that had much smaller shafts branching out radially. Hanna chose one directly across from the cavern road entrance. After a few short steps, the shaft ended at a natural cave system. Although the Canadian Shield was mostly granite, this pocket was made of limestone. The limestone had been extensively eroded by water. Stalactites hung from the roof of the chamber and the torch light reflected off the glistening, mineralized projections. There was an even larger chamber beyond, with a huge stalactite forming a column in the room. The columns sparkled in the torch light. Minerals in the water produced beautiful reds.

Hanna sighed and turned. "This is so beautiful. Still, if we go back and try another passage, we might learn more about the mine."

Retracing their steps, they expected to see the mine shaft appear at any moment. After twenty minutes, Hanna turned to the others, her face pale in the torch light. "I've never seen this chamber before. I'm, I'm hopelessly lost." She sat down and put her face in her hands.

"Let's not panic," said Jacob. "The worst that could happen: we might have to spend the night here. Tomorrow the workers will hear our shouts."

"We don't even know if they visit this particular cavern every day," said Hanna.

"Let's try to find our way out systematically. Imagine you were back home in your house," said Jacob, "and were blind or there was absolutely no light. How could you find your way out? If you picked a wall and put your hand on it and kept touching that wall as you followed wherever it led, then even though it may take you through many rooms, if it's an outside wall, you'll eventually reach one of the doors out of your house."

"What if it's not an outside wall?" asked Zeke.

"Well, my home in Leslieville had an interior wall that made a closed loop near the kitchen. If I'd the misfortune to pick that wall, then I'd eventually complete a circuit and end up where I had started—back in the kitchen. The same applies here. If we pick the wrong wall and return to our starting point, we should've chosen the wall across the passage."

"Your house is small, and you could complete your search in minutes," said Hanna. "This cave system could be huge. Your solution would work, but it might take years to complete."

"True, it's not perfect, but it's a plan. If you have a better idea, let's do that," said Jacob.

"No, searching is better than sitting."

"If we mark our starting point and decide we don't want to continue our search any further, we can always reverse direction and come back here."

"I agree with Hanna. I'd rather do something and keep walking than sit here and freeze," said Zeke.

"Okay, let's guess this is the outside wall. We pile three rocks on top of each other next to the wall so we'll know if we complete the loop."

They started out. In every new chamber they encountered, they placed two stones on top of one another. It took so long that on two occasions they debated whether to go back. Finally, hours later, they saw what they thought was the huge pillar they had seen earlier. A short time later they were relieved to find the shaft entrance.

Hurrying out of the mine, they came into the night. "What time is it?" asked Hanna.

Jacob looked at his watch. "Two a.m.," he answered. A helicopter lifting off a short distance away, droned. But it flew without lights.

"What's going on?" whispered Hanna.

CHAPTER 15
DEADLY HIDE-AND-SEEK

"I'M NOT SURE WHAT'S GOING ON," SAID JACOB, "BUT SINCE COVENTRY doesn't have any helicopters, it can't be good."

Branches snapped. Zeke brought them to ground by the side of the road.

About a dozen soldiers wearing night vision goggles came into view. Their rifles on ready, they trotted toward the mine building. Luckily, the three friends were not seen.

"Do you think they might be searching for us?" whispered Hanna.

"I'm not sure, but I don' think so," said Jacob.

With Jacob in the lead, they quietly and cautiously picked their way back to the compound, listening for any sound. Soon, they heard a loud rat-tat-tat that sounded like gunfire. After their agonizingly slow creep along the road, the greenhouses came into view. Jacob signaled his friends to stop. He crawled forward to the corner of the greenhouse and then crawled back.

"I think they have our compound surrounded," whispered Jacob. "I saw flashes of gunfire around the side of the building. No hope going for the main entrance."

They continued to hear sporadic gunfire with the occasional boom of much heavier ordinance.

"What are we going to do?" whispered Zeke.

"We could give ourselves up until this blows over," said Hanna.

"No way," said Zeke, "I like where I am. What if they ship us out somewhere else?"

"I think I know of a way in," said Jacob. "If they catch us, I doubt they'll treat us differently than if we'd surrendered."

Jacob led them into the central greenhouse. The lights were off, but Jacob could smell cabbage and heard the quiet gurgle of the water in the central stream. They felt their way along the warm water canal, moving from one greenhouse unit to the next, until they reached the end of the last greenhouse, right next to the mining building.

Jacob tried a heavy door. Locked.

"Now what do we do?" asked Zeke.

Jacob thought a moment. "There's a reservoir in a large room behind this door, fed by the pumps that bring up water from the depths. There's an emergency exit inside to the main foyer of the mining building.

"We're right up against the back wall of the compound. There's an underwater tunnel that connects each of the greenhouse canals to the reservoir that collects the hot water pumped up from the depths. I'm pretty sure the central tunnel is the shortest. I'm hoping if I swim through the tunnel, I can open the locked door from the inside."

"Pretty sure?" sputtered Zeke.

"If I don't come back, go to plan B." Jacob took off his heavy coat and boots, and climbed into the water. It was quite warm, a few degrees above body temperature. The current in the central canal was almost imperceptible. He began to swim. A pale light shone in the distance. He swam at a steady pace but thought about turning back. He was just about to do so when the tunnel walls disappeared, and he found himself in a pool, with light shining above him.

Breaking the surface of the reservoir pool, he breathed hard. In the far corner he saw a disturbance in the water caused by the water coming out of the pump like a small fountain. He swam to the edge of the pool and climbed out dripping.

Maybe it would have been smarter to strip down.

He was just on his way to try to unlock the door, when Hanna's head broke the surface of the pool, followed immediately by Zeke. He helped pull his two friends out of the water.

"We heard voices in the greenhouse and thought we'd better take a chance and follow you," said Hanna.

The reservoir was on the main floor and Jacob opened the emergency door to the main building a crack. He heard a shout through the door, "They've sealed the stairs to the lower levels with some kind of blast door."

"Then blast the damn thing open! Get on it now. Bring in the twenty millimeter with armor-piercing shells and blow a hole in it."

"Sir, there's someone in the room at the end of the hall. I saw the door open."

"Get them now. Try not to shoot them. I want intel."

"Can I at least wing 'em Sarg?"

"Knock yerself out. Just bring me back some intel about the place."

Jacob shut the door and heard it lock.

"We're trapped." said Zeke.

"Maybe not, I worked in here remember?" said Jacob as he led them to the end of the room by the pump. He stopped at a corrugated metal plate flush with the floor. Placing his fingers in a slot at one end, he pulled up on a hinged metal trapdoor. Inside was a vertical tunnel with large, gleaming stainless-steel pipes and an access ladder that led into the depths. Hanna, then Zeke climbed down the ladder. Closing the trap door behind him, Jacob followed. A pump hummed quietly. In the dim light, Jacob could see the floor about ten meters below them. At the bottom was a second door, but it was locked with a push bar and a sign "ALARM WILL SOUND."

"This is an emergency door, it should be open," said Jacob. Jacob tried it but it was locked from the other side

"We're trapped," said Zeke.

Jacob heard voices upstairs. "Where are they?"

"Search everywhere. I want prisoners!"

Jacob looked around franticly. There was a rack of wrenches beside the pump. Grabbing a large hex wrench, bent at a right angle, he made his way the ladder. The bottom of the trapdoor had a handle. Jacob worked the wrench through the handle, took off his sweater, and wedged the wrench in place with the soggy garment.

Just then someone tried to lift the trap door. The wrench jammed into the frame.

"It's jammed," said a voice.

"Open up down there or we'll pepper you!"

Zeke began pounding on the downstairs door with a second wrench, calling for help.

Jacob half-climbed, half-slid down the ladder as the trap door was raised a few centimeters and a rifle muzzle was thrust through the gap.

The three friends ducked into the corner as bullets ricocheted around the room. Some bullets hit the metal piping but didn't pierce it. Just then, the bottom door opened. Captain Hodgkins appeared, pulled them through the door, and then closed it again.

"I was wondering if my three intrepid snoops would get back in after the attack began," said Hodgkins. He looked at the three of them, bedraggled, making puddles of water on the floor. "Follow me. There's very little time left before we seal this level up. They're going to blow through the upper blast doors at any moment."

He led them down another floor and along a side corridor to a series of tubes, which were open, like the tubes on a water slide.

A man in uniform was in charge. "Use the first tube Hodgkins. I'll evacuate the last of my men using the other tubes, then we'll seal all the tubes up."

"Zeke you go first," said Hodgkins.

"I thought it was supposed to be 'ladies first'," said Zeke.

"It is," said Hodgkins. "That's why I'm sending you."

Zeke smiled, said "Here goes nothin'," and jumped into the tube. Hanna went next. Finally, Jacob, holding a convenient handle above the tube, slid in feet-first, crossed his arms on his chest and lay back. He descended at an alarming pace, as if he were in a steep water slide. The tube was coated with a substance that provided almost no friction. After about twenty seconds, which seemed a very long time, the tube became horizontal and he slowed. The top half of the tube dropped away and the friction increased until he was able to step out of the tube and join his friends. Hodgkins arrived shortly after Jacob.

Hodgkins told them to follow him. He led them to a cavernous hangar-like structure, large enough to hold everyone from the top levels. All of F Company was assembled to one side, partitioned from the other companies. Jacob, Zeke, and Hanna sat at the back of their company, miserable in their wet clothes.

Hodgkins cleared his throat to get their attention. "The upper levels of Coventry Penal Colony have just been attacked by government forces. At least two dozen 'inmates'—who we believe were plants by the security forces—disabled elevators, blocked stairwells and generally disrupted our movements.

We weren't sure how violent this takeover would be. Because of probable casualties, the decision was made to move you to the lower levels of Coventry.

"The forces taking over the prison know we've barricaded ourselves into the lower levels. However, the Coventry Penal Colony is much bigger and has many more levels than has been revealed to you. We don't think that the security forces have any idea of how deep our levels go. You won't be told how big our facility is now. You'll be given a chance to join us. If you choose not to, we'll give you safe passage to elsewhere in Canada or even to contacts we have in the United States. They'll help you seek refugee status there if you so choose.

"If you decide to stay, that will be an irrevocable decision since we have secrets which, for our own collective safety, must be kept from the authorities."

Jacob could see that Dennison, but not Rousseau or Litch had evacuated with them. Dennison was giving Hodgkins his full attention.

Hodgkins continued. "You'll be given temporary quarters and I will await your decisions no later than tomorrow at noon. Indecision or no decision on your part will be taken as a choice to return to the surface. Until then, I ask you not to imperil the generosity we've shown toward you by trying to discover our secrets." Here he looked at Jacob, Zeke, and Hanna.

"If you stay, you'll become full citizens of our community with all the rights and privileges that entails."

Hodgkins continued. "We're preparing a room with cots to get you some sleep. Tomorrow we'll interview you individually and help you determine what makes the most sense for you. Your questions will be answered as fully as we are able during the interview. Dismissed."

Jacob was about to leave with the others when Hodgkins called. "Jacob, I owe you some thanks. Your heads-up on Rousseau and Litch proved critical. They led the way to enable the incursion forces to get into our building quickly. If we hadn't been watching them and if Dennison hadn't warned us what they were doing, I think all of us on Level 2 would have been captured. As it was, we had enough time to block off Level 2."

"So Rousseau and Litch are gone?"

"Yes."

"And Dennison?"

"He wanted to get away from Rousseau's influence, and as I said, he helped us significantly. He couldn't go back after informing on them and didn't want to."

Jacob joined the others. Their sleeping quarters were in a large gym, which had been partitioned in half with a moveable, fabric wall. Jacob and Zeke were assigned cots next to each other near a partition door.

Hanna, who had gone to the women's quarters, returned. She had changed. Jacob saw a neatly-folded set of fresh clothes and shoes on the end of his cot.

"So, what's going on?" asked Hanna sitting on the side of Jacob's cot.

Zeke sat down opposite Hanna, realized his clothes were still damp and hastily got to his feet. "From speaking to Hodgkins and some of the senior cadets," said Jacob, "I think that the prison security forces have taken over the top two levels of the prison in one of what sounds like one of their periodic attempts to reassert their dominance and control over the prison population."

"So, what happens next do you think?" asked Zeke.

"I think the plan is to barricade ourselves in the lower levels, wait them out, and then negotiate a return to the status quo. After all, we make them a lot of money, do everything they want, offer them no opposition, and generally make ourselves the most well-behaved prison population the security guards will ever have to manage. Why wouldn't they want to return to that situation?"

"I suppose that makes sense," said Zeke. "What are you going to do about the interview?"

"I plan on staying," said Jacob. "I was expecting to land in hell-on-earth and found something much better—with you guys, it feels as if I have part of my family back. I was even treated better by the prison old timers than by my co-workers in Toronto. If I did get out, I'd be on the run hiding from my old boss, Connaught. If he ever found out I was loose, he'd be out to frame me for something again. I have no future there."

"I think the same," said Zeke. "Whoever sent me here in the first place would still be searching for me."

"Then it's unanimous," said Hanna. "We're staying."

CHAPTER 16
TO GO OR TO STAY?

The next morning, they were called to be interviewed in alphabetical order. Hanna went first. Jacob had not yet seen her return when he was called. He entered a room with a long table and an empty chair facing the table. Hodgkins, another man, and a woman approximately Hodgkins' age were sitting on the other side. They were each studying documents as Jacob came in. The woman had a prosthetic hand extending from the end of her sleeve.

Hodgkins waved Jacob to the empty chair. "Hello Jacob, this is Brigadier General Suzanne Penner and Professor Martin Friesen of our training college. We're here to help you make a decision about where you ought to go next."

Hodgkins continued. "You were brought down here without your agreement or permission. You likely have a lot of questions. Why don't we answer them first?"

"Sir, what actually happened upstairs?"

"Well," said Hodgkins, "what I had indicated to you when we last talked about Rousseau's suspicious behavior has transpired. The security forces, not content with simply dictating their wishes to us from outside, have once again attempted to take over our penal colony, much as they would a regular prison. This has happened many times before. We don't want any bloodshed. But we also don't want to subject our people, almost all of whom were born here and were never incarcerated by the government in the first place, to the predations of the security forces.

"We had a bit of intelligence that they were building up forces for the invasion at the warden's compound so we made our plans days ago. Sometimes they build up and then don't attack. Other times the attack comes weeks after the initial buildup.

"In this case, thanks to a key informant, we had about twenty-five minutes warning before the actual attack began. As soon as we knew it was imminent, we evacuated as many as we could to the lower levels.

"Since you were out of the building when the evacuation began, we weren't able to give you the same warning as the others.

"The invaders captured about two dozen of our rear guard who were searching for stragglers. These captives will negotiate on our behalf. We'll tell them what we've told them when this has happened before: almost all of our people were born in captivity. This is now their home. They want to stay. They definitely don't want to rejoin Canadian society. We pose no threat to Canada, and wish nothing more than a return to the status quo, where we work for power and food from Canada while running our own affairs peacefully.

"If this plays out as it has previously, they'll try to starve us out. They don't know how to operate any of the equipment upstairs. The plumbing and heating have been shut off. We deliberately designed the controls for the mine shaft ventilation to be beyond their easy reach. They'll be very uncomfortable living in a cold building with no lights. If everything goes to plan, after a few months at most, they'll agree to our terms and retreat across the causeway. We'll take over the upper levels again and, after a cleanup, we'll resume shipments."

"I understand that there's a lot of money in rare-earth metals, but a military operation like this must cost them even more. Why do they even care about taking over the means of rare-earth production?" Jacob asked.

"I don't think they do care especially. Having us work for power, medicine, and food is one way of exercising control over us 'Cretins' as they call us. What they do care about is keeping us under control. The protest of 2051 still frightens our government. We represent an unknown to them. That adds to their concern."

Hodgkins looked at Penner questioningly. She gave a slight nod. Hodgkins continued. "Since you reported Rousseau, I ... we think you ought to hear this. We would appreciate it if you kept this to yourself."

Jacob nodded.

"We think there's now more behind this than just the Canadian government. All major countries have intelligence and security forces that share intelligence. We think this informal arrangement over the last dozen years or so has transmogrified into something much more substantial. In other words, although Rousseau is part of the Canadian intelligence establishment, he's taking orders from an international group that's identified Coventry as a special enemy of note. That's partly why we suspect and fear this may not just be a temporary takeover as usual."

General Penner added, "Since you are new here Kraiser, and Rousseau was part of your company, we thought we owed it to you to tell you, because it may influence your decision whether or not to stay."

"Wow!" said Jacob. "An international conspiracy. How did you find out about it?"

"We can't tell you any more than we already have," said Hodgkins. "Let's leave it there. Do you have any other questions?"

Jacob thought for a moment, trying to remember the questions he had prepared. "So, how big is this place? How deep do the levels go?"

"We won't tell you that until you become a citizen of Coventry. Even then, there are few people who know the full extent of our delving. We offer no threat to Canada; indeed we still consider ourselves citizens of both Coventry and Canada, but we don't trust contemporary Canada much. The average Canadian doesn't recognize how much Canada has changed over the past hundred years, because the changes happened incrementally and slowly. We've been isolated here, and from our perspective, we think Canada's changed so much for the worse that we're better off if the powers that have marginalized us know as little about us as possible. We mean them no harm, but we've no illusions about how aggressive they might become if they knew more about us."

"You've raised more questions than you've answered," said Jacob. "Thanks for telling me more about the attack. So, what happens next?"

"Well, Jacob, here is the choice before you: this decision has come much quicker than we would've liked. We usually allow about two years of time upstairs before we offer citizenship in Coventry.

"If you decide to join us, you have to pledge to keep our secret. We'll then tell you many things about us you currently don't know: our achievements, our history, and our plans for the future. We'll expect you to honor your pledge to us, even if you decide you can't stand life underground. If it came to that we'd move you out of Coventry and find you a place somewhere else, but still expect you to honor your pledge."

"I would be in a sort of witness protection program?"

"I suppose that's a good metaphor. Our surface operatives would stay in contact with you and warn you if your identity were compromised. It almost never happens. The government cares so little about the rural areas.

"If you do join us, you'll be enrolled in Klemhofer College, headed by Professor Friesen." Professor Friesen nodded in acknowledgement. "You'll find our education here quite different, and hopefully much more uplifting than what you experienced on the surface. You'll work for your tuition, room, and board. You'll learn skills which will enable you to become a productive and free citizen of Coventry. Because of our history, we are at core a collection of faith communities; we'll not force you to join one of them (although we hope you would). But we do ask you to respect our history and our faith traditions."

"I've been thinking about this question since yesterday. I want to become a citizen of Coventry."

General Penner spoke for the second time. Jacob looked at her more intently than he had before. She was a woman in her fifties with close cropped gold-blond hair with a touch of grey. "You understand you will likely not be able to see or perhaps even contact your family and friends again. Have you thought about that?"

Captain Hodgkins looked uncomfortable. Jacob said, "If you knew my history, you would realize this decision is an easy one, General. Really, it's the only decision for me to make. I grew up in a small town in Alberta. We were a close-knit rural family and pretty independent. Then everything changed in an instant. My whole family—brothers, sisters, and parents—was killed in a car accident. I was an orphan in shock, too young and alone to manage the farm. The accident caused another change: it changed my Victimization Index. Do you know about those?"

General Penner looked sober. "I'm sorry. I should have known about your loss." She cleared her throat. "Yes, I know about Victimization Indices."

"Well, because of the trauma of the accident, I went from an index of zero, which is as low as you can get, to three. That entitled me to free education, job training, and a well-paying job in Toronto. So, I moved to Toronto."

Jacob knew he was rambling on, but he spoke as if it had to come out. He was surprised that all three seemed to be listening intently.

He gulped and continued. "The culture was so different in Toronto from Leslieville. It was bewildering and alien to me. It was as if everyone was lying to me and deceiving me all the time. Everyone had an angle. Nothing was ever what it seemed. After my brief schooling, it all came to a head.

"I'm doing my job in Toronto and one thing after another went wrong. I could never reconcile what people were telling me with what happened to me.

"The next thing I knew, I was facing a string of fines on traffic violations I never even knew I was committing, I was accused of stealing government equipment and embezzling money from my operation. A woman in my department who'd asked me for help with a transfer she didn't want, turned around and accused me of behaving inappropriately. Finally, I was accused of being a 'Cretin' even though I had no religion, and so I was shipped to Coventry. All my bridges have been burned. I have no family to miss, no friends to go back to, and no future in Canada, now that I've been designated as a subversive. I don't see that I have a future outside."

General Penner spoke again. She seemed too motherly to be a general. "Leslieville is a quiet place and the people would know you well. It's out of the government eye, and we have strong connections with rural communities. You've earned some money here. We could set you up with your family farm. You could hire some help and make a life for yourself. We'd watch you for a while to make sure the government didn't grow suspicious, but I don't think …" Here she looked at the notes in front of her … "Connaught or anyone else cares, as long as you don't show up in Toronto."

"General, my friends are here. From the first day, Coventry never felt like a prison—actually, I realize that living in Toronto, with all of its oppression, was the prison."

Professor Friesen spoke for the first time. "Had you had a chance to learn our history, you would've realized that most of the thirty thousand that were imprisoned here in 2051 belonged to various Christian faith traditions, denominations, if you like. Although we often had theological differences, our survival depended on cooperating for the common good. Still those different communities continue to exist today. You've been told some rather horrific stories about us at school. Aren't you troubled about joining our ranks?"

"Since I came to Toronto, I've come to realize that everyone there talks spin. They don't even believe truth exists. They tell you whatever helps them most. The locals are sophisticated enough not to believe it. I did believe the spin and that was my mistake. I thought people were basically honest without thinking about it. I don't want to go back. I don't fit in. I don't know if I fit in here, but it was so refreshing after I crossed the causeway that people here said what they meant and meant what they said. I truly want to stay."

"If you'll step outside for a few moments, the three of us will need to confer," said Hodgkins.

CHAPTER 17
A BREATH-TAKING RIDE

THE CITIZENSHIP OATH CONSISTED ONLY OF A HANDSHAKE AND REQUIRED JACOB TO verbally affirm that he wished to join the Coventry community, and in good conscience before God, that he would abide by their rules and requirements.

After Jacob and his friends were accepted into citizenship, they were given some money to purchase basic supplies, then were herded with many others to what appeared to be a train station or tube-car station at the north end of the sixth level (Levels 3, 4, and 5 had been taken over by the Coventry Defense Forces as a buffer zone, ready to be isolated and shut down if the attackers pressed to lower levels).

One of the platforms had "Klemhofer College" marked as its destination. Entering the large train-like vehicle with his two friends and about one hundred other people, all carrying gear, Jacob figured everyone else had also been accepted for citizenship. Storing his dunnage in sealed overhead bins, he strapped himself into a chair on gimbals. The doors closed and the tube-car began to accelerate horizontally, quickly enough to push Jacob firmly into his seat cushion. He felt his chair tilt as the tube-car turned more steeply downward until they were dropping at an alarming rate. He was about one third of the way up the train car and it felt like he was hanging in a seat on an amusement ride. His stomach felt queasy as he became nearly weightless. A rock-lined tunnel flashed by at breathtaking speed. After a few seconds of the steep descent, they began to decelerate and level out. What followed was another twenty minutes of horizontal travel that felt like being on a train. Brightly lit caverns flashed by as the train hummed through them. Some were farms, others villages, one was a large lake with fishing boats on it as the train skirted the cavern wall. *Where do they get all the power for the lights? Where does all this sophisticated technology come from?* He wondered.

The doors opened onto a covered platform with a sign that read "Welcome to Klemhofer College." From the platform, a lawn extended to a small lake with a fountain at the near end. Beyond the lake were pine woods climbing up to the far cavern wall. In wonder from the trip and the vista before them, Jacob, Hanna, and Zeke stepped off the platform and looked up at the smoothly-arched roof. It was a continuous expanse of white light approximately the intensity and color of sunlight.

"Did you see what I saw on the train ride?" asked Jacob. "There are only maybe thirty thousand people working for forty years. How did they carve out those caverns? How did they manufacture all those lights?"

"Where did they get the technology?" asked Hanna. "This doesn't seem like a penal colony."

"You don't seem as surprised as we do, Zeke," said Jacob.

"Well," said Zeke, "I suspect many of those caverns were discovered by Iron Isle Mining while they cut their extensive shafts. Coventry repurposed them and made them livable with their technology. They now have virtually limitless energy and robots that can carve rock twenty-four hours a day. It's surprising but not beyond the realm of possibility if you think how motivated they were to work hard after the Years of Tears."

Zeke thought for a moment and stoked his chin. "Oh, I'm flabbergasted, but I guess there was a part of me that suspected something like this. On our farm, power was always an issue, especially as the government became less and less able to provide it for rural customers. When the outages became too frequent, we contracted a company, Rural Heat Pump Systems, to build us a heat pump system to make us independent of the grid. We're still hooked up, but the installed heat pump system worked a little bit too well. My father is a smart man and he realized Rural Heat Pump Systems was owned by Coventry, through an American holding company. He never asked any questions, but figured there was more to this power system than met the eye. They buried some components underground as part of the installation process. Now, that

I've seen this, I'm willing to bet there's some device down there that augments what we recover from the heat pump."

Most others who had been on the train were also standing around looking at the wonders of the place, and talking about the extraordinary ride. A man in a jacket and bowler hat moved among the gawking newcomers and urged them to move to the College.

Everyone else had already begun to move toward the buildings when the man approached the three friends.

"Please move along to the College buildings. We need to find you accommodations. We have several more trainloads arriving today."

There was a paved road that ran across the lawn to what appeared to be a series of buildings, or perhaps it was just one building with many wings, corners, arches, and alcoves. The building, with its wings and extensions, looked ordinary in the sense that it had a roof, windows, and doors.

"Maybe in addition to light from the cavern roof, they also have something that approximates rain," said Hanna as they walked on.

When they reached the building, Jacob asked the man chaperoning them, "How is this possible?" gesturing to the lights, the plants, and the lake.

"Later," said the chaperone. "We're evacuating the upper levels and I have to get you settled now. The rapidity of your induction into Coventry society means there will be many surprises awaiting you." The chaperone marched them off through a side door. They joined a queue and talked about how they might contrive to stay connected.

Eventually Jacob was led to a table. The advisor at the table asked Jacob a series of questions about his interests and the type of work he would like to do. After some discussion, Jacob selected "Natural Sciences" as his faculty.

"We know this is a rush. You can change your selection later, if you really feel out of place."

Following the chaperone's directions, Jacob, Zeke, and Hanna arrived at a common room labeled "Natural Sciences Faculty." Together with the rest of the recent inductees who had chosen the same faculty, they were greeted by Professor Daniel Whitefeather. The arrangement of the faculty room was similar to the F Company facilities. The common room was larger, with many more alcoves and sitting areas. There was also a door for married quarters, in addition to men's and women's dormitories. Jacob and Zeke went to the men's dormitory and found neighboring rooms, just as they had before.

"At least, it looks like we don't have to put up with the three stooges, since they sabotaged the first floor." said Zeke.

"That should make life a bit more pleasant, although we might see Dennison again. Apparently he had a change of heart and ditched Rousseau at the end," said Jacob.

Supper was held in a common cafeteria. After that Professor Whitefeather gave each of the new arrivals in the Natural Sciences Faculty a temporary timetable for the following week.

Jacob's time was taken up with test after test. Some tests were written, others required problem solving, many puzzles he was asked to solve made no sense to him at all.

The next week, in the middle of yet another written examination, the building started to shake. It felt like a minor earthquake. Everyone stopped what they were doing and looked around. The proctor left the room. Jacob overheard him conferring with someone outside. When he returned, he was white-faced, as if he had just heard about a death in the family.

That afternoon Jacob met with Daniel Whitefeather, his newly assigned faculty advisor. As soon as Jacob sat down, Whitefeather took off his glasses and rubbed his eyes. "Before we begin talking about your aptitude tests," said Whitefeather, "I need to tell you about a development that occurred this afternoon. In the weeks since we evacuated you, our defense forces have been holding Levels 3, 4, and 5 from the Canadian Forces that had been brought in to take over Coventry Penal Colony. We had long anticipated this incursion and had effectively sealed the levels off to prevent as much loss of life as possible; both theirs and ours. They tried blowing holes into the third level, but each time, we simply sealed them off.

"With their repeated failures, they began broadcasting a broadband message warning us that continued resistance would mean they would purposely and permanently seal us in. This warning was wholly new. In all previous attempts to take over Coventry, they'd never made such a threat since they have a strong interest in maintaining rare-earth metal production. Clearly, this attitude has changed."

Jacob said to himself, *Rousseau and the international intelligence cabal!*

"However, this afternoon they carried out their threat and set off a massive explosion that effectively shattered Level 3, sealing off our access to Iron Isle. Level 4 was also damaged and is no longer considered structurally safe."

Jacob felt panic rising. *We're trapped. We're buried alive.*

Eyeing the expression on Jacob's face, Whitefeather raised his hand in admonition. "No! No! Don't jump to any unwarranted conclusions. We're not trapped. We don't actually depend on the Penal Colony for water, power, or anything else. This has all been a ruse and subterfuge for twenty-five years now. We are self-sufficient, as you probably surmised from your train ride. Our underground holdings are much more extensive than anyone in government believes, and we have many exits to the surface."

Jacob swallowed and tried to regain his equilibrium. "Were many killed in the explosion?"

"None. I can't tell you how—it's classified—but, in addition to the broadcast ultimatum, we learned that the sealing explosion would likely be coming about thirty minutes before they set it off. We evacuated everyone to the lower levels and monitored the event via our robots."

"We have robots?" asked Jacob.

"We have a lot of things that you don't know about, Jacob."

Whitefeather cleared his throat and continued. "The Canadian government will believe they've effectively removed the threat (whatever they conceived that to be) and, on the short term, we think they'll not pursue the matter further. We have contingency plans for the long term that will unfold as part of your studies here. Indeed, you'll learn a great deal as part of your studies, and I think the learning will answer many of your questions. Let's talk about your aptitude tests."

Whitefeather looked through a sheaf of papers. "Well, you certainly are suffering from what our provincial governments pass off as education. You know almost nothing of chemistry, physics, or mathematics even though you appear to have a strong aptitude in those fields. You've read few of the great works that make up English and western literary tradition. Like most in your generation, you have been reading and watching the propaganda that the government passes off as literature as they seek to make you into their version of a model citizen. I can see we have our work cut out for us."

With those remarks, Whitefeather handed Jacob a packed timetable for courses and job assignments, which he explained, would help Jacob pay for his education. When Jacob compared notes with his two friends, it looked as if for the next six months, the three of them could expect to be working harder than ever before. Gone were the essays such as the one Jacob had written for his Chemistry 12 final on "Why are there so few Nobel Laureates in chemistry from the South Sea Islands and what do you propose we do about it?" for eighty percent of his high school chemistry grade. Instead, at Klemhofer, it was all about bonding, orbitals, thermochemistry, chemical kinetics, reaction mechanisms, and structure proofs. Looking up from his timetable, Jacob said, "Back in grade twelve I think I would have rebelled if someone had given me this much real work. Now, although I know it will be a lot of work, I like it because I'm really learning something."

CHAPTER 18
SURPRISES IN HISTORY

I had the privilege of interviewing Drs. Klemhofer and Kinsinger as I prepared my notes for *A History of the Coventry Penal Colony*. They were good friends—each with a thoroughgoing sense of humor. Surprisingly, they did not take themselves too seriously even though everyone at Coventry knew them.

The two friends reminisced about a particularly rancorous meeting held in the Colony just at the time when the new ion space drive had been developed and Torchship Coulsen was making her maiden voyage boosting at 0.66 gravities. Special trees called Travel Oaks, used for transporting people and equipment long distances, continued to function normally even when the ship achieved relatively high velocities mid-voyage. Distance did not seem to make a difference. The kinetic energy of the Coulsen at those relatively high speeds did not seem to disrupt the Travel Oak transfer.

As the meeting progressed, Kinsinger thought a fight was going to break out. The physicists insisted that since energy was not being conserved, some chemist must have made a measurement or calculation error.

The chemists insisted that since the transport was likely quantum mechanical in nature, these kinds of weird effects were unsurprising.

The biochemists smugly pointed out that living organisms are constantly doing seemingly amazing transformations beyond what chemists with flasks and physicists with their instruments and devices can achieve. Therefore, it should be no surprise when one more near miraculous biological effect is added to a long list of biochemical achievements that plants and animals manage to exhibit.

In the end, it turned out energy was conserved in that if the Travel Oaks could not match energy deficits with chemical energy, enough water was exchanged between the sister trees to maintain energy balance.

"Curiously enough, everyone came away feeling vindicated," said Klemhofer, smiling. "The physicists thought, 'Ah ha! We knew the chemists had made a mistake, missing the energy-balancing water transfer.' The chemists felt justified in their belief that the transfer was quantum mechanical in nature. Finally, the biochemists were happy to add one more amazing biochemical process to their catalog, making the achievements of physicists and chemists seem mundane."

Christian Mutembe, *Personal Notes on Klemhofer and Kinsinger.*

IN CONTRAST TO JACOB'S SCHEDULE WITH F COMPANY, WHICH HAD consisted of four workdays and two study days, at the College, Monday and Tuesday were 'earn your pay days' while Wednesday through Saturday were study days. Much as Jacob loved the technical courses, the most interesting course was *A History of the Coventry Penal Colony,* since it was so relevant to his current situation and the many questions he had about Coventry's history and technological development. Edward Mutembe, their teacher on this subject when they had first arrived at Coventry, had been recruited to teach their introductory course at the College. Jacob's favorite day was Saturday, which was a question-and-answer free-for-all when everyone submitted written questions to Mutembe. It was the one day when instead of answering a question with another question, Mutembe would give definitive answers.

What is Coventry's long-term plan? This question was discussed on the first Saturday. The students seemed to think that at some point, with its technological superiority, Coventry would rise up and right the many injustices across the world, everything from the intellectual manipulation in the west to the periodic and devastating Single Nuclear Exchanges, which had for years now, plagued the less-developed world.

"But that's not our plan," said Mutembe. "If we imposed our political system on all those governments you've spoken about, we'd merely be replacing one tyranny with another. We have enough trouble not becoming tyrannical as we govern ourselves during this time of prosperity. It's so much easier, when you're fighting for survival, to keep a clear head about your priorities. When things become easier, it's natural for people to want to meddle in each other's affairs and even their freedoms.

"No, our long-term plan is three-fold. First, we want to maintain our own freedoms by making sure that people who don't want to be here can leave without jeopardizing our continued existence. Second, we want to help those outside who are looking for help by contributing where we can without becoming politically involved. Third, and this may surprise you, like the pilgrims of old, we're looking for a new world where we can live out our faith in peace and without harassment."

That created a buzz in the class. There were several calls for more information.

"First of all," said Mutembe, "it ought to be obvious to you, given what happened with the huge detonation sealing off the third level, that we can't assume that we'll continue as we have over the past twenty-five years."

He crossed his arms and leaned forward, "Indeed it's prudent that we assume that at one point, perhaps in the not-too-distant future, we'll need to conduct a wholesale evacuation, and we'd better have some place to go."

A student at the back put up her hand. "So, we have another underground refuge under construction then?"

"No, that wouldn't be very safe or effective. Any power that could attack us here would be looking for just that kind of a refuge."

Mutembe began to pace in front of the class. "It may not be immediately obvious to you," said Mutembe, "but the very problems we had to solve in order to live underground are exactly those problems that must be solved for very long space flights or for living in hostile environments. We live and grow crops by artificial light. We have to effectively recycle everything, including converting carbon dioxide to oxygen. If you read the history of that ill-fated project called Biosphere 2, you'll realize that the technical problems that have to be solved are not trivial. The sociological problems of people living together in a small space for years are even more challenging."

A rising murmur filled the class. Mutembe raised his hands for silence. "What you probably don't realize, because of the spin to the contrary, western governments have almost completely lost their ability to conduct scientific investigations as they conducted them in the past. Since the rise of postmodernism, when people no longer believe in Truth but view all statements as expressions of power designed to convince or urge others to action, no one even asks if something is true or false but only 'what motivations are they trying to engender?'

"We still believe in Truth and that truth matters and is connected to reality, apart from the language in which it's clothed. Pretty well all of the recent technological underpinnings of the surface society have their origins in Coventry. We interact with the outside world through a series of multinational corporations that we control. For a while before The Big Crunch ruined most economies and most corporations, there were a few companies dabbling in space flight. We acquired their assets over time, including an artificial island off Aruba that was designed as a launch site. Through these multinationals, we continue to launch orbital vehicles to maintain satellites for pretty well everyone around the globe. Without us, most global communication would have shut down. So our companies are indispensable. But we've done much more with our orbital program. In 2072 we launched three, what we call 'torchships', toward Alpha Centauri. These three ships, the Copernicus, the Faraday, and the Aquinas, were outfitted for a very long voyage, were self-contained, and began boosting at 0.66 gravities toward Alpha Centauri. At the halfway point they flipped and begin to decelerate. They were scheduled to arrive in 2087."

"What do you mean 'were'?" asked an overeager student.

"In 2080, when the three ships were near maximum speed, we lost contact with the Faraday, the ship launched by our sister colony, Coventry Baikal, which is established near Lake Baikal in the Central Asian People's Republic. In 2084, we received a short distress call and then radio silence from our other sister colony, Coventry Victoria, near Lake Victoria. We believe they were overrun by the military of the North African Democratic Republic, the NADR. Since all contact with the Aquinas went through Coventry Victoria, we don't know what happened to the Aquinas torchship."

Mutembe eyed the class. He had everyone's attention. "Alpha Centauri is a triple star system. But one of the stars, the red dwarf, which we call Proxima Centauri, is in such a distant orbit from the system barycenter, it has almost no effect on the other two stars, Alpha Centauri A and B. A and B are of comparable size and revolve around a common center of gravity. Both stars have planets that revolve around them."

Mutembe cleared his throat and continued. "We do know that our vessel, the Copernicus, made it to Alpha Centauri A-3 in 2087. After several months of mapping and orbital reconnaissance we realized that we'd discovered an earth-like planet in the habitable zone with a large moon, a strong magnetic field, and water covering about seventy percent of the surface. The atmosphere, about six times the pressure of our own, has enough oxygen to sustain life and about 2000 ppm carbon dioxide. However, the planet is a completely barren rock with no life whatsoever. Not so much as a microbe—that is until we arrived."

Jacob and the rest of the class sat in stunned silence. Finally, Hanna raised her hand.

"Miss Heidel?"

"Sir, you said that the mapping and analysis took place in 2087. Have we landed? Is there a colony there?"

"Yes, Miss Heidel, we landed and established a ground colony, the town of Kinsinger. Although it's completely barren, the planet is so Earth-like that some organisms we released were able to establish themselves right away. For the others, we've worked to build up some soil and begin to establish an ecosystem that can sustain the plants and animals we've come to depend on here on Earth. We've named the planet Canaan."

Mutembe turned on the wall-sized monitor. "Here's what you really want to see." He showed them image after image of a world with two large continents and many smaller islands. Later there were pictures of a green oasis beside a river, next to a small mountain. Pictures taken at the edge of a small town that had been established showed a rocky landscape that looked like a desert.

One picture of the night sky raised questions. "What is that small bright disk? It's so much brighter than a star, but looks too bright for a planet."

"That bright disk is Alpha Centauri B. For observers on Canaan right now, it looks about as bright as our sun looks on Uranus."

When the hour was done, Mutembe shut down the monitor and again turned toward the class. "You haven't asked me the critical question. Can anyone think what it is? Any ideas Mr. Kraiser?"

Jacob looked around and then asked, "If I remember correctly, Alpha Centauri is about three light years away. Even if one had a very powerful transmitter, it would take three years to get a message back to Earth. How did you get these pictures? How can we possibly even think about moving our colony to this new world?"

"All good questions. Before I answer your question, Jacob, let me tell you a little bit about Alpha Centauri. Actually, Alpha Centauri A and B are about 4.37 light years from Earth. Alpha Centauri A is a bit bigger and brighter than our sun. So, the third planet, which we've named Canaan, is a bit further from A than Earth is from Sol. Alpha Centauri B is a bit cooler and smaller than our sun. It orbits a common center of gravity with A in an elliptical orbit that has it roughly at the distance of Saturn at its closest, and at the orbit of Pluto at aphelion. To give you an idea, on Canaan right now, B is about at the orbit of Uranus and so B would appear as our sun would appear at Uranus, except that it's about half as bright, since it's a bit cooler. In short, it doesn't have much of an effect. Canaan orbits A and gets a bit more light from B. It looks like we have a habitable system."

Mutembe raised his hand as Jacob was about to speak again. "So to answer your question about communication, let me begin by saying you are right, Jacob. Transmission of pictures and messages by radio waves would be completely impractical as you correctly pointed out. To tell you how we received these pictures and messages, I have to give you a bit of history that's mostly been covered up. In the first half of the twenty-first century, shortly before the Big Crunch, a university off the coast of North Carolina conducted a force field experiment that moved them to a parallel world. After they came back, much of what they'd experienced was hushed up, but we were able to talk to some of the students who returned after the dislocation. This other world was in some ways not as technologically advanced as ours, but in other ways, particularly in the development of novel organisms, they were far ahead of us. At least, in times past they'd had an ability to use and mold organisms that significantly exceeded our own capabilities, even when our biochemical research was at its height.

"As any botanist or biochemist will tell you, plants and animals are able to do things in chemistry and materials science that to us appear miraculous. Think of amazing navigation feats shown by migrating birds or spawning salmon, echo location by bats, powerful electric discharges in water by electric eels, or the remarkable ability of fish to withstand huge pressure changes.

"It should perhaps not be too surprising that this trip to a parallel world brought us into contact with an amazing plant. This plant, called a Travel Oak, grows as a tree-ring about three to ten meters in diameter. Travel Oaks produce two kinds of fruit. The more frequent is a daughter acorn, which when planted, forms another Travel Oak ring that's linked to the parent. As the returning students from the University of Halcyon reported, if you spend sufficient time in a linked Travel Oak, or place an object inside of it, you are—or it is—transported to the linked ring in about six to eight hours. After we were able to collect a few specimens, which had been smuggled back to our world, we made a remarkable discovery: *this transport mechanism is not limited by the speed of light*. We planted two Travel Oaks on the Copernicus and have been rotating crews to the vessels throughout the flight. It was a bit tricky near the middle of the voyage when the Copernicus was near light speed because of time dilation. Time dilation meant that the relativistic passenger only spent minutes in the Travel Oak while travelers at this end spent hours. But other than that caveat, the transfer is quite straightforward. As long as these plants are alive and linked, you can spend time (overnight is usually most convenient) in our Travel Oak and arrive on the Copernicus orbiting Canaan in eight hours or less. That's how we received reports that would've taken years to reach us, even if we had had a transmitter powerful enough to give us a discernible signal at this enormous distance. Now we have a tree ring at Kinsinger as well, and you can go there after spending one night in the sister Travel Oak in our solar system."

"So, we do have an exit plan," said Hanna softly to herself.

"A *potential* exit plan. What we have so far in Canaan is not sustainable. We have a lot of work to do until we have a community that can survive on its own."

"So, how do I join up?" asked a fellow in the back of the class.

"Well," said Mutembe, "first you have to learn a useful skill by completing your studies here. Then it's simply a matter of signing up for the Space Academy and the Canaan Program, and working with them until you're pronounced ready to ship out."

Another student raised his hand.

"Yes?"

"Professor Mutembe, something bothers me about these plants ..."

"You're not alone, Daniel. A great many of our physicists are very bothered about this factor than light transfer. But I digress. What's your question?"

"When the Copernicus was traveling at a fraction of light speed, wouldn't the bodies transferring out of the Copernicus have enormous kinetic energy? How can the plants make conservation of energy work? Seems impossible."

"Excellent question, Daniel. Travel Oaks use the transfer mechanism to provide food and oxygen to the linked organism when it's stressed, and can do so by using chemical energy to balance the conservation of energy requirements. At relativistic speeds, chemical energy wouldn't be enough. Travel Oaks thrive and operate most efficiently when they're planted near water. It turns out that whenever they effect a transfer that overwhelms the chemistry, energy is always balanced by an amount of water that participates in the transfer, which is exactly equal to the difference in energy balance required between the two locations. In other words, at high speeds, when the kinetic energy difference between the two tree rings is enormous, when a one hundred kilogram person transferred to the Copernicus, about one hundred kilograms of water was simultaneously transferred back.

"To summarize, Travel Oaks help us get around the limitations of relativity. They act like biological star gates of popular science fiction. For next week I want an essay describing what we know about the University of Halcyon's disappearance and return."

CHAPTER 19
A CONTEST LIKE NO OTHER

The Alelli Space Exploration and Mining Company (ASEM) was the culmination of a multi-national industrial dream to use robot miners to harvest metals from the Asteroid Belt. This consortium built an artificial island near Aruba as a launch site and commissioned a fleet of freighters (half airplane and half rocket) to supply a geostationary, orbiting assembly hanger. Assembly of the huge robot miner craft was to have taken place in the hangar.

With the bankruptcy of the consortium after failing to construct and launch a single robot miner, ASEM's assets were purchased by Coventry's Gibeah Space Exploration and Mining operation. The two stage chemical freighters were refitted with Coventry's new Matrix Fusion power source, the new ASEM soon had eight freighters a day delivering supplies to the orbiting hangar. The construction of the Coulsen, the starship prototype with its new ion drive, had begun in the confines of the orbiting hanger   .

From *Class Notes on Coventry Space Exploration* by Edward Mutembe

KLEMHOFER COLLEGE TURNED OUT TO BE AN EVEN MORE MARVELOUS place than it had appeared at first sight. As the three friends had seen from the train platform, the College itself was in a large cavern. At one end were the buildings and classrooms. The bulk of the College cavern was taken up with a lake and a beach, with woods on a hill on the far side of the lake. They called the lake, Lake Klemhofer, and in their spare time, of which there was very little, students could swim, fish, lie on the beach, sit on the lawn, hike in the woods, or even spelunk in the passages beyond the woods. In a neighboring cavern, the College had sports fields for the house-league teams.

The cavern roof was taken up with matrix-fusion-powered lights, which gave a near approximation to sunlight. Huge fans, built into alcoves of the main cavern, provided artificial air circulation.

In addition to the Faculty of Natural Sciences, Faculties of Literature, History, Theology, Philosophy, as well as Engineering, and Mathematics completed the complement of College faculties. Physical conditioning, as well as training on machinery of various types, competed with their theoretical studies.

After Mutembe kindled the three friends' interest in the Space Academy and the space program, all three signed up for flight training. The training centered on a series of game contests called Fleet Fight. For this event, a third, multi-chambered cavern at the College was hermetically sealed. It contained an atmosphere of ninety-six percent carbon dioxide, slightly above atmospheric pressure for added buoyancy. Each team had a squadron consisting of four fighters and a mother ship. The objective of the contest was to disable the other team's mother ship before they disabled yours. The fighters were ultralight weight, almost neutrally buoyant, pliable, single-seat vehicles, with low-powered infrared lasers as cannons. A computer-games master kept track of hits and damage, and progressively disabled both fighters and mother ship as laser hits accumulated.

The skin of the ships was a soft silicone rubber derivative that allowed them to sustain low speed collisions with the cavern walls with minimal or no damage.

The Natural Sciences Faculty had twelve intramural teams, which practiced and then played one another. The best Natural Sciences team overall, fought against the best team from each of the other faculties.

Jacob, Zeke, and Hanna were joined by three new recruits. Together, their team was coached by Flego Zimmer, the captain-graduate of last year's master team. At their first training session, Zimmer explained the process.

"I'm here to train you into a competent flying squadron. We'll do that using Fleet Fight to hone your skills. We have twelve intramural squadrons: four entry-level, four intermediate, and four high-level squadrons. The top high-level squadron will represent our faculty at the inter-faculty competition for the Klemhofer Cup. We also have any number of teams that play on our simulators. Periodically we swap out two of the low-level teams back to simulators and let the best low-level team move up to intermediate, switching with the lowest team there.

"At each level the speed of your fighters and mother ship is regulated. At your level, the speed is low enough that even if you bounce your way around the cavern like a pinball, the soft skin on your ship will keep you from sustaining damage.

"At the higher levels, the speed goes up and the danger increases. For the intra-faculty contests, there's no speed limit. You can push your machine as fast as it'll go. Frankly, we've had fatalities when flyers became too aggressive. Now mount your simulators."

The controls were relatively simple: a stick for maneuvering, a pedal for speed, and a pedal to activate the air brake. A button on the stick fired the laser forward down the centerline of the small fighter. Jacob caught on quickly and managed to hit Zeke with his laser only to be nailed by Hanna, who had snuck up behind him while he was lining up Zeke.

When the three friends returned to their dormitory, they sought out Professor Whitefeather and asked why they were practicing on this odd simulator under these strange conditions. "They don't really have anything to do with flying topside on Earth."

"Oh, with the rush to get you started here, I guess no one has told you that we have a colony on Venus?" He replied.

"On Venus?" asked Hanna. "I thought the surface of Venus was hot enough to melt lead."

"It is," said Whitefeather, "but our colony isn't on the surface. As you rise from the hot surface into the clouds and the pressure drops, you pass a temperature and pressure zone that is nearly Earth-like. On Venus we have a giant dirigible city called Galilee that forms our living quarters. The Venus atmosphere is about ninety-six point five percent carbon dioxide. Nitrogen, oxygen, and, of course, helium are all buoyant gases compared to carbon dioxide and keep the dirigible city afloat. Some day you may be sent to Venus.

So everyone here who hopes to enroll in the Space Academy, trains on the basic flyers until flying becomes second nature."

One day, as Jacob was studying by the lake, he saw Dennison walk by. Dennison saw him too, and came over and held out his hand.

"I owe you an apology, Kraiser. Or, may I call you Jacob?"

Jacob stood up and shook his hand. "I heard that you had saved our bacon to keep us all from being snatched by the incursion forces. We'd all be in prison now, if it hadn't been for you."

Dennison looked sheepish. "I knew Rousseau for a long time. Since school, actually. I thought he was my friend when he recruited me to join him in infiltrating Coventry. I thought I was doing a public service. But I was increasingly called on to do things that, frankly, made me a bully and disgusted me. When I saw what he was planning and how it would affect everybody, I couldn't stand it.

"I'm enrolled in Coventry now. It took a while for Coventry to decide to trust me. I guess I gave them so much information that they decided they could.

"See you around. I'm in the Natural Sciences Faculty. I heard you were too."

"See you around. Hope it works out for you," said Jacob, turning his attention back to his book.

Jacob was looking at his book but not reading. *So, Dennison is back. Has he really turned over a new leaf?*

CHAPTER 20
THE FLIGHT OF THE DRAGONS

THE NEWLY-FORMED FIGHTER TEAM DECIDED TO NAME THEMSELVES THE Dragons. They met once each week late in the afternoon in one of the simulator rooms. Zimmer would teach them a new maneuver, which they would first practice against each other. Then, they would play against one of the other simulator teams in a virtual cavern. Each week, four teams from the simulator pool were selected in rotation to compete in the flight cavern against one of the four entry-level intramural teams. The Dragons' first contest with real fighters came three weeks later. Zimmer looked quite worried.

Jacob, Zeke, and Hanna climbed into their fighters and waited for launch. Everyone was chattering excitedly. Jacob had enjoyed the simulator. He'd had a measure of success and couldn't wait to pilot a real fighter.

Zimmer's voice came over Jacob's headphones. "Listen up. You've never flown before, and the Falcons have. Concentrate on navigating the linked caverns of the gaming area. It'll be the same as the simulator, but the lighting is different every time. Stay away from the Falcons for the first half of the contest. Your job is to stay round the mother ship and hide from the Falcons as long as possible. Then, after you've developed a feel for your ships, we might try taking a shot at the Falcons, just to gain experience when they do locate you. Safety first at this stage."

Zeke came over the local line-of-sight channel. "Zimmer doesn't have much confidence that we're going to beat these guys, does he?"

"It's only once in a blue moon that a simulator team beats a practiced team in the cavern on their first try," said Hanna. "Even then the win usually comes against a practiced team that's recently been promoted. I read up on it."

"Of course you did," said Zeke.

"At entry level contests," cut in Zimmer, "I'll be giving you commands. I have all of your cameras up on my screen. Okay. Launch in five, four, three, two, one, … launch!"

Jacob's ship, like all the others, had a cockpit the size of a motorcycle. The silicone copolymer was clear. Two stubby wings, a short fuselage and a tail completed the structure. All of the non-pliable equipment, such as the engine, instrumentation, and Jacob's seat were insulated from the skin so that the ship could sustain significant collisions without damaging the core components.

The fighter had a programmable team symbol and name, as well as colored lights that helped identify the team. Jacob proudly programmed "Rattler" onto the bow and hoped to add a few "kills" if he managed to convince the flight computer he had tagged an opponent's ship in a vital area.

Once launched into the game cavern, he saw that they were in an area of shadow. He could see the flashing green lights of three teammates in the fighters and the double flashing green lights of the mother ship manned by the final two Dragons.

"I think I know where you are," said Zimmer. "Mothership: move to starboard and climb to the ceiling. Rattler and Blade: follow the mothership. Leopard and Werewolf: get in front of her."

Jacob maneuvered Rattler to station about thirty meters behind the Mother Dragon. Zeke joined him in Blade.

"See that shadow to port?" asked Zimmer. "We're going to hide in there. Here's a trick. Find a cavity in the ceiling and maneuver your ship so the flashing green light is in the cavity. That will make you harder to spot. We call it 'wall hugging.' Hopefully a single scout from the Falcons will come along and we'll try to swarm him."

"That we should be so lucky!" Zeke said over their private communications line.

While they were clumsily maneuvering their fighters close to the wall, four Falcon fighters zoomed in at high speed, strafed Leopard, and veered off.

"Move it! Move it! Move it! Get out of there. Mothership—lead away from the Falcon fighters," shouted Zimmer. "Dragons—take up rear covering positions." The Mother Dragon began to accelerate. The three fighters followed. The Falcon fighters had circled and were coming in at relatively high speed for another strafe.

Jacob pulled out of formation and accelerated directly at the enemy fighters, firing his laser haphazardly. The Falcons fired back, but weren't able to hit him either. After a near collision, Jacob was through the pack. Close to the wall, he slowed down and tried to make a turn.

Not exactly the same as a simulator. I'm afraid of scraping the wall. I'm too cautious.

Three Falcons were on him, maneuvering him nose-first into a crevice in the cavern wall, so tight that the silicone polymer of his canopy bulged. He could not use his engine to dislodge himself since the thrust would force him deeper inside and might rupture his canopy.

"Just sit tight, Kraiser. Those jackasses were just showing off," said Zimmer, before shouting orders to the rest of the team as they tried to hide the Mother Dragon.

Jacob was so angry he could feel his face flush. *No way am I going to sit here*. He undid his seatbelt and detached his oxygen bottle from his seat. Attaching a tether to his seat frame, he wormed his way along the fuselage to the emergency exit near the tail, where he entered the escape code. His console flashed red and a voice warned of a life-threatening oxygen depletion.

"Kraiser, what do you think you're doing, you idiot? Do you have a death wish?" It was Zimmer's voice.

The escape hatch swung open and Jacob climbed out onto the tail. Closing the hatch and hugging the fuselage with his arms, Jacob wedged his helmet onto the vertical tail fin and pushed on the rock wall with both legs.

I think it moved a centimeter.

"I can't see you on the camera anymore. Where are you? What are you doing?"

"Don't worry about me, coach. Help our Mother Dragon survive. I'll call if I get into serious trouble."

Taking a few deep breaths, Jacob tried again. The fighter popped out of the crevice like a cork out of a bottle.

The fighter immediately began to sink very slowly since the cabin had filled with carbon dioxide when Jacob had opened the emergency hatch. The autopilot kept the fighter on the level with a few stabilizing bursts and began inflating the helium bags in the wings until neutral buoyancy was restored.

Jacob crawled back into the cabin, punched the purge button, removed his oxygen mask and resumed his seat.

"Rattler calling Zimmer, what's going on?"

"Don't bother me now, Kraiser. Leopard is down and the Falcons are toying with Blade and Werewolf before they take down Mother Dragon."

"So, what should I do? Come and help?"

"Kraiser, you're free? What did you do? Never mind. Find Mother Falcon. I know just where she'll be. Turn starboard and go low. Now, head through that opening to port. Do you see her yet?"

"I see her. She's making a lazy circle high up, watching for trouble."

Zimmer was getting excited. "Now Kraiser, flip your ship on its back to hide your light and get right under her and then make a vertical climb."

Jacob almost fell out of his seat—he hadn't reattached his seat belt.

Zimmer must have realized his near disaster but said nothing until Jacob had secured his seatbelt. "Now line her up. Unless they're being careful, they won't see you if you're coming directly from below. Wait until you're within forty meters and can't miss. Hold steady. Line her up midships. Now fire! Keep firing! That yellow light flash meant you hit her with medium damage."

The Mother Falcon picked up speed and headed for the next cavern.

"Don't get on her tail. With her turret gun and a gunner, she outguns you," said Zimmer. "Dive and come up from below. That's it. That's it. Two of the fighters are heading your way at top speed. Come on, finish her off."

There were a couple of red flashes on the Falcon Mother and the gaming computer announced, "Contest over. Dragons win. Head back to base."

Everyone at launch-base was ecstatic and clapped Jacob on the back. Hanna hugged him. Zimmer was trying to be angry, but couldn't contain his grin. "Kraiser, that was the dumbest stunt I've ever seen. Don't do it again."

"Unless it'll win us another victory," said Zeke.

"You were really worried when you heard we were playing the Falcons, weren't you?" asked Jacob.

"Yeah, I was. Three weeks is not nearly enough time on a simulator. I also knew the Falcons tend to be stinkers and enjoy humiliating their opponents. That trick of wedging your ship into a crevice is the kind of thing I mean. Now the Falcons have been kicked out of the entry tier and are back in the simulator pool. That's got to deflate their egos a bit."

"So, what does that mean for us?" asked Hanna.

"We take their place and every week we have two games instead of one. Our next contest will be against one of the teams in the entry tier. Then next week, we play another simulator team and another entry-tier team all in the cavern."

CHAPTER 21
HOBSON'S CHOICE

THINGS WERE GOING WELL FOR THE THREE FRIENDS. AFTER THEIR SHAKY start, the Dragons won their next three games against simulator-level opponents, but could not win against the three other entry-tier teams. Although inexperienced, the Dragon fighter pilots had a natural feel for their craft and under Zimmer's excellent guidance their individual aptitude and team play increased measurably with each game.

Their courses were also going well. Professor Mutembe's *History of Coventry* class was the only one Jacob shared with Dennison who had transferred to the Faculty of Engineering and Mathematics. That choice had puzzled Jacob ever since he heard of it, since none of the three stooges had ever expressed any interest in working hard at their academics. But then, Jacob reasoned, Dennison had always been under Rousseau's thumb and may have adopted Rousseau's cynical attitude toward Coventry studies while he was with him.

"Well class," said Mutembe, his dark face serious, yet animated with pleasure at a subject he enjoyed passionately, "I told you last week that at about 2020, Canada's population was almost forty million people. Now our population is just under twenty nine million and dropping. What happened? What did your research tell you?"

As usual Hanna was the first to have her hand up. "Miss Heidel."

"Since about 1971, the number of live births per woman in Canada dropped below 2.1, the value one needs to keep the population steady. Since then, that number has continued to drop."

"Correct as usual, Miss Heidel. The birthrate dropped precipitously after the postwar baby boom. The drop, beginning in the early sixties continued until it was below the replacement rate. It leveled off at about 1.5 live births per woman. So why did the population keep rising until the 2040s? Yes, Mr. Cranmer."

"Canada made up the difference with immigration."

"So, why did that change?" asked Mutembe. "Mr. Kraiser, I think it is time you volunteered an answer."

"Sir," said Jacob, "I believe the answer lies partly in Single Nuclear Exchanges or SNEs."

"Please elaborate, Mr. Kraiser."

"From my reading, in the 2020s, a number of regimes began selling low-yield nuclear weapons to anyone who could afford them. Dictators in many poor countries had these weapons at their disposal. Local conflicts, which used to drag on for years using conventional weapons, now ended quickly but devastatingly as these belligerents nuked each other's capital cities and set back their fledgling economies and infrastructure by twenty years. The devastation and privation were unprecedented. It was as if the world faced a Hiroshima and Nagasaki every two or three years. Most other developed nations, had an even lower birthrate than ours and had no one to send to us. Fear of nuclear terrorism eventually shut our borders to many countries that had high birthrates."

Hanna put up her hand. "Miss Heidel?"

"Didn't the pandemic of 2020 also slow immigration?"

"Good observation. The rapidity with which the pandemic of 2020 spread around the world through travel, meant that the developed world became much more cautious about travelers in general and immigrants in particular. That along with the SNEs were the main reasons immigration was insufficient to offset the low birthrate.

"Well stated. Please do the math everyone. With a birthrate of 1.5 livebirths per woman, considering that the replacement value is 2.1, three generational reproductive cycles of twenty to thirty years in duration, a low birthrate means the population will contract to about one-third. We have essentially completed two cycles of low birthrate and hence our current population of about twenty nine million."

Professor Mutembe left his desk and moved to the wall-sized monitor. "There is something else I want you to think about and then write about in your essay: the marked divide between rural and urban populations in Canada now. Currently our rural birthrate is close to the replacement value. However, very few tax dollars find their way back to rural communities and so there is a general movement of young people to the cities where they begin to mirror the behavior of other urbanites. Comment on these differences and, in particular, on the challenges young people might face moving to an urban environment."

Jacob felt that Mutembe was looking at him when he said this. Being reminded of the difficult time he had experienced after he had come to Toronto agitated him so much that he felt he had to be alone. "I need to go out for a walk," Jacob said to Hanna and Zeke. Hanna looked surprised.

Jacob collected his books and dropped them off at his room. Heading back downstairs, he saw Dennison walking briskly following the left path around the outside of the lake. Wishing for some time alone, Jacob instinctively took the deserted path on the right. In his mind he went over the strange things that had happened to him in Toronto. He felt like a naïve fool. He couldn't read the signs, the political machinations. He had been duped and played by pretty well everyone and then they had taken his life away and sent him here to rot in Coventry.

Then it dawned on him, he hadn't rotted in Coventry. Instead, for the first time since that tragic day when he was told about the car accident and the death of his whole family, he had found a new home and new friends. He had landed on him feet!

He was walking through the woods on the far side of the lake and the cavern roof lights were being dimmed for twilight when he heard Dennison's voice off to one side, but very close.

"Are you sure you weren't followed?" whispered Dennison.

"I checked," said another voice which sounded familiar to Jacob. "I saw no one on the path and doubled back a couple of times to make sure no one was trailing me. Besides everyone heads back before it gets dark and the sprinklers come on. So, what's the big secret?"

"You and I are here to find out how these Cretins have managed to come up with their remarkable technology."

"Yeah, I know," said the other voice.

"Have you also noticed how none of our courses have moved us a millimeter closer to the answers we seek?"

"I suppose," said the voice, "but we're still getting our feet wet with the simple stuff."

"But we can't even find books in our library that have the answers we're looking for. I know, I've tried in ways that are untraceable."

"What are you saying?"

"I'm saying they may suspect that agents have penetrated this far into their infrastructure and they are deliberately keeping their vital secrets hidden from us."

"If that's the case, why not just arrest us?" asked the voice.

"They may not be sure, we're agents yet. After all, if we're legitimate and are truly on their side, we can help them a good deal. They're still giving me a bit of slack."

"But if they find out who we are …" said the voice anxiously.

"That's my point. If they're suspicious now, they will find out. There is no doubt about that." said Dennison.

"But I'm in deep cover and have never done anything to make them suspect …"

"Yes, you're likely safe if you keep your head down. But I think we may be the last hope for our side to get some real intelligence. Our handlers are starting to indicate that our time and their patience is at an end. The Canadian government is getting restless. They expected Coventry to capitulate a week after Iron Isle was sealed. They now know that is not going to happen. Cobra is also getting impatient. They want us to take some kind of definitive action."

"When?"

"Tonight."

Jacob could hear tension and fear heighten in the timbre of the other fellow's voice. "Then our cover will be blown and we need to get out of here!"

"We're going to get out tonight. But before we do, we're going to get the information we need. I've been holding off until I had stolen a password and found the keys to the desk that has what we're looking for in Engineering.

"After we steal the information we need, we're going to meet an operative I know who will transport us outside of Coventry and has arranged for us to be taken to headquarters."

"You're springing this on me now? You could have told me sooner," said the familiar voice.

"Look Conrad, as you said you're under deep cover. I wanted to leave it that way until now. You work for me and I share information on a need to know basis. Until now, you didn't need to know." Dennison's voice turned deadly cold. "Are you in or out?"

Of course! Conrad is a fellow student in the Natural Sciences Faculty. That's why I know the voice.

There was a long pause. In a quavering voice, Conrad said "I'm in."

CHAPTER 22
CHOICES UNDER PRESSURE

WHAT IS COBRA? SOME KIND OF COVERT CANADIAN SPY AGENCY? JACOB'S thought distracted him.

It was now very dark in the woods. Jacob stood stock still at the edge of the path by a conifer and prayed that they would not come in his direction. The two conspirators crashed through the undergrowth and rejoined the path. He heard their footsteps recede.

Jacob thought furiously. *If I follow them, when I leave the forest while trailing them, the night roof lights will mean they'll see me. I have to get back before they do!*

Jacob turned the opposite direction and broke into a run. The path was smooth and although the forest was very dark, the path glistened like a luminescent ribbon in front of him. When he left the trees, he sprinted for the Engineering Faculty building.

The main doors were locked. Jacob was looking around wildly for someone to warn when he had to take cover as Conrad and Dennison approached. There was simply no one else around.

Dennison went to a side door and entered. Jacob hesitated for a moment then decided to follow. The door was unlocked.

He entered just as he saw an office door close up the hallway. He crept up and saw the name H. Breitkreutz on the door. He was about to turn and look for help when he sensed movement. His head seemed to explode. He felt himself falling to the floor. A strong hand covered his mouth as he felt a needle jab into his neck.

CHAPTER 23
FEELING LIKE A FOOL

JACOB WOKE IN THE DARK WITH A GAG, TAPE AROUND HIS MOUTH, THE cloth of a hood over his head, and his hands and feet tied. His head was throbbing. He tried to remember what had happened. He was covered with loose packaging material which was coarse enough that he could breathe. His coffin, for so he thought of it, was being transported somewhere. He heard faint noises and perhaps faint voices.

He was very thirsty. He began to remember almost regaining consciousness before but each time he had sunk back into unconsciousness. Only now did he seem able to stay awake. He didn't know how much time had passed. His fear was palpable. He knew he had been kidnapped by Dennison. *What a fool I was to follow! What else could I do? Idiot, you could have just gone for help. If they hadn't believed you, that would have been their problem. If they had believed you, maybe Coventry might still have prevented their escape, no matter how well they had planned it.*

What seemed days later, although afterwards he learned it was only a few hours, the lid on his box was pried open. Jacob was roughly jerked to his feet, but he immediately fell to his knees, too weak to stand. Arms on either side jerked him back to his feet and dragged him for several meters. His hood was removed and as his eyes adjusted to the dim light, he saw that he was in some kind of a cell. The first face he saw belonged to Litch. After Litch cut his bonds, Jacob was thrown on a musty mattress in the corner.

"Enjoy your solitude while you can Kraiser. Rousseau is not known for his gentle interrogation techniques. We'll see if you're still a smart-ass after he gets through with you." The door clanged shut and Jacob was left in complete darkness. There was no window.

He found some drinking water and a toilet in the corner and then fell asleep again. He woke to the noise of his cell door opening. It was Hodgkins and another man.

"Sir, am I glad so see you!"

"Hush, Jacob. Let the doctor examine you. I am so, so glad we found you. But hold your questions. We're in a hurry."

The doctor examined Jacob quickly, asked a few probing questions, and pronounced him fit to travel.

"What's going on?" asked Jacob.

"Your friends reported you missing for the Dragons' late-night training session. We put two and two together and followed the trail after the Breitkreuz break-in. It's very bad. They took a huge amount of information and we couldn't get it back. At least we found you. Now we have to move before Rousseau returns. The exit route Dennison used will have to be pruned."

Hodgkins and the doctor helped Jacob into a waiting vehicle and drove him out of town.

"Where are we?" asked Jacob.

"We're now leaving Thunder Bay. We'll drive north and west to a lumber camp that belongs to Coventry. It's one of several exit ports that we work hard to keep secret. When one is compromised, such as the one Rousseau's operative used, we shut it down, seal it up, and sell the business that operated it on the surface to someone else within the week. We can't have any entry points for an assault on Coventry."

"What did Rousseau get?" asked Jacob.

"I think he got quite a lot of information. What I don't know—what we don't know is how well they will be able to use it. Science and engineering education have been so politicized and degraded that it's hard for them to understand and implement what they will read. At least that's my hope. In any case this is very bad for us."

"By the way," said Jacob, "what's Cobra?"

"Where did you hear that?" asked Hodgkins, alarm in his voice.

"This whole thing started when I accidently overheard a conversation between Dennison and Conrad. They talked as if Cobra, more than the Canadian Government, was behind this intelligence work."

"We don't know much about Cobra. With Single Nuclear Exchanges plaguing the world, everyone has an intelligence agency heading off the next attack on their own soil. Canada, the U.S., what's left of Europe, the Central Asian Democratic Republic, and the North African Democratic Republic regularly share intelligence. We think that these channels of cooperation between the intelligence agencies has harden into something like a functioning organization that's looking to be a puppet master for the countries that are supposed to be their masters."

Hodgkins looked at Jacob intently. "I don't know how many plants Rousseau has in your class year. The one that Dennison used for this escape, was one we didn't know about. We're lucky he had to take you along. It gave us a bit more warning.

"Since this is the second time you've caused Rousseau trouble, he may think you're an unacceptable risk to his plans and try to eliminate you."

"But I don't really know anything about Rousseau's organization," protested Jacob.

"That may be, but Rousseau may decide to have you silenced to make sure you didn't learn anything injurious to him during the kidnapping. I think he can be quite ruthless.

"In any case," continued Hodgkins, "you need to leave the College immediately."

Jacob felt the bottom drop out of his world. Leave Klemhofer College and his friends!

"I'll send you, Heidel and Rempel to the Space Academy early. That will get you away from your classmates for now. You can pick up the missing courses on the side."

CHAPTER 24
SO FAST THEIR HEADS SPUN

JACOB, ZEKE, AND HANNA WERE HUSTLED OUT OF KLEMHOFER COLLEGE so quickly they could not say "Good bye" to their classmates or even their Dragon team mates. The Space Academy was an underground extension of Penner Aerospace, another company secretly owned by Coventry and renowned for launching communication satellites. Penner Aerospace, a division of Gibeah Space Exploration and Mining, had bought an artificial island near Aruba that had been constructed in the late 2020s on top of a sea mount when multinationals still believed they could make money from orbital launches. Since 2040, world-wide engineering capability had so degraded that this site had been abandoned and the owners were only too happy to unload the island.

The subterranean Space Academy, tunneled into the sea mount under the Penner Space Port, was planned on a design very similar to Klemhofer College. It even had a flight cavern very much like the one at the College.

The multi-cavern cave system of the academy could be isolated from the space port by closing huge blast doors. It had its own gardens and farms and could sustain its atmosphere independently.

After a thorough physical examination, the three friends were inserted into the first year of study which was already underway. Jacob, Zeke, and Hanna felt at home in most of the courses which were similar to what they had been taking in Coventry. The three were assigned a tutor, Dr. Reuben Rosenthal, in order to make up the gaps in their training.

In addition to the regular college courses, they were given detailed instruction on the maintenance of the Torchship Coulson. Everything from astrogation, to powerplant basics, life support, and computer troubleshooting. Although the Coulson was in orbit around Venus, most of the subsystems—as well as a comprehensive torchship flight simulator—provided all of the cadets with hands-on experience.

Everywhere there was a sense of urgency. Although almost no one knew about the details of the break-in, everyone knew that Coventry needed to be ready to move at a moment's notice and everything that would facilitate the migration had been accelerated.

The three friends signed up for the Canaan Program on Alpha Centauri as soon as they arrived. Their applications were accepted and they were told to finish their studies at the Space Academy and continue their flight training.

The common room and dormitories in the academy seemed eerily familiar.

"Doesn't it strike you odd," said Jacob, "that we've lived in three places within Coventry and that the floor plan of our dormitories are almost identical?"

"I find it kind of nice," said Hanna. "It makes me feel as if I haven't moved twice."

"It does seem odd," said Zeke, "maybe they have particularly unimaginative architects in Coventry."

Jacob was unconvinced.

CHAPTER 25
GOING WITHOUT GOING

THEY ENCOUNTERED ONE OF THE MOST INTERESTING NEW TRAINING courses early in the first week. It was a class that students lovingly referred to as "Mech Class."

The three friends were ushered into a room which contained a series of glass cylinders about three meters tall and two meters in diameter. The class was divided into two groups. Half of the class were "pilots" and half "monitors." Since Jacob, Zeke, and Hanna were new, they did not know enough about the equipment to act as monitors, so they had to be pilots.

Jacob changed into his bathing suit and climbed shivering into his empty tank.

"Don't worry, Kraiser," said the monitor. "When the tank fills, it will be 0.9 percent saline at thirty-seven Celsius and you'll be as comfortable as we can make you."

With the monitor's help, Jacob's head was covered with a custom helmet, specially constructed for him.

"Breathe normally," instructed the monitor, "check your comm and then give me the thumbs up."

Jacob did so. Gauntlets and leggings were attached and then finally, a tether strapped to his upper body.

The monitor climbed out of the tank. "Filling now," he said.

The tank filled rapidly. "Oh, by the way, can you feel a switch at your waist on the left side?"

"Yes," said Jacob.

"That's your emergency switch. Lift the flap and carefully feel the switch underneath. If you're ever in trouble, just lift the flap and punch that switch. The siren will sound, a red flashing light will activate, and the water will immediately drain from your tank. Even if all the monitors were raptured …"

"Raptured? What's that?"

"Oh, forgot you're new. Coventry joke … if all the monitors were to disappear in a moment, you could still drain the tank, remove all your equipment without outside help, and climb out of the tank."

Weird! Thought Jacob.

Jacob felt the tether lift him off the bottom of the tank. There was a pause, then the monitor continued. "Everything looks good on my panel. Everyone else is already connected to their mechanical avatars and Colonel Tsang is getting impatient. Connecting now …"

Jacob saw the whole inside of the visor light up. He looked around. His mech-avatar was under water. On every side he saw humanoid-shaped mechanical contraptions. Each had a panel on chest and back with names of his classmates. Colonel Tsang's mech-avatar walked over and checked his mechanical readout. "Everything okay Kraiser?" said Tsang over the comm. "I've already checked Heidel and Rempel."

"Copy, sir!" answered Jacob. "I'm okay."

"Now listen up everyone, we're going to walk over to the closest hydrothermal vents. Stay together. I don't want you to walk your mech into a crevice and have to call for emergency services to recover it."

They were in a lighted metal-plastic structure. Tsang headed toward the door with six cadets following. Their footsteps made no noise but sent up little eddies of sand and mud. Next came Jacob, Zeke, and Hanna. Finally, the last six cadets. There were additional mech units in the shed that were not activated.

"Switch on your lamps."

"The switch is by your jaw. Alternatively, you can say 'lamps on!'" said Jacob's monitor.

Jacob switched on the lamps. He noticed they shone wherever he wanted to look, so the helmet was monitoring his eyes. They followed a solid, well-engineered path. When Jacob moved his legs or arms in the tank, the mech-avatar copied his movements. Actuators in his leggings pressed on his feet when the mech foot made contact with the underwater path. Jacob lost himself in the experience and he believed he was walking on the sea bottom.

"For you first-timers," said Tsang, "be careful about leaving the path. Some of the sediments here are very soft and you could sink in over your head. If you do, don't panic, just inflate your buoyancy tanks until you're clear and call for help."

The path ran straight ahead into the gloom of the deep ocean. A two meter, snake-like fish swan into Jacob's light beam. Jacob almost stumbled in surprise. The fish darted off in panic.

"Just a cusk-eel. They're attracted by the light. Nothing down here messes with a mech!" said one of the cadets behind him.

They had walked ponderously for fifteen minutes when large columnar structures rose from the sea bed like stove pipes or factory chimneys. Hot water, filled with what looked like soot, streamed out of the vents and then, as the hot water cooled, the black dust settled over a wide area. Tsang took them over to older deposits which were being mined. He ordered half of the crew to break up the rock-like deposits with picks while the three friends and others loaded broken nodule fragments into a pick-up truck-sized metal box.

Tsang walked over to Jacob, Hanna, and Zeke. "Quite amazing aren't they!" said Tsang gesturing at the large vents spewing sulfides.

"Yes, sir," said Jacob.

Tsang continued. "Many hydrothermal vents team with life. Not this one though. For us we're interested because it's particularly rich in manganese, vanadium, chromium, niobium, and molybdenum. You'll get a chance to see some of the more interesting ones during other excursions."

Tsang walked away from them and then broadcast to the whole group. "That's enough. Let's head back. We'll leave the ore wagon for the recovery craft to pick up."

Once back in the shed, Tsang ordered everyone to return their unit to the storage rack. They were clamped in place so that the units didn't fall over in case of a sea quake.

Jacob's monitor said, "Disconnecting." The whole procedure was reversed. Jacob had completely forgotten about his body floating in the tank. When he had walked, he had moved his legs and the feedback from the mech-avatar made him believe he was actually inside the machine. This would take some getting used to! He couldn't wait to talk to his friends.

CHAPTER 26
REUBEN ROSENTHAL

THE THREE FRIENDS HUDDLED IN THE ALCOVE IN THEIR COMMON ROOM, each drinking a cup of coffee. They had just begun talking about their mech-avatar class when a man, wearing a *Yarmulke*, spoke to a student and then approached.

They looked up expectantly. "My name is Reuben Rosenthal and I'm your tutor."

Shaking hands, they introduced themselves to Dr. Rosenthal.

"Would you care to join us, sir?" asked Zeke as he slid over to make room.

"Yes, thank you."

Rosenthal sat down. "I'm sorry to intrude. I thought it best that I make contact immediately. Everyone else is in the midst of their class year and I'm here to help as you try to catch up. Which class so far is giving you the most difficulty?"

The three friends looked at each other, then Jacob said, "Probably Torchship Coulson maintenance. For most of the courses, there is a lot of overlap with Klemhofer; Coulson is completely new."

"Well," said Rosenthal, "I'll clear my desk and take the first few classes with you and give you individual instruction. That way you won't have to disrupt the class and ask the instructor questions that everyone else already knows."

They spent another hour reviewing their various courses and Rosenthal answered their questions competently. He knew the information inside out.

Jacob couldn't take his eyes off the head-covering that Rosenthal was wearing. "Sir, may I ask you a personal question?"

"That depends on how personal," said Rosenthal, smiling.

"Well, I'm a new arrival here and I'm still learning about how Coventry operates. What's the significance of that head-covering you're wearing?"

"It's called a *Kippah* in Hebrew or a *Yarmulke* in Yiddish. It's a head-covering that is often worn by Jewish men."

"Forgive me if I'm overstepping myself, sir, but isn't Coventry a Christian community? How did your people come to be here?"

"Well, originally we came to be here like everyone else. We had family members who took part in the protest of 2051 and were then sent to the Coventry Penal Colony. Those who remained outside, did what they could to help the starving inmates and from time-to-time would also be sent here."

"But you could leave. Wouldn't you want to go back to a secular society?"

"You might think so, Jacob. But I think you're missing an important point and possibly making an unwarranted assumption. I think you're assuming a secular society will automatically be more tolerant than a religious one."

"That's what I've been taught. Isn't that true?"

"Not necessarily. What matters is not whether a society is secular or religious, but rather how it treats outsiders. In other words, what matters is tolerance. Even though Coventry is decidedly Christian as its default position, people here work to make room for others.

"For example, my community has its own cavern and we work there together. We're given the ability to manage our own customs as we like. Locally, we honor the Sabbath, the seventh day of the week, but we recognize that's not the default practice of the whole community."

"But I've always been taught that secular society was important because it headed off religious strife. Isn't that true?" protested Jacob.

"It can be true," said Rosenthal. "Especially, initially when the argument was made, when religious views were very influential, governments were careful to be seen as tolerant. But as public education, as the secular message of the media took hold, that careful tolerant stance became less necessary.

"You see all governments face the same difficult problem: in order to provide peace, order, and good government, they have to, in some measure, keep the populace content. This is easier to do when everyone has the same world view, that is to say, sees the world through the same glasses. It doesn't matter so much to government what that world view might be, as long as it's the same.

"Freedom of speech and especially freedom of religion allows people to have very different world views. Governments then may find themselves in the awkward position of satisfying one segment of the populace while alienating another. That drive for homogeneity inevitably leads to intolerance."

"Is government here different?"

"For now, it is. We're in survival mode and that galvanizes everyone's attention on getting to a place of safety. Secondly, we're a very modular society. We live in small caverns and that allows a lot of self-government. A lot of the friction points are alleviated by local custom and control. If you don't want services shut down on the Sabbath, you probably wouldn't move to our cavern. But religious people also have a difficulty. Some don't really believe in freedom at all. Others ostensibly do recognize that they disagree with others about important things, perhaps *the* most important things. Then, as one worries about one's children, there is great danger that the end begins to justify the means and then intolerance of speech and action creeps in and one finds oneself doing very intolerant things because the stakes are so high."

Rosenthal looked at his watch. "I should go. I enjoyed our discussion very much. I'll see you this week at your Coulson class. I'm not in uniform this evening. I'm a Colonel, so in class you should refer to me appropriately. Shalom."

CHAPTER 27
TORCHSHIP COULSON

CLASSES AND TRAINING SESSIONS WENT ON AT A BLISTERING PACE. Rosenthal was an excellent teacher and had the three friends able to handle the theoretical work and hands-on exercises in the Coulson simulator class within two weeks. For other classes, they would drop in to see him evenings if they encountered a deficiency in their background knowledge. Rosenthal was such an excellent teacher, that he invariably discovered the gaps in their knowledge after a few focused questions and then would fill in the missing information with a few minutes of instruction and some suggestions for follow-up references.

Their work with mech-avatars and flight training also went well. June was examination time: practical, oral, and written.

At Coventry, concern over the stolen data continued to mount. The decision was made at the Space Academy to move their group on to practical cadet duties early, and double the size of the first-year class. The day after their term ended, they were ordered to report to the Canaan Program operations center on Venus, a division of the Coventry Space Academy.

"Something has bothered me for a while," said Zeke, "Venus is hotter than a blast furnace isn't it? Why are we even going there? It sounds as if almost anywhere else would be more hospitable than Venus."

"Oh, on the surface it is incredibly hot," said Hanna, "but Venus Base Hebron is not on the surface."

"What then?" asked Zeke. "Is it a space station orbiting Venus? What's the sense in that."

"If you'd read the material the Canaan Program sent us when we first enrolled, you'd know that Venus Base Hebron is a giant carbon-fiber dirigible. It floats high up in the Venusian atmosphere at an altitude where the temperature is about twenty-one degrees Celsius. You sign up for a program and don't even read what you're getting into?" Hanna rolled her eyes.

"You're my friends, okay? Hanna, I knew you, at least, would read all about it and tell me if there's something I should know."

"Really Zeke, sometimes you think I'm your mother. You need to check these things out for yourself."

It turned out they were not going directly to Venus Base Hebron, but to the Torchship Coulson. Coulson, had been the prototype for the Faraday, Aquinas, and Copernicus interstellar craft and was now in a permanent orbit around Venus. It served as a training center for cadets, an emergency evacuation vehicle for Venus Base Hebron, and also as the construction depot for the second Venus base, Venus Base Galilee. It also served as the only "local" transport for an emergency evacuation of a Coventry base. In the event of an emergency evacuation of Coventry at Iron Isle, Coulson would boost at 0.66 G to Earth, be crammed full of people while in Earth orbit, and augment the slow Travel-Oak-mediated transfer of people to Hebron by boosting back to Venus. For those reasons it had to remain operational and in a high state of preparedness.

Unlike the three interstellar ships, Coulson was a cylinder, two kilometers in length. As a Torchship, it was designed for long term, multi-year acceleration needed for interstellar travel. In acceleration mode, the apparent direction on the ship was down toward the engines. However, while in orbit, artificial gravity was induced by spinning around the short axis, across the middle of the cylinder. Then the centrifugal acceleration gave rise to an apparent "down" towards the two ends of the spinning cylinder with zero gravity at the middle of the cylinder.

Jacob, Zeke, and Hanna were instructed to transfer to the Coulson with a dozen other cadets. They carried their gear to the Travel Oak grove at the Coventry Space Academy and prepared to spend the night. After they entered the Travel Oak ring, they all sat on the ground, leaning on their dunnage, and talked about what they would find the next morning. Finally they drifted off to sleep. Jacob had an unusual dream in which he felt as if he were floating. He woke with a start as a stranger's voice urged them to get up and get moving. As he tried to rise, Jacob realized something was different. It took a few seconds, but it became clear that he weighed less and that made him uncoordinated.

"You're at 0.75G," said the stranger. "Give yourself time to get used to this. Pick up your gear and follow me."

The stranger led them through a garden containing grove after grove of trees and other plants. The ground was covered with netting to hold the soil in place.

"I'm Sergeant Kim," said the stranger. "You will call me, 'sir.' You're now in the bow of the Coulson. When underway, apparent gravity is induced because of the boost acceleration and 'down' is towards the stern of the ship. Since we now have artificial gravity by a head-to-tail spin, for everything in the forward half of the ship, what used to be the floor during boost, is now the ceiling. You'll see every room and compartment in the forward half of the ship is designed to be switched over quickly if we have to return to boost."

"What about the garden?" asked a cadet.

Kim stopped and glared at the questioner.

"I mean, *sir*," stammered the student.

Kim's features relaxed and he resumed walking until he reached a large blast door and stopped.

"To answer your question," he stared pointedly at the student, "this garden and a second one like it near the stern, are the most protected parts of the ship. They reside in a sphere enclosed by twenty-five centimeters of the best blast-resistant armor plating we can make. The bottom half of this sphere contains all the power and equipment to maintain life support and plant support indefinitely. In case of an emergency, if you hear 'evacuate to the garden' this is where you will come. We can always get home from here.

"In answer to your specific question, cadet, this sphere is loaded on two sets of gimbals and will rotate as we begin to accelerate. It has freedom of motion in three dimensions and can rotate to keep the soil and tree roots pointing downward even if the ship were to crash and lie over on its side. We can't have the trees ripping out of the soil because they're on the apparent ceiling!"

Kim stopped on the outside of the hallway after descending a small stair and pointed to huge gimbals which anchored the sphere containing the garden to the main frame of the ship. "When we move from orbit to boost, the spin is stopped and the engines accelerate the ship. This whole sphere in the bow will rotate. So during change-over, the plants and trees are at zero gravity only for a short time. The netting and ground cover hold everything in place. The pools you see are covered with a lid at zero gravity. I've often wondered what the carp think as they float around in these giant blobs of water held together by surface tension."

Kim led them to a spiral staircase. As Jacob walked up the first steps, he was surprised to note that the ceiling also had steps. It dawned on him that when the Coulsen stopped spinning and began accelerating, he would be walking on the ceiling when using these stairs. Their weight gradually increased as they passed deck after deck. Finally, they were stopped by a door with a big "No Unauthorized Personnel" sign.

"The next floor is flight control and navigation. We have a duplicate set of flight controls next to the engines. We only use this flight control when we're boosting. It will be a while until you're allowed past this door."

They exited to the deck and after several turns found their rooms. As in all Coventry ships, men's and women's dormitories, and married quarters were strictly separated by a common room. Jacob saw what Kim had meant as he examined his room. He had a bed, a desk, and a closet. There were brackets on the ceiling for transfer during free fall to prepare for boost. Even the shower had two heads and two drains. Every drawer snapped shut and locked. Even the mattress was fastened to the bed frame.

I suppose they would first stop the spin and then I'd have the task of unclamping the furniture floating it to the ceiling and re-clamping it there. Seems an impossible task, thought Jacob.

After storing his dunnage, Jacob returned to the common room to meet with his friends. They handed him a sheet entitled *Academy Expectations and Course Schedule — Torchship Coulson.*

"So," said Jacob, "I read that while the Coulson is the prototype for the three interstellar ships, they look quite different. Is that true?"

"Yes," said Hanna. "Come over here. I saw a model of the two ship types in a cabinet in our common room."

Zeke and Jacob followed her to an alcove. In one glass case, was a cylinder with ion engines at one end. So, this is what we look like." She pointed to the cylinder. "Cadets are housed in the forward section, while the crew and flight officers are near the engines, at near one gravity when we are *'spun up.'*

That way they can get us underway as quickly as possible, while we have to rearrange our rooms and our common rooms for boost. Apparently in a severe emergency, a klaxon would sound and they would boost and kill spin at the same time."

"Well, what about us?" asked Zeke. "We just become plastered to the new floor?"

"I think," said Hanna, "that it's the price we pay if we don't immediately react to the klaxon or we leave stuff lying around our room which is against regulation. Every time one of your books zaps you on the head, Zeke, it will be saying 'you should have put me away.'"

"Alright, Hanna don't rub it in, I get your point."

Jacob pointed to the other model, which had a central flattened hull and two nearly semicircular wings. "So, that model depicts the modifications made for the interstellar craft?"

"Yes, I think so," said Hanna. "The central flattened cylinder is nearly the same as our ship. The stubby wings and aerodynamic nose are different. My reading suggests they wanted these ships to have the added capability to land in an emergency on the planet surface. They couldn't take off again, but they could glide to a landing if they needed to.

"But notice," continued Hanna, "they are symmetrical enough to induce artificial gravity by spin around the central axis. The wings also let them carry extra water to fuel the ion drive virtually indefinitely and also by electrolysis to generate hydrogen and oxygen to work the maneuvering jets, the shuttle craft, and the supply pods in case of an emergency landing."

"What are the supply pods?" asked Zeke.

"In case of an emergency landing, many of the supplies are jettisoned in pods that can complete re-entry on their own. That way if the ship is damaged, any survivors have a chance to recover equipment and supplies. Not everything depends on one successful landing."

After stowing their dunnage in the rooms off the cadet common room, they met Sergeant Kim in the cafeteria for the rest of the orientation tour. He took them to the control room, the shuttle bay, and finally the engine room to show them the propulsion system.

"I am the second assistant propulsion engineer on the Coulson," said Kim. "Our captain needs three things for this ship to function. We need an astrogator to make sure we navigate to the correct destination and we need life support including food, water, and oxygen to make sure everyone is still alive when we arrive. However, without a propulsion system, we're not much better than an expensive bit of space debris."

Kim seemed to swell with pride. He placed his hand on a cylinder the size of a pickup truck, surrounded by instruments in the center of the huge room. "This is our plasma chamber. It generates a plasma, the fourth state of matter—a collection of positive ions and electrons. We eventually strip all of the electrons off under high vacuum and feed both electrons and positive ions into our two relativistic plasma accelerators. Those huge acceleration rings are spirals located in the floors below us. With fusion power, we ought to be able to accelerate these ions to near light speed and achieve any kinetic energy we desire. At least, that's in principle. In practice we've never achieved a thrust bigger than 0.66 gravities. When firing, the relativistic electron beam exits at near light speed from the central engine nozzle while the relativistic positive ions exit the three nozzles near the rim of the space craft. As you can imagine even a slight imbalance in the charges would quickly lead to an enormous and dangerous buildup of electrostatic charge on the Coulson making us an interstellar Van de Graaff generator. We use a simple electrostatic feedback control that minutely adjusts the electron beam to keep the ship's charge neutral."

A cadet raised his hand. "Sir what fuel do you use?"

"Good question son. We normally use water. We have tried other fuels by way of experiment—ammonia, methane, chlorine, carbon dioxide—but water is the safest, will always be present in large quantities on the ship for life support purposes and has worked well. Water has carried the Copernicus to Alpha Centauri."

After that tour, they were given their timetables. What followed was a grueling schedule of zero gravity training, hours in flight simulators and, finally, sessions with an experienced instructor in the Viper, a training two-seater all-purpose space and upper atmosphere vehicle. Except for the ion drive controls for space flight, these ships looked to be larger, more powerful versions of the ships they had flown in Fleet Fight.

The Viper had a long-range ion engine that could achieve an acceleration of about 0.66 G for very long periods of time when operating in vacuum. For atmospheric operation, the fusion cells were used to decompose a raw material into fuel. In Venus' atmosphere, the fusion cells converted atmospheric carbon dioxide into carbon monoxide and oxygen. Conventional thermal rocket engines used this combustible mixture to generate thrust, but burned through prodigious amounts of fuel. When the Viper entered the denser Venusian atmosphere, the fuel tanks were recharged automatically.

Zeke was a natural flying the Viper, while Jacob had great trouble handling his ship in vacuum, but was much better when operating in the atmosphere. Hanna was the opposite of Jacob, handling space docking with ease, but often stalling when trying atmosphere maneuvers.

However, their mech-avatar class was even more amazing.

CHAPTER 28
STAYING COOL IN A HOT PLACE

IN THE FIRST WEEK ON BOARD THE COULSON, THEY WERE ASKED TO REPORT for a mech-avatar class. Their instructor took them to a repair shop which housed a three-meter-tall mechanical-avatar.

Master Sergeant David Chandaka loved working with the machines and had helped to design them.

"These mechs, mechanically and electronically are unlike anything you've encountered before. Everything had to be redesigned for high temperature operation. Even the lubricants are solid at room temperature and the joints are frozen at ambient temperature. Once on the surface, they'll work properly. We do have an oven here for testing before we send them back to the surface to make sure our repairs are effective.

"For those of you that are new here, we have two operational areas on the Venus surface. One is on the top of Maxwell Montes, the highest mountain on Venus, while the other is near the lowest point in Diana Chasma."

He displayed a large map of the surface. "Compared to the Earth with her oceans, the surface of Venus is rather featureless. We've used false color to separate the highlands from the lowlands, so to speak. The demarcation line is the average altitude."

A hand went up. For once it wasn't Hanna asking a question, but a young man.

"Yes?"

"Sir, I've read that the carbon dioxide at the surface is like an ocean. Is that true?"

"Good question. Unfortunately, the answer is not simple. My answer is 'sort of.' Every liquid has what is called a liquid-vapor critical point that occurs at a particular temperature. The critical temperature of pure water is about 374 degrees Celsius. At that point, liquid water ceases to exist. That is to say, water will always be a gas, no matter how high the pressure becomes and expands to fill a container as a gas does. But here's the kicker—one can put as much pressure on the gas as one wants and can achieve densities that are close to liquid water."

He opened up a silicone rubber dish, donned some gloves and picked up a large marble-sized piece of what looked like ice. "This is dry ice or solid carbon dioxide. At our pressure, carbon dioxide sublimes directly into the gas phase without passing through the liquid phase. Carbon dioxide has a critical temperature of 31 degrees Celsius, so of course the surface of Venus is far above the critical temperatures of both water and carbon dioxide. I'm trying to say that the density of the atmosphere at the surface is quite high, almost like a liquid, but there is no ocean, no shore, no phase separation into liquid and gas. In some sense it has the properties of both liquid and gas."

"Any other questions?" For a change there were none. "Okay, I can see I've confused you. No matter, the best thing would be to experience the surface through your mech-avatars first-hand. You know who your partners are. The one with their first name later in the alphabet, works the mech-avatar first, while the other is the monitor for this trip. Later, we'll switch places."

Jacob and Zeke were paired together. Zeke could have claimed his name was Ezekiel and made the first trip, but was content to let Jacob take the first mission. Jacob, after changing into his bathing suit, climbed up onto the scaffold, attached the familiar elbow-length gloves, leggings, body harness, and the helmet with its oxygen-nitrogen tubes. Zeke attached the tether to the back of Jacob's harness, checked the instruments briefly and gave Jacob the thumbs up. Jacob climbed into the tank, made sure breathing was adequate and the comm was active and then returned the thumbs up.

Jacob felt the sensors on his hands and feet connect and saw his helmet view screen light up with a strong reddish cast. As he focused on the sense of touch imparted by the sensors and the image on the screen, he began to forget about his body suspended in the tank and focused on his mech-avatar. Looking through the mech's optics, he was standing in a metal-framed warehouse with some two dozen mech-avatars secured in small metal frames around the periphery of the warehouse space to keep them from toppling over when unoccupied.

Chandaka's voice came over the comm. "Remember to unstrap your mech and follow me."

Jacob unstrapped his mech and followed the others out of the hanger in single file. The size of the mech and the viscosity of the supercritical carbon dioxide on the surface of the planet made the motion of this mech quite different from the underwater models he had used at the academy.

He stepped outside and looked at the alien landscape. "Are you seeing this Zeke?"

"Yep. Quite a rugged landscape. At least there's very little wind according to the instruments."

"Cadets follow me," said Chandaka. "We're in the Diana Trench, some of the lowest terrain on Venus. It's also some of the most rugged. An empty ore hopper has been floated to ground about three kilometers from here, on a landing area near mine C. We avoid the landing area, unless authorized, to prevent accidents. We'll have to drag the hopper to the mine. Senior cadet, bring the hauling cables."

Chandaka led the way, periodically checking his mech's wrist for directions. The trench looked like a narrow valley about two kilometers in width with very rugged sides. In places, large slab-like rocks had broken off the walls and fallen into the valley. Jacob looked around, amazed at the rock formation. He knew the odd colors were false colors produced by the optics using a combination of visible light, infrared, and microwave. He felt cool and comfortable. He had never seen colors or rock formations quite like this. *What an odd way for me to think about it? Here I am thinking that 472 degrees Celsius is cool!*

The mechs were able to cover the distance quickly and when Jacob topped a shallow rise, he saw a box-like contraption in the distance.

"Good!" said Chandaka. "The parachute-balloon has automatically retracted. That will save us some time."

Chandaka held his mech's hand in a fist indicating 'Stop.'

"It's safe to proceed. Please note, you always call Mission Control to confirm that there is no in-coming shipment in the air before we enter the landing area. When we've left, I will also send them the 'all clear'."

The hauling cables were attached to a metal-wheeled hopper about the size of a dump truck and then everyone took their place at equal intervals along one of the cables. On the senior cadet's command, they began pulling the hopper off the landing area. The senior cadet rode on the back of the hopper and applied brakes as needed. As they learned to pull together, the immensely powerful mechs made the hopper pick up speed.

They came to the entrance of mine site C and pushed the hopper under a scaffold there. A number of ore-boxes, about one cubic meter in volume were lined up at the entrance. Moving in pairs, the mechs seized these boxes, hauled them up to the scaffold, and dumped the contents into the hopper. When the hopper was filled, they refastened the lid and dragged the hopper back to the landing site. After Master Sergeant Chandaka had chased everyone off the landing field, he inflated the enormous metallized balloon and watched it rise with the red warning beacon flashing actively.

When Jacob had climbed out of the tank and changed back into his clothes, he helped Zeke don his equipment and helped him connect to the mech at the Mount Maxwell mine. The Mount Maxwell operation was quite different. The mechs collected bismuth sulfide snow with large shovels and metallic wheelbarrows and added the snow to the hopper for transport. When Zeke finally finished, they were both tired.

"That was quite something, wasn't it?" said Zeke.

"Those mechs were so much bigger than the ones we used under water, it took me a while to get the hang of it," said Jacob.

"We can't say playing 'space cadets' hasn't been interesting. I only hope it doesn't get too interesting," said Zeke, frowning.

From then on they had classroom time, exercise in the gym, more class time, two sessions a week on mech-avatars, and finally training time on flight simulators.

Finally, the day came when they graduated to senior cadet and were able to fly on their own single-seat Vipers.

CHAPTER 29
EARNING THEIR WINGS

THE VIPERS WERE MUCH LARGER, MORE POWERFUL VERSIONS OF THE fighters they had flown as part of the Fleet Fight game. The larger size of the fighters gave them near neutral buoyancy at the lower altitude of their Venus operational range.

When the three friends started their first Viper mission, they followed some senior cadets to pick up one of the torpedo-shaped mining balloons from the Mount Maxwell mine. Jacob maintained a safe operating distance from Zeke and Hanna who along with their commander, Paul Nkomo, made up their wing.

"Look sharp," said Nkomo, "we're approaching the beacon coordinates." Dense sulfuric acid clouds doted the skyscape, but not nearly as dense as the bright layer below them.

Far below, Jacob saw one of the robot harvesters that collected sulfuric acid and converted it into water, sulfur, and oxygen. "Kraiser reporting. Robo-harvester bearing 87 degrees at minus two thousand."

"I see it, Kraiser. I just spotted the target. Change course to zero five and climb 500 meters. Maintain formation and match my airspeed. Don't worry about the harvester, it's programmed to avoid obstacles like mining balloons."

Jacob could see the hopper underneath the torpedo-shaped balloon. They were slowly approaching the balloon when Nkomo said, "Full stop and hover while I secure our line."

Jacob saw Nkomo's Viper change direction and approach one end of the balloon. Two mechanical arms detached from recesses in the body of Nkomo's Viper and one of the arms seized a large ring at the end of the balloon. The other mechanical arm clasped a heavy-duty electromagnet attached to the end of the tow line that was unreeling from underneath the Viper. The mechanical arm was strong enough to bring the balloon and Viper into closer alignment and the electromagnet snapped home onto a flat magnetic plate on the balloon. The mechanical arms retracted into their nacelles and Nkomo's Viper began to move away unreeling the tow line as the distance increased. Nkomo pulled gently on the balloon. "I'm ready for you. Umbrella formation about a third of the way back along the tow line. Rempel you attach first."

Zeke moved his Viper about two hundred meters behind Nkomo's and extended his Viper's mechanical arms. Jacob upped the magnification on his view screen. Although Zeke had done this maneuver one hundred times on the simulator, this was different. The mechanical arm kept missing the tow line.

"Rempel, take a deep breath. Activate the camera inside the palm of the mechanical hand and approach the line slowly. The air is calm and we have time."

Zeke attached his carabiner to a loop in the line and slowly extended his tow line until told to stop. Nkomo then had both Vipers pull on the load gently to keep the lines taut. Hanna attached next and finally Jacob. Both he and Hanna had more trouble than Zeke.

Finally, Nkomo had them slowly turn the load to an intercept course with Galilee. Then they gradually gained speed. Jacob, Zeke, and Hanna were the spokes of the umbrella and Nkomo was the handle.

When they approached Galilee, several of the local Vipers took over the much trickier operation of maneuvering the load onto the landing platform, re-tracting the balloon and then moving the ore hopper into the manufacturing bay.

After flying back to the Coulson, the three relaxed in their common room. Zeke and Jacob had an ice-cold beer, while Hanna had a cranberry juice. They talked over their day, elated over their successful mission.

Finally, they grew quiet and more contemplative. Zeke asked, "What was it like living in the big city?"

"You've never been to Toronto, Zeke?"

"No, I've never been. In our case, the nearest big city was Winnipeg. My parents and other parents in our community would go, but they regarded the city as dangerous, a 'den of iniquity.' They kept people my age away, and frankly sometimes some in our community wouldn't come back."

"What! They decided to stay?"

"Don't know. Maybe they were grabbed and sent to Coventry although I haven't seen anyone I know yet. It was the rumor in our community that the Canadian Child Protection Department was always on the lookout for teenagers who had not been brought up according to their regulations. They have the power to take any action they see fit without consulting the parents."

"My family was the same," said Hanna. "They were very unwilling to let me go to Ottawa. There were a couple of girls my age who went to Ottawa on a lark, disobeying their parents. They disappeared and even though their parents searched for them for a year through the police, they never found the girls. I remember my parents spoke to the parents of one of the girls and came back thoroughly frightened. When I asked what troubled them, they simply told me the MacDougals didn't think the police were being honest with them. They were convinced police had a sham investigation going only to keep the parents off their backs. But they wouldn't quit searching. The girl was their only child. Eventually the MacDougals disappeared from our community as well. We were all too frightened to ask what had happened to them."

"Well," said Jacob, "at first, in my case, when I came to Toronto, I was convinced I had landed on my feet. I had a nice apartment. My Victimization Index card gave me special privileges and I seemed to have kind, friendly co-workers who seemed genuinely interested in me. Then, to my horror and shame, I realized that everyone around me was an accomplished liar. They told me what I wanted to hear. Everyone had an angle, such as getting me to treat them to the privilege of a better restaurant table that someone with my Victimization Index could demand.

"It all started to unravel as their real motives and agendas became clear when my supposed friends abandoned their facades and openly criticized me. It ended with my being sent to Coventry to make me disappear."

"Even after you trusted them! What an awful betrayal," said Hanna.

"When I look back now though, it almost seems as if someone was looking out for me and turned all that malice, planning, and rank treachery to my advantage. By sending me here they did me good."

Jacob thought for a while. "Now let me ask you something. Do you believe in God like many of the people here do?"

Zeke shrugged, "I guess so."

Jacob caught himself smiling at Zeke. "You guess so? What does that mean?"

"I believe in God," said Hanna. "I could see how that belief was a rock in my parents' lives and now I see how it makes this place function, even though everyone here doesn't believe."

"I haven't believed in God, but I wonder if I'm starting to. I keep re-reading the Curdie books by George MacDonald and there's a great-great-great-grandmother in there. I think she is something like what God is like or should be like if He's truly good. This grandmother is very careful about people's beliefs. She doesn't reveal herself unless someone truly wants to find her. There seem to be many people in the book who take quite a while before they want to find her. Some even try to keep others from looking for her."

"Are you looking for your 'grandmother'?"

"I think I am," said Jacob, "but I'm not exactly sure what 'looking' involves."

CHAPTER 80
THE FLOATING REFUGE

FOR JACOB'S FIRST EXTENDED VIPER MISSION HIS CLASS WAS commissioned to ferry supplies to Venus Base Galilee, a new base, very similar to Venus Base Hebron. The apparent annihilation of their sister colony in Africa had impressed upon the Council of Elders, the elected governing body of Coventry, the need for an escape plan if a serious invasion of Coventry was undertaken.

Venus Base Hebron was not large enough to hold Coventry refugees if a rapid, mass evacuation became necessary and so a second giant floating city, Venus Base Galilee, was being constructed using readily available materials in the atmosphere. The coal-black, four-kilometer-long flattened dirigible was made from carbon-fiber composed of the carbon in carbon dioxide so abundant in the Venusian atmosphere. Oxygen was used to fill several huge flotation bags to keep the structure from plunging to the very hot surface. The three friends were observing the delivery the last of four engines to the Galilee by flight instructors.

The engines had been shipped from Earth in pieces small enough to fit into a Travel Oak grove and then assembled in the large cargo hold of the Coulson. For transport to the Galilee, each engine was wrapped in plastic with self-regulating buoyancy tanks to keep it at neutral buoyancy—and towed by eight Vipers flown by the instructors. The senior cadets were under orders to keep station, but to stay well clear of the cargo. They trailed behind within sight of the engine-towing crew.

The convoy dropped from orbit to the polar flow, a strong current of carbon dioxide that flowed from the equator to the poles. Jacob, Zeke and Hanna were three of the twenty students trailing the payloads.

"Kraiser, Rempel, and Heidel: keep station!" It was Lennard, the most senior cadet telling the most junior cadets to remain at the back of the grouping. Lennard's course corrections continued intermittently with Jacob, Zeke, and Hanna receiving more admonishments than the others.

They had been flying for six hours and Jacob was tired. He could have switched to autopilot but was not sure that doing so would be acceptable except in an emergency. The light was quite bright in this region. Above, the ionized ionosphere emitted some light and below, the sulfuric acid clouds reflected about seventy-five percent of the incident sunlight.

Up ahead a massive glowing column rose rapidly. He called out a warning over the communicator as the unexpected updraft engulfed his Viper, the punishing winds and dense sulfuric acid clouds whipping his craft from side to side. His visibility was zero and even the radar appeared erratic with the rapid change in composition within the cloud. He wrestled with his joy stick to regain some stability and decided it was safest to maintain course and speed and hope he passed through this cloud without any collisions.

Hanna's tension-filled voice came on their private channel. "Jacob, Zeke, can you hear me?"

"I can hear you, Hanna"

"Jacob! You're there! I can't see anything."

"I think, we're fine if we maintain speed and heading. Are you still reading the Global Positioning Satellites?"

"My heading is still zero. My ground speed is 400 kilometers per hour and my altitude is still 71,424 meters."

"I'm about a thousand meters below you. It looks like the clouds are clearing. We should be back to three-thousand-meter visibility soon."

The clouds ended abruptly. Jacob saw the rest of the senior cadets, but not the package and the instructors which should have been ahead and well above them.

Then he spied them, well below him, losing speed rapidly.

Another smaller cloud bank rose and the rest of the cadets disappeared from view.

Jacob's communication receiver lit up with the red emergency light. "Mayday, mayday, mayday. Does anyone hear us?"

"Kraiser here. How can I assist?"

"Three tugs collided with a water harvester that was swept up in the updraft. They've all dropped to the equatorial flow to limp back either to Coulson or Hebron. We need three new tugs. Can you assist?"

"Will confirm," responded Jacob.

Jacob contacted Hanna and Zeke. Zeke had just rejoined Hanna after being blown off course. The other senior cadets were presumably streaking for Galilee far ahead in the next sulfuric acid cloud. The three friends dropped into position. Zeke went first, launching his magnetic grapple and locking onto the engine payload, making the maneuver seem effortless.

Hanna went next and looked very erratic at her approach, but the grapple connected well. Jacob was not so lucky. His approach was okay, but he shot his grapple wide. Now he was nervous. His second approach and shot were even worse than the first. Zeke called him up on their private channel and talked him in, coaching him on how to correct for the cross draft. The third grapple landed and held.

Hanna, Zeke, Jacob, and one instructor were part of the rear echelon, which was the most difficult of the tug positions. The front echelon consistently pulled the load forward with cables arranged like the spokes of a flipped umbrella. When pulling forward, the rear echelon, also fanned out, the cables connected to the back of the engine and pulling, adding their thrust to keep the back of the engine from fishtailing. Most of the time, they pulled forward along with the front echelon, but in an emergency, if they needed to decrease the speed of the load rapidly, the back echelon had to change from towing to braking. That meant moving their ships as a counterpoint to the first echelon and pulling to slow the load's speed.

Jacob prayed he wouldn't have to try to flip his craft to brake. If this maneuver was done expertly the load would go slack for a few seconds as the rear echelon repositioned for braking. If the transfer took too long, the turbulence would cause load fishtailing. If someone missed station, the braking would be off-center and havoc would ensue.

They passed through another dense sulfuric acid cloud where visibility was almost zero. Jacob had his eyes glued to the radar readout in the Heads-Up Display (HUD) and kept an eye on the tension to make sure he was keeping station. He was sweating when they finally left the cloud and he was able, once again, to see the others.

At long last the command came to change altitude and reduce speed. Now began the trickiest part of the maneuver. They had to match speeds with the Galilee, but avoid stalling. Luckily Venus at this altitude had almost as much light reflecting off the inner clouds as came through from the sun. Jacob saw the huge flattened dirigible shape of the Galilee towed slowly by several large tugs.

Several Vipers climbed up from the spaceport at the underside of the Galilee.

"Senior cadets Heidel, Kraiser, and Rempel, retract your grappling hooks and land in the Galilee spaceport. Thanks for your help. Well done."

Jacob breathed a sigh of relief. He retracted his grapple and followed Hanna in. The black, carbon fiber bulk of the Galilee was awe inspiring. The ship was not moving quickly, but Hanna wisely avoided the wash and turbulence created by the massive ship. Finally, they were below it, and they entered the huge kilometer-long box-like spaceport attached to the bottom of the Galilee. They coasted to the far end, where robot porters grappled onto their vessels and cleaned the sulfuric acid off for water recovery and carried them through airlocks to the interior storage area.

Large sections of the Galilee were still under construction and open to the outside atmosphere. There were only two habitable parts: the crew and spaceport quarters just above the spaceport and the forward control module which would operate the engines and steer Galilee once the four massive engines were operational.

All the critical tasks such as installing the new engine and attaching the motors for the flight control services were handled by the veteran crew. The senior cadets spent many hours delivering carbon-fiber beams, newly manufactured from carbon dioxide in the Venusian atmosphere which had been converted to elemental carbon and oxygen in the small robot manufactory in the forward part of the Galilee hull. Still Jacob found this task tricky. They used inflatable neutral buoyancy tanks on the Vipers filled with an 80-20 helium-nitrogen mixture to allow them to float their loads through the interior of the

Galilee. Once unloaded, their Vipers quickly compensated for the loss of the load and only needed the minimal amount of thrust to maneuver their vessels through the constrained quarters of the Galilee superstructure. But after all that hauling, Jacob's confidence had grown. Six months later Jacob and his class were ordered to return to the Coulson to make room for a new cadet class on Galilee.

CHAPTER 31
ANOTHER SURPRISE

JACOB SHOWED HIS SUMMONS TO HANNA AND ZEKE.

"What does this mean?" asked Hanna.

"Don't know," said Jacob. "All I know: I have to visit Commandant Schneider."

"Maybe they recognized your stellar leadership qualities and are promoting you to admiral of the fleet," said Zeke.

"You think?" said Jacob.

"If they do, I'll have to spend a lot more time on my knees praying for safety and protection," said Zeke with a twinkle in his eye.

"I've seen your knees," said Jacob, "there aren't any callouses on them. It would do you good to spend more time on them praying."

"Stop it, you two! This is serious." said Hanna.

"What???" said Zeke.

"Lummox, don't you see that Jacob is worried?" said Hanna. "He needs encouragement."

"What's wrong with beating it out of him with verbal barbs? See Hanna, we're a team. You encourage and reassure. I stoke the fires of worry and doubt. Between the two of us, we'll make Jacob a better, tougher, and more resilient person."

Crossing her arms, Hanna huffed, and turned her back on Zeke.

"Well, I'd better go," said Jacob as he rose and picked up his tray. He made his way to Commandant Schneider's office, and knocked. He was worried, but somehow Zeke's light-hearted kidding had helped him to laugh at his situation rather than worry about it. Now, however, as he faced the meeting, the uncertainty about his future settled like a shadow over his thoughts.

"Come in."

An adjutant placed a report on his desk, folded his hands, and frowned at Jacob as he entered. Jacob saluted. "Senior cadet Kraiser reporting to Commandant Schneider as ordered."

"At ease, cadet. You may head in, since the Commandant is expecting you." The adjutant tilted his head to indicate the door at the back of the office.

Jacob knocked on the door, took off his cap, and hearing an acknowledgement, entered. Commandant Schneider was a balding man with a fringe of grey that made him look like a medieval Franciscan Friar.

"Senior cadet Kraiser, reporting as ordered, sir."

"At ease cadet. Sit down." Schneider waved toward a chair directly in front of Jacob.

Jacob sat, holding his cap in his hand and waited for Schneider to speak. The commandant was looking at a file on his electronic tablet.

"So, you were one of the three who helped bring in the engine after that near disaster?"

Jacob wasn't sure he was meant to answer but said, "Yes, sir," to be safe.

Finally, Schneider shut his tablet off, folded his hands, intertwining his fingers, and leaned across his desk. His eyes were sharp as an eagle's and transfixed Jacob with their intensity.

"We control the number of settlers on Alpha Centauri A-3 very carefully so that we don't over tax our colony. Your class is not scheduled to transfer to Kinsinger on Canaan for another six months when additional housing will have been built and new fields brought under cultivation to accommodate the additional population."

Schneider stroked his chin. "However, one of the sons of the Canaan pioneers has been lost and is presumed dead and I've received an urgent request to replace him. I've picked you, Kraiser. Your file says you come from a farm in Leslieville, Alberta and you've worked with horses. The colony has as little technology as possible, since it's hard to get it there and even harder to maintain it. So, they use a lot of horses. You'll find they use a curious hodgepodge of nineteenth century and twenty first century's technology."

Schneider continued, "Get your dunnage together and head to Hebron for transfer to Kinsinger immediately. Don't look so shocked. You signed up for the space program and now you get your wish—perhaps a little sooner than you expected."

Jacob was flabbergasted. His mouth must have flapped wordlessly until he finally stood up, straightened his back, and saluted, mumbling "Yes, sir!"

His heart was racing as he turned and left the office. He didn't even respond to the adjutant's wish of "Safe journey."

Hanna and Zeke were waiting for him back in the dorm common room.

"So, what's the story?" asked Zeke.

"I'm off to Canaan as soon as possible to replace a colonist who is missing and presumed dead."

"That's exciting then, isn't it?" said Hanna working to form her mouth into a smile.

"By all accounts, it's an empty world with no real dangers," added Zeke. "Of course, you're going there because somebody died on a world that has no real dangers."

Hanna elbowed Zeke in the chest.

After grunting, Zeke resumed. "It seems to me it's a great opportunity for you. Maybe I was right. Perhaps you will make admiral of the fleet before you graduate as a cadet." Halfheartedly, he clapped Jacob on the back as Hanna gave Zeke a blistering stare.

"How do you feel?" asked Hanna.

"Feel?" said Jacob. His mouth twisted into a quirky smile.

"Is that so difficult? How do you feel?" asked Hanna again.

"I'm going to really miss you two. You're my family now. In fact, you're the only family I have."

"Maybe we'll be part of the next contingent when the additional housing is built and the new fields are under cultivation as Schneider suggested," said Hanna.

"Maybe," said Jacob. His voice sounded dubious.

He went up to his dorm room and Zeke helped him pack his dunnage.

Hanna was waiting for him downstairs. She had tears in her eyes as she hugged him goodbye.

Jacob made it to the shuttle bay. It was faster to take the shuttle than to spend a night in the Travel Oak that connected to Hebron.

The two-hour journey was uneventful. Hebron was huge and he had to ask directions twice until he rode the correct magnetotube to the Kinsinger Garden. He reported in and was sent directly to the appropriate Travel Oak. Two young men were there returning to the colony. They had a border collie and a half dozen sheep with them. They were just settling down to spend the night for the transfer.

"Oh, you must be the new recruit," the older of the two said to Jacob. "My name is Takeo Yamamoto and this is my younger brother Makoto. We were one of the original families sent to Canaan."

Jacob moved his dunnage into the circular grove and placed it on the ground beside the two young men sitting on their bedrolls. They shared the grove with sheep, which kept to the other side. Jacob took out his bedroll and sat on it, with his legs folded. "Anything you can tell me about Canaan?" asked Jacob.

"I know you've been taught some things about Canaan in class," said Takeo, "but I'd better review them since these facts will affect your day-to-day life there.

"Canaan is a little larger than Earth although the gravitational acceleration is only ninety-six percent of Earth's. The day is twenty-four Earth hours, thirty-seven Earth minutes long, so our day ends at 24:37 local time every night to keep our minutes and seconds in step with Earth time. Alpha Centauri A is a bit hotter than Sol, and Canaan orbits our star a bit further out. Our year is four hundred nineteen Canaan days long, and we added two months of twenty-seven days each into the calendar. We try to keep winter and summer solstice the same, so we wedge the extra months in—one after March and one after September. We call one spring and the other fall."

"Very imaginative," said Jacob.

Takeo and Makoto laughed. "Absolutely," said Takeo. "Canaan's orbit is almost circular, like Earth's, but the tilt axis of Canaan is only twelve degrees so seasons are less pronounced. Atmospheric pressure is quite a bit higher than on Earth with a higher concentration of carbon dioxide."

"So, we really won the lottery finding Canaan so close to Earth."

"I suppose," said Makoto, "if you believe in lotteries. I think we were given this as a way of escape from our situation on Earth. Still, I know finding an Earth-like planet so close was astoundingly improbable. Finding one with oxygen in the atmosphere and liquid water on the surface caused a great deal of head scratching among our scientists."

"Dad says a lot of scientists would rather obliterate the planet from the space charts than revise their favorite theories about the origins of life," said Takeo. "Dad was joking."

"Anyway, it's a completely barron world and that has its own problems for colonization. It's not easy starting agriculture from scratch. There is no loam. Soil consists of pure clay and sand. We brought quite a bit of fertilizer from home and had to work hard to get grass and then especially trees to grow in the very barren soil. Thankfully, Travel Oaks are quite resilient. We think when one member of a pair of Travel Oaks lack nutrients, the other one can use the transport properties to resupply the lack. So, our Travel Oaks flourished even when most plants need to be coddled. As you'll see our aquaculture has done particularly well and we regularly harvest water plants as soil-starters. We are pretty well self-sufficient for our small population and we're bringing new fields into cultivation as fast as we can. We have a pasture, an orchard, grain fields, and a vegetable garden. It's been fun to see it grow."

"What I can't get over is the Travel Oaks themselves," said Jacob. "How do they manage to move large objects light years in a matter of hours?"

"I certainly don't know," said Takeo. "I'm not sure anyone knows. But haven't living things always surprised us? Birds that can migrate thousands of miles. Who would have predicted the incredible chemical complexity of living organisms? Electric eels who can generate enough energy to stun a horse in water without stunning themselves."

"You know what was really amazing to me when I read it," said Makoto, "when the Copernicus, in the middle of the journey, was speeding along at a large fraction of the speed of light, the Travel Oaks worked fine even though time dilation was noticeable. How did they compensate for the huge difference in energy between the Travel Oak on the Copernicus and the sister Travel Oak at Hebron? What we learned is that they always transmit water the opposite way from the cargo so energy is always conserved between the two sets of trees. That's why we always plant them near water."

Jacob couldn't completely stifle a yawn. "Let's catch a bit of sleep," said Takeo. The two brothers climbed into their bedrolls and were asleep within minutes. Jacob remained awake. The Border Collie came and curled up beside him. The smell of sheep reminded him of home and his missing family. He found himself overwhelmed with a sense of loss and loneliness. He thought of calling up Doc Giesbrecht and then realized that Doc would be light years away from him by tomorrow. He was very much on his own.

CHAPTER 32
NOW THIS IS REALLY DIFFERENT!

Kinsinger, the colony founded on the barren, but habitable world Alpha Centauri A-3, was named after Josiah Kinsinger, the Overseer of Coventry during the period known as The Years of Tears. The inhabitants of Kinsinger call their world Canaan since to them and to all of us it seems like the Promised Land, but a land with no Philistines.

Canaan is in all respects Earth-like but had no life on it whatsoever—not so much as a microbe—at least not until we landed. Once we arrived, we were carefully bringing in what was needed and we worried that there might be something on the world, not yet discovered, which could wreak unimaginable havoc on our home world.

For that reason, Venus Base Hebron was established as the expedition was planned. It serves as a quarantine buffer between our world and Canaan. If a pathogen were discovered and made it back to Hebron, Hebron would be sealed off from Earth until a cure had been found.

However, after the Coventry Base near Lake Victoria in the North African Democratic Republic went silent in 2084 there was real concern that Coventry's Victoria base had been discovered and that an attack would be imminent on the other two Coventry sites. At that point Venus Base Hebron and the planned future base Galilee were repurposed to serve as vital evacuation sites in case of attack.

Christian and Edward Mutembe. *The Continuing History of the Coventry Penal Colony.*

JACOB AWOKE AS TAKEO SHOOK HIM GENTLY. "WE JUST TRANSITIONED. It's still night here, but we use this ring of trees constantly so the next set of passengers heading to Hebron are already waiting to enter."

Jacob gathered up his dunnage and followed Takeo out into the night. The transition to the denser atmosphere had been gradual and all Jacob noticed was a sense that the air was somehow thicker. The sky had many constellations similar to what he had seen from Earth, since Alpha Centauri was a near neighbor. The most striking aspect was a bright star, brighter than any he had seen on Earth. "That's Alpha Centauri B, the second star in our three-star system," said Takeo. "It's about as far away from us as Uranus is from Earth. At this time of the year it makes our nights brighter than a full moon and is quite handy if we have work or travel at night."

"So, where's the third star?" asked Jacob.

"Proxima Centauri is a red dwarf that's so far from the bary-center—that is the center of gravity of the whole planetary system—that it's hard to see unless you know where to look."

Takeo pointed to an unfamiliar bright star. "See that moderately bright star just south of the constellation Cassiopeia? That's Sol, our sun. If we had a small telescope, we could see Proxima Centauri, the third star in the Alpha Centauri system, as a very faint red star approximately between us and Earth's sun."

Takeo led the way from the garden toward a series of buildings. The village was dominated by two large stone structures, surrounded by a series of small buildings. Takeo led Jacob to one of the small stone cottages. "This is the unmarried male dormitory. You'll stay in Joel's room."

"Joel is the young man who's missing and presumed dead?" asked Jacob.

"Yes," said Takeo, "we're a small village and we know everyone. We still can't believe it. I still expect him to come ambling into town with some story about how he'd hurt his leg and had to lay up for a long time before he could return home."

"I can see how Joel's disappearance has been hard on everyone."

Jacob could see Takeo smile in the light of Alpha Centauri B. Takeo entered the dormitory and switched on the hall lights. Passing a kitchen and living room, he opened a door at the end of the hall. Whispering he said to Jacob, "We've put Joel's things into storage. These rooms are small, but none of us have much stuff."

"Do you and Makoto live here too?" Jacob found his voice too loud in the stillness.

"No, we came as a family and still live with our parents. We're the next cottage over. Get some rest. I'm sure the town council will put you to work tomorrow. I think you saw where the bathroom is when you came in." Takeo quietly left and closed the door with a click.

Jacob's bed consisted of a plasti-wood frame and a foam mattress. He removed his light sleeping bag and pillow from his dunnage, put on his pajamas, and climbed into bed to resume his interrupted sleep. If there was one thing he'd learned from the Space Academy—you always caught your shut-eye when you could. You just never knew when you might be called upon to stay awake three days running.

He woke to the sound of rat-tat-tat on his door. It was Takeo. "The others are already off to work. Mom sent me over to bring you back to our house for breakfast. I'm to take you under my wing and tell you about our village and how we operate. Later this afternoon, we're going to head out and continue our search for Joel on horseback."

Mrs. Yamamoto was a diminutive, pretty woman who looked as if she were in her early thirties. She had a ready smile and, wiping her hands on her flowered apron, pulled Jacob into a hug. She sat Jacob beside her and brought out fried rice mixed with goat's cheese and one egg, chiding Jacob when she decided he did not eat enough. "My husband, Hideo and I are aquatic biologists. We manage half a dozen fish ponds that we've set up in the village to establish a flourishing eco system that's self-sustaining. We hope to eventually release aquatic plants and then fish into the barren waterways in this planet beginning with the Jordan River."

She beamed in pride at their contribution to Kinsinger. "You'll see our work when Takeo takes you for a tour of the village."

A look of concern flashed across her face as Jacob couldn't handle the second helping and had stopped eating. "I'm sorry," said Mrs. Yamamoto, "we have very little meat."

"This is wonderful Mrs. Yamamoto. I had a big meal before I left and my excitement at arriving at such a wonderful place has left me with little appetite, but an insatiable curiosity."

After breakfast, Takeo took Jacob to the center of the village. The village consisted of one long street. At the midpoint was a wide, arched stone bridge that crossed a creek. The creek was surrounded by trees and grass and dammed to form a series of six ponds each about half a hectare in size. Under the bridge was a little waterfall flanked by a reed bed and a series of barriers.

Apparently noticing Jacob's interest in the screens, Takeo said, "We try really hard to keep the minnows from getting swept into the next pond. It's Makoto's job every day to replace the screens and clean the used ones."

Above the large pond at the level of the village, three ponds resided on a series of terraces so that they formed a series of steps above the village, climbing toward a cliff-face, which formed a backdrop to Kinsinger. On the river side of the village, the water successively fell into two larger ponds before emptying into the Jordan River.

"Mom and Dad have worked hard to establish an eco-system in each of these ponds. The top two nearest, The Rock, as we call it, are trout ponds. The middle two are bass and the bottom two are carp ponds. They'll likely cordon off a section of the Jordan River with netting and introduce aquatic plants and see if the carp can survive inside the pen."

"Why are there so few of you here?" asked Jacob.

"I guess we always have a crisis mentality because the years of deprivation are etched into our psyche. We always make the worst-case assumption that Coventry could be overrun or that Hebron might be destroyed. Given that mindset, the decision was made early on to only have enough people here, so that they could survive on the limited food supply that we have available if we were completely cutoff from home. As we bring more fields into cultivation and as we build more houses (since we have no wood yet, we have to use stone, and the building process is very slow), we'll bring in more people."

Takeo stopped and gathered his thoughts. "Our atmosphere has almost 1600 parts per million of carbon dioxide. Back home, on Earth, greenhouse owners would deliberately increase the carbon dioxide to get higher growth. Here we get it for free and, once we improve the soil, we get very high yields."

Next Takeo took Jacob to the large building beside the church. "This is the first building we constructed. We brought a fairly large contingent from home to set it up and equip it. It serves as cafeteria, restaurant, store, blacksmith shop, hospital, administrative offices, and courthouse. The church next door serves as a school and library as well as a place of worship.

"With that in place, we brought in farmers and biologists like my parents to begin the work of establishing a self-sustaining colony. Each time we plant a new field and build some new housing, we bring in additional people."

Takeo took about an hour showing Jacob the big building nicknamed The Manor. Afterwards they briefly looked into the church since school was in session. Everything was tidy and well organized and looked like something from a western novel set in the late 1800's.

When the village tour was complete, Takeo took Jacob back to the ponds. The series of ponds served as a park and garden with walkways and flower beds. The center garden above the stone bridge and very close to the manor, contained two familiar rings of Travel Oaks.

"You have two Travel Oak rings," said Jacob.

"The older ring links us with the Copernicus which has six rings that connect home. When we first arrived on the surface, we transplanted a ring that lets us travel to the Copernicus. In those days, before our ring was functional, we would make a two-step voyage from Hebron on Venus: first to the Copernicus and then to Kinsinger.

"Now we have it much easier but still make frequent trips to Copernicus."

Takeo led Jacob up the terraces until they reached the cliff wall. The stream flowed out of a large opening.

Takeo waved at the cave mouth. "This is why the expeditionary team chose this location initially. Inside is a large cavern that serves as a storage area and barn. This is where we keep horses, sheep, and goats when the weather is bad or in the winter. The tunnels and caverns are quite extensive and have not been fully explored. We have lots of room for expansion if we need the space.

"Let's head back for an early lunch and then we'll set out to look for Joel on horseback."

Mrs. Yamamoto was waiting for them with fresh baked bread, butter, and goat cheese. It tasted so good. After spending so much time underground at Coventry, it was a delight to be above ground and smell the fresh air of outdoor fields, meadows, and waterways.

CHAPTER 33
THE SEARCHERS

AFTER LUNCH TAKEO PULLED OUT A LARGE MAP OF THE SURROUNDING area. There was also a stack of color images of the terrain taken with a high-resolution camera from space.

"Our mother ship, the Copernicus, has taken up a geostationary orbit above our colony. These maps were generated during the initial survey when the ship had a much tighter orbit and briefly surveyed the whole planet looking for a suitable colonization site."

"So, the Copernicus couldn't land on the planet?"

Takeo thought for a moment, stroking his brow. "The interstellar ships were assembled in orbit and optimized for interstellar travel. In an emergency she could make a landing on the planet, but then she would never be able to lift off again. We chose to leave the Copernicus in a geostationary orbit over Kinsinger and ferry the landing party down using the on-board shuttles. We then planted Travel Oaks at Kinsinger for the Copernicus. Now we use Travel Oaks for pretty well all of our travel and keep the shuttles for emergency use only."

Takeo returned his attention to the map. "These pencil lines indicate the searches that have already been conducted."

"Wow," said Jacob, "there's a lot of territory to cover yet. I presume you're searching where Joel was last seen."

"That's part of our problem. Joel left that day without telling anyone where he was going, although someone saw him follow the river downstream. He's an experienced explorer and probably knows the barrens better than anyone else. I guess we'd grown complacent. The only danger here is the terrain and the weather. Now everyone logs their planned route."

Takeo pointed to the left bank of the Jordan on the map and traced their proposed route with his finger. "We'll follow the river downstream to Maranatha Creek. My plan is to follow the creek as far as we can. It leads to the Storm Mountains; very rugged and inhospitable terrain with rapidly changing weather patterns. As I thought about my conversations with Joel, it occurred to me that he'd talked about exploring the foothills leading to the peaks. We can't travel too far. As soon as we leave Kinsinger, the land will be as barren of life as the most inhospitable desert terrain on Earth (except for abundant water). We have to carry fodder for the horses since, of course, there is nothing to graze on. Still, all we're looking for is some evidence that one of us has been there before. That would be enough to mount a major expedition to look for him."

"Is there much hope of finding him?"

"I think," said Takeo, "we're getting into the danger zone. You've heard of the rule of threes?"

"I think so," said Jacob. "Three minutes without air, three days without water, and three weeks without food. After that survival would be threatened."

"That's it!" said Takeo. "We're hoping that whatever happened to him, he has access to water. It's been almost three weeks since Joel disappeared so he's likely on the edge of starvation."

He turned and, stroking his horse's neck, spoke quietly. "So Senshi we go on another trip into the barren lands."

After saddling two horses and loading up two pack horses with fodder, Takeo mounted and followed a well-traveled trail down the Jordan River.

"What's my horse's name?" called Jacob.

Takeo turned back smiling. "He's called Wanderer."

"So, Wanderer, put up with me as I try to remember what it means to ride. I'm a greenhorn." Jacob felt like a sack of potatoes in the saddle. He knew he was going to be very sore by evening, but Wanderer behaved himself and seemed content with Jacob bouncing around on his back.

Soon Kinsinger had disappeared as the Jordan River bent to the left and only the occasional patch of scrawny grass appeared as it tried valiantly to grow in the crushed rock and sand. Before long even that disappeared and all Jacob saw was rock, gravel and sand.

The first thing Jacob noticed was the lack of the smell of growing things. Even the air had become barren and sterile.

Takeo pointed to some lichen on the rocks. "Lichens have spread out well ahead of our colony and have started breaking down the rocks. It's a slow process, but will generate soil over time."

The water of the Jordan River was crystal clear and the banks were either rock or sand. It looked like a river high up in the Rockies where the water was so cold that aquatic weeds did not grow.

Judging by the sun, they reached Maranatha Creek by midafternoon. Takeo stopped for lunch in the shade of a large rock. After feeding and watering the four horses, they broke out their lunch.

"Now we leave the well-traveled path and head into the unknown."

"Has no one gone this way before?" asked Jacob.

"I wouldn't say that. I'm pretty sure someone has explored this creek for a couple of kilometers, but then the country starts to climb toward the mountains. I don't think anyone, with the possible exception of Joel, has bothered to explore further."

Takeo's prediction came true. Soon the creek formed a series of cataracts as it climbed a steep, rocky hill. Takeo left the creek and picked his way around boulders as Senshi threaded his way up the hill. The horse showed excellent sense as it picked out their route. Wanderer seemed content to follow Senshi. After an hour they crested the hill and found a barren valley with a small nearly circular pond in it.

The sun had clouded over. Again they watered and fed the horses.

"I think we should search this little valley thoroughly. If Joel came this way, it's likely that he would have stopped here. If we can find any trace of a camp, that would be important. I'm sure no one else has searched this far up the creek. If we find something, it's almost certain to be Joel."

They split up. Takeo skirted the edge of the pond, looking for a likely campsite. Jacob decided to follow a little rivulet that wound through the valley. He hobbled Wanderer who began to eat contentedly from his feed bag. Jacob began exploring on foot. He saw nothing but rocks, gravel and sand. He began to climb a hill on the other side of the valley following a tiny stream of water, which splashed from rock to rock. The sound was comforting in this barren landscape. He was part way up the steep hill, when the clouds parted momentarily and a flash of light from something caught his eye as if reflected off a mirror. The clouds closed in and the flash vanished. He looked carefully to pinpoint the source of the brief reflection. Maranatha Creek plunged down the hill in a series of cataracts at the base of a cliff, more than one hundred meters high. He was pretty sure the gloom had come from the top of that cliff. *What could it have been? Ice? Water glistening on a rock face? Or was it an injured Joel, in desperation, signaling with a mirror?*

As stupid as it may sound, I'd better tell Takeo.

Jacob climbed down the way he had come. He couldn't go very quickly without tripping or turning an ankle. When he reached the valley, he began to run toward Takeo, calling. When Takeo heard him, he also began moving rapidly to close the distance between them.

Jacob was out of breath. "I saw …" He put his hands on his hips and took a few big breaths.

"Catch your breath and tell me what you saw."

"I saw a reflection … like a mirror … from the top of that cliff." Jacob pointed.

Takeo studied the cliff. "We can't get up there from down here without climbing equipment. Maybe if we follow Maranatha Creek up the next hill, there will be a back way to the top. If Joel is up there signaling, he must have reached the top without a technical climb."

Takeo looked to the west. "We'd better hurry. I don't like the look of those clouds." They mounted up and resumed their ascent with Senshi picking their route up the hill. After a while, they entered another valley. Here Maranatha Creek split into two branches. The much smaller creek came out of a cave opening from the very cliff they were hoping to scale. It was now about fifty meters high.

"Look!" said Takeo. There was horse manure and a scattering of oats among the gravel. "We must be on the right track."

Just then the first thunderclap rang out and the roiling black clouds swept in to cover the valley. The horses whinnied in fear and began to pull at their tethers.

"We have no shelter from the lightning here. The horses are going to bolt. The creek is broad and shallow. Let's cross over to that cave and see if we can get away from the lightning."

Takeo led Senshi and his pack horse and walked across the creek. The water only came up to his calves. Jacob followed with the other two horses.

Another jagged bolt of lightning rent the sky and the horses reared. Jacob pulled on the halter and moved across the creek as quickly as possible. Takeo had taken out a flashlight and was already climbing the far bank and leading the horses into the cave mouth. Jacob entered the cave as the third lightning flash appeared, followed almost immediately by thunder.

That was close!

Takeo switched on the flashlight. The passage was just wide enough to lead two horses. After fifty feet the cave opened up into a small cavern with barely enough of a flat gravel space for the six of them. A rock fall formed a steep slope behind them. They sat with their backs to the rock fall looking at the creek.

"Hopefully the thunderstorm will move on quickly so we can get home. We found what we were looking for. I'm pretty sure Joel came this way."

Jacob heard a curious rumbling sound. "Look at the creek!" shouted Takeo. "Let's get out of here!"

The water was rising rapidly and already spanned the width of the tunnel. They untethered the horses. Senshi pulled the lead out of Takeo's hands, plunged into the creek and was swept down the tunnel. The other three terrified animals followed unwittingly. Jacob was about to plunge in after them when Takeo grabbed his arm. "No, the water is already too high and fast. The creek outside will likely be a raging torrent. We'll be swept over the cataracts and drowned or smashed. Up the rock fall!"

Takeo began climbing the rocks. Having now filled the exit tunnel completely, the water continued to climb, dogging their heels. By the light of Takeo's flashlight, Jacob could see a rapidly-rising pool. The tunnel was at the bottom of the pool.

The water wet Jacob's boot. Ahead the rock fall ended and Takeo was inching up a narrow chimney. Jacob was exhausted. "Put your left foot on that ledge." Takeo's light illuminated the way. Jacob did as he was told. Fear increased.

I'm trapped! Drowning was one of his greatest fears. He could imagine himself trapped in a dead-end chimney with water covering his mouth and his hands scrabbling on the rocks, tearing his fingernails on the stone, hoping to get out. Then he would gulp water when he couldn't hold his breath any longer.

Then another terror struck him. *We're trapped in an enclosed space. When we run out of oxygen we'll suffocate.*

"I think the water is receding," said Takeo. "Thank the Lord." Jacob, in his terror of drowning or suffocating, had not realized the water was no longer up to his knees. Takeo squeezed past Jacob and followed the water back down as it receded. Takeo drank by cupping his hands. "One good thing about a barren planet, there are no pathogens in the water." Realizing how thirsty he was, Jacob joined him.

It seemed hours later when they reached the bottom of the rock fall. Now there was about a one-meter air gap in the tunnel. Takeo waited until the water was ankle-deep before he waded into the tunnel, fastening the flashlight to his forehead. "The current's not too bad." Jacob followed half-walking, half-swimming through the deeper depressions in the tunnel. When they exited the tunnel, it was night. Alpha Centauri B was just over the horizon and illuminated the landscape more brightly than a full moon on earth. Jacob found himself in a sizable pond, which was dammed with a weir made of a rock ledge at the point where the water plunged into the next valley. They swam across the pond and heard the friendly whinny of horses. They found three horses on the far side, well away from the water's edge. One of the packhorses had disappeared.

Takeo and Jacob unloaded the horses and fed them oats from the remaining packhorse. Everything was wet, so they spread the rest of the oats out on a rock to dry. They were too tired to do much more and promptly fell asleep.

The next morning, they searched but found no sign of the second pack-horse.

"Now what do we do," asked Takeo. "We know Joel was here. He may have gone on and just crossed the next rise. He's probably hurt."

"So, why don't we go on?"

"Jacob, you're a recent arrival. We've had a catastrophe and lost a horse. My father will be worried. We're out of supplies. We've always been taught to go back and avoid the point of no return by a large margin."

"But as you pointed out, Takeo, Joel must be close to the end of his tether. By the time we go back and mount the next expedition, we may be too late. How far can we go before we hit the real point of no return?"

"We could take a chance and keep going today if we unload the pack horse and stash any extra supplies here."

"I vote we do that," said Jacob.

The cliff they would have to scale, if they tried to find the source of the puzzling reflection, was part of a mesa and decreased in height as the land around it climbed toward the Storm Mountains. Eventually the mesa bent to the east and again increased in height. Maranatha Creek ran past the mesa in a deep gorge. Takeo went to examine the mesa wall at its lowest point. Jacob saw that it was less steep and looked climbable here. Several rock bridges crossed the narrow gorge, but they wouldn't want to take their horses across. Jacob kept looking up to where he had seen the reflection, but did not see any more.

The shallow valley ended in a ridge. A rock fall had filled the gorge and created a series of waterfalls. Crossing the ridge, they came to a small lake.

"Look!" said Takeo. On the rim of this valley was a makeshift camp with a tattered tent. The trail was treacherous and the narrow valley was strewn with debris.

"Look at all the mounded sand and gravel. A flood came through here," said Takeo.

As they approached the tent, Takeo called Joel's name. They heard a muffled cry.

As they finally reached the tent and opened the flap, Jacob saw a pale young man lying on a ragged sleeping bag, with a crudely splinted leg.

"Joel!" said Takeo.

"Takeo," said Joel, "I thought you'd never come. Where's my father?"

"Joel, he hasn't stopped looking for you since you disappeared. No one knew where you were. He's searching north of Kinsinger."

Takeo introduced Jacob and began to examine Joel. "You've broken your leg. What happened?"

"I had made camp here and heard a funny sound."

"What do you mean a funny sound?"

"It was a humming grinding sound. Like a machine. I left my tent and took my horse and packhorse to investigate when a sudden storm from the Storm Mountains flooded the creek. We were washed downstream. I managed to pull myself out of the water near the tent, but I saw the horses wash over into the gorge."

"We didn't see any carcasses downstream, so they must still be wedged in the gorge."

"I'm sorry to hear that. I had hoped against hope that they had made it through and wandered home."

After giving Joel something to drink and eat, Takeo and Jacob worked to stabilize his leg.

"Without wood around here, there's very little to work with," said Jacob. "We'll have to use the tent poles."

"Yes, we just have to do the best we can."

Takeo gave up Senshi to Joel and the three headed back. They stopped briefly at the cairn to eat and then continued on into the night. At about midnight, they reached the mouth of Maranatha Creek and met an expedition led by Takeo's father. Takeo rushed to embrace him. "We found him, father."

Takeo's father examined Joel's leg. "We have to get back. This has not set very well. He'll need to be sent back to Hebron since we don't have the medical facilities here."

They continued to travel back to Kinsinger and Mr. Yamamoto called to the Copernicus to let Joel's family know that Joel had been found. Joel's father met them on the way home and embraced his son with tears in his eyes.

When they reached Kinsinger, Joel was rushed into the Travel Oak circle and the doctor and his staff worked on his leg there so that they could travel back as soon as possible.

Looking at Jacob, Mr. Yamamoto said, "Jacob, welcome to Canaan. It looks like you have experienced first-hand the terrible storms we sometimes have here. We may not yet have any dangerous wildlife, but you can die here in the wilderness just the same."

CHAPTER 34
A PERILOUS REFUGE

THE MAYOR ASKED JACOB AND TAKEO TO EXPLAIN THE DETAILS OF THEIR rescue. Takeo took the lead. He told how Joel had talked about hearing an unusual noise, which had prompted him to get closer to the Storm Mountains than he had initially intended.

"He shouldn't have done that," said the mayor. "I'm glad he's safe, but he's cost us three horses, and we've had to send him, his father, mother, and the colony doctor back to the hospital in Hebron at a time when we can't afford to lose anyone."

"There's more," said Takeo, "we saw a reflection on the mesa, as if something metallic was up there. That needs to be investigated."

The mayor objected. But Takeo and Jacob were so insistent, that Mr. Yamamoto chimed in with his support and the mayor had to yield. He took down an exact statement of location and time of day of the sighting, and reluctantly promised that an expedition would be sent immediately.

"These boys need to be examined," said Takeo's father. Takeo's protests were of no avail.

The nurse prodded, x-rayed, and scoped the two, and finally sent them to bed where they were kept under observation.

The next morning, Jacob learned that an expedition had already been sent away with provisions for a week.

The two kept busy with chores, but their minds were constantly on the expedition. A week passed. Then ten days. Finally, the searchers returned—exhausted, but with no new sightings. They had not seen the reflection, even in bright sunlight and at the same time of day that Jacob had reported seeing it. They found the same traces of Joel's camp, however, and even the carcasses of two horses in the gorge. Takeo's packhorse was not found. In the meantime, the mayor had requested an optical scan of the mesa from the distant orbit of the Copernicus. It showed nothing suspicious.

In the debriefing, which the whole village attended, the rescue team leader explained their trip in detail. He concluded: "We found two of the missing horses. We searched the whole area for a week, but saw no further trace of the reflection or heard anything suspicious.

To warn travelers off about the uncertain weather in that region, we left our supplies in a cairn. We put a flag by the cave entrance you found, Takeo, along with a warning sign about the danger beyond. We left as much fodder and food there as we could afford. Then we hurried home."

"Did you climb to the top of that cliff where we saw the reflection?" asked Takeo.

Jacob was glad he had said "we."

"No. We searched all around that area. Those cliffs form a mesa. There was no way to get our horses up there, especially with that gorge in between."

Jacob saw the blood drain out of Takeo's face, then watched him turn his back on the expedition members and stomp out of the room. His father followed quickly.

Jacob stayed for a brief question-and-answer session with the expedition leader. When that was done, Jacob wandered off looking for Takeo. He found him sitting on a stone bench near the lower bass pond. He looked angry.

"So, what's going on, Takeo?

"I had a disagreement with my father." He looked at Jacob shaking his head. "Don't ask."

"So, what do we do next?" asked Jacob.

"I think we take up the tour where we left off before we headed off to look for Joel."

He continued to show Jacob the operation of the colony. He gave him an extensive lecture on the ecosystem of the fish ponds and how they were going to begin a trial in the river with carp. Takeo showed Jacob where his mother already had plants growing in the river in an area confined by nets to keep the plants from drifting downstream.

Jacob could tell by Takeo's distracted demeanor that his heart wasn't in the tutoring.

"So, what's eating you, Takeo?"

"I'm sure this metallic reflection and the noise Joel heard are significant. No one believes us."

"They sent out an expedition."

"They should have sent us out again. We would have climbed to the mesa."

"So, what are you going to do?"

"What can I do? My father forbade me from searching."

"You're going out on your own, despite your father's words, aren't you?"

Takeo looked searchingly at Jacob. "How did you know?"

"That's what I'd do if I'd been here longer. I'm with you. I know something funny's going on. My intuition is flashing warning lights. Parents often stop their children from taking risks that they themselves would take in a heartbeat. It's because they love their children so much they can't bear the thought of losing them. Let me come along."

"I thought I read you were an orphan. How come you know so much about how parents think?"

"I became an orphan late in life when my parents and siblings were killed in an accident. My parents were good to me. I know how they would've reacted."

"So, you want to come along? You know I'm going to be in a pack of trouble no matter how this comes out. They can't send me back to Hebron since my whole family is here. But in your case, they'd likely send you back with a giant black mark on your record. I can't let that happen."

"Takeo, that's my decision to make. If my gut feeling is correct, it's more important to get to the bottom of these odd occurrences than to risk having a black mark on my record. Besides, two will always be safer than one. I've done some technical climbing in the Rockies, so I can help you there as well. We'll need at least two packhorses if we want to stay more than a couple of days."

"What you say means a lot to me. You'll know by tomorrow morning what I decide to do."

Takeo made them quit early. Jacob wandered around Kinsinger for a while and then he started reading *Mere Christianity* by C. S. Lewis. It was one of the few books on his bookshelf in his dorm room. He found the first chapter especially interesting. He had never seen this book in his school or in the public library, and certainly not at the Technology Ministry in Toronto.

He was so engrossed in Lewis' discussion of The Law of Human Nature and the universality of Right and Wrong, that the time slipped by.

But I've always been taught that right and wrong is something we invent, and the important thing is to let people invent and choose what they like. But Lewis seems to be saying that by their very speech—when those who believe in moral invention appeal for 'fairness'—they're tacitly acknowledging that we all believe there's a common standard that we ought to support. How can we all invent the same standard?

It looked to be time for supper. He walked over to Takeo's house. Takeo's father was grave but said nothing. Takeo also said very little during the meal and then asked if he could go to his room. Jacob was anxious to leave as soon as politeness would allow. He felt that if he had not been there, Takeo and his father would have had much more to say to each other.

While thinking about how he could leave without being rude, Takeo's father rose from his place as if to follow Takeo.

"Let him go, dear," said Takeo's mom, "he's very upset about his friend Joel's injury. It's hard waiting for news."

Jacob excused himself. On the way out, he saw Takeo carrying a sack to the stables in the cavern.

————————

At three o'clock in the morning a noise woke Jacob. Jacob was up in the hayloft of the cavern-barn and he heard the slap of shoes on the stone floor. Peering over the edge, he saw Takeo with his shielded flashlight, carrying his saddle to Senshi.

Jacob crept down quietly. "Here let me help."

Takeo stifled a yelp and then almost collapsed when he realized it was Jacob. "What are you doing here?"

"Well, I *was* sleeping in the hayloft thinking that if you were going to sneak out, you'd have to saddle up Senshi. Now I'm thinking I'm setting out in the middle of the night on an expedition to put some of our questions to bed."

"But Jacob, it's too dangerous from several perspectives."

"I could threaten to holler if you don't let me come—but I won't. I still say it's my decision. But if you're going to be a bone-headed idiot and tell me to stay, I'll go back to my real bed. Don't be a bone-headed idiot!"

"I give up. Take Wanderer and help me load up the pack horses. I'm planning to double the load and store the extra at the cache. Have you brought your climbing equipment?"

"Yes, I saw from the pictures back in Hebron that Kinsinger had a rock wall near the town, so I brought my equipment. Besides, it's all about survival when you're colonizing, isn't it?"

In thirty minutes, they had loaded the animals. Takeo turned off his flashlight, and on foot, led two horses along a path that avoided the town buildings and skirted the bottom of the cliff.

In the bright starlight of Alpha Centauri B, Jacob could see reasonably well. After twenty minutes, their trail joined the path they had taken previously. Takeo mounted, and led them rapidly away from town.

Jacob felt a slight ground tremor. *I didn't know this was an earthquake zone.* He looked up. Takeo seemed lost in thought and appeared not to have noticed.

They were just out of town, when Jacob, who was leading his horse along a side path close to the bank of the Jordan River said, "That's funny."

"What's funny?" asked Takeo edging Senshi close to Jacob.

"Look at the water," said Jacob. The level is dropping rapidly. It's like a bathtub draining."

Takeo looked at it for a moment and then said, "This is bad. Very bad. We have to get back."

Takeo handed Jacob the reins to the second pack horse and headed Senshi back to town at a gallop. Seeing Takeo disappear around the bend, Jacob tied the second pack horse to the first and also headed back to town. He increased his horses' pace to a trot. When Jacob came up to the Yamamoto cottage, Senshi was puffing. Mr. Yamamoto appeared in his pajamas, disheveled, with the glazed look of someone who has been woken out of a sound sleep. He looked at the saddled horses and scowled. "Takeo, say again what's going on? What's the emergency?"

"The river's dropping, fast," said Takeo.

"What?" said his father.

"We felt an earthquake. The river must be blocked upstream. It's almost empty."

His father grabbed his coat and ran down to the river in his pajamas, followed by Jacob and Takeo. What used to be a river was now a series of pools.

Mr. Yamamoto rushed back into town to the main building. Within a minute Jacob heard a loud bell ringing.

The mayor, bleary-eyed, appeared from his own cottage and asked what was going on. "The river's blocked upstream. When the dam breaks loose, we're going to face a flood. We need to get everyone to higher ground and have the Copernicus optically check out the river channel back to the source in the mountains," said Mr. Yamamoto.

Mrs. Yamamoto didn't wait for a decision from the mayor but began urging the gathering women to lead their children to a ledge on the rock behind town. Seeing everyone responding to the emergency, the mayor rushed to the main building to contact the Copernicus. Fifteen minutes later he joined the working men, white-faced and shaken. "There's been a massive landslide in the mountains. The Jordan is dammed up and a lake's filling behind it. When the lake fills up and starts to overflow, Copernicus thinks it will wash the sand and gravel away quickly and we could have a major flood."

The colonists put a lookout on top of Kinsinger rock while everyone else began to bring animals, supplies, and possessions into the cavern.

CHAPTER 35
THE ONLY QUESTION—HOW HIGH?

THE MEN WORKED FEVERISHLY FOR TWO HOURS HAULING AS MANY supplies, tools, and valuable documents away from the town as possible. A parade of women, having made sure their children were safe, also came back to their houses to collect precious keepsakes the men had missed.

About four in the morning a flare went up from Kinsinger Rock. The water was rising! Jacob rushed back to the foot of The Rock. A wave of water perhaps three meters high was racing down the river bed. This flood continued to swell. It overflowed the river bank and kept rising. It swallowed up the lower pond and kept rising. It reached the second and third ponds, swallowing up the cottages near to the bank. The water kept rising.

Jacob climbed up to the ledge. Mrs. Yamamoto was crying softly. The men looked grim.

The water's advance slowed but not before the fourth pond was swallowed up. The water lapped around the stone walls of the village's main building and surrounded the mound on which the Travel Oaks grew.

"If it reaches the Travel Oaks, what will we do?" asked the mayor. "We'll be cut off!"

It was sunrise and an orange light flooded the landscape. The Jordan had crested, leaving devastation in its wake. The stone houses near the river remained standing, but they had been flooded.

When the lower ponds flooded, the fish had escaped. Silt and gravel had filled the lowest pond. Thankfully, the top two trout ponds were intact. More importantly, the Travel Oaks were spared.

As the villagers surveyed the damage, the doctor, Hanna, and Zeke emerged from the Hebron Travel Oak. The doctor appeared stunned by the devastation. Hanna and Zeke were merely curious until they heard of the disaster they had just missed. Hanna went pale when she learned how close they had come to being swept away.

Jacob introduced Hanna and Zeke to the Yamamotos who had returned from the river bank where they had been assessing the damage.

"How did you manage to swing your trip here?" Jacob asked his friends.

"When your doctor arrived along with the injured young man and his family, the decision was made to send replacements. Since you were already here, Hanna argued that we made a great team and should be allowed to go," said Zeke.

"I can be very persuasive when I want to be," said Hanna with a smile.

"No kidding," said Jacob.

After the introductions were over, the conversation turned to the work at hand. "The net's been swept away," said Mrs. Yamamoto. "Many of the aquatic plants went with it, although a few remain. So much for controlled release. There are now plants and fish downstream. Who knows which ones will survive?"

The Yamamotos procured a new net from stores and re-established a holding area in the Jordan. Zeke, Hanna, and Jacob helped the Yamamotos net carp as they came up to feed, and transferred them to the holding area in the Jordan. That took most of the day.

One of the colonists brought out a digger from the cavern and removed silt and gravel from the lower two ponds. Takeo worked with Jacob and Zeke to place screens at the pond drainage sluices, and after a week the ponds were ready to hold fish and plants again.

The next two ponds had also overflowed and many bass had escaped, but without silt damage, these ponds, although depleted of fish were still usable when the water receded.

As the days passed, more and more help came from Hebron. Once the ponds were established, the town council proposed plans for a second garden on higher ground behind Kinsinger Rock. The colonists set to work. They ground rock down to a powder as a precursor for soil. They added silt from the river. They redirected a stream from the backside of Kinsinger Rock through the new garden. Travel Oak cuttings from Hebron and the Copernicus arrived and became the center-piece of the new garden on a high northeastern terrace beside Kinsinger Rock.

CHAPTER 36
RESOLVING A MYSTERY

THREE WEEKS PASSED. MANY OF THE TEMPORARY WORKERS HAD RETURNED to Hebron. The cottages near the Jordan had been cleaned and repaired. Work continued on the new garden, with additional plants arriving daily.

One afternoon, Takeo approached Jacob as he worked in the new garden a few meters from Zeke and Hanna. Looking around, Takeo whispered, "Still willing to check out our mystery?"

Jacob was startled that he had forgotten about their quest in the heat of the village's emergency. "Yes, I'm ready to go."

"Should we tell Hanna and Zeke?"

Jacob thought for a moment. "I'll write them a note explaining what we're doing. If we tell them now, they'll want to come. Why jeopardize their careers? One career casualty will be enough. When do we leave?"

"Tonight at one o'clock. I think, rather than an extended expedition, we'll travel light and make our way up to the top of the mesa. We'll either find something interesting or not. If we don't, I'll be satisfied and leave it at that. I'm supposed to scout down river to determine if any of our escaped water plants have taken hold or if some of the fish have survived. By starting early, and making a fast side trip, we should get back about the time they expect us."

That night, Jacob snuck out of the dormitory and met Takeo in the cavern. They filled their saddle bags with provisions taken from the kitchen stores and by 1:30 a.m. they were on their way. The smell of cut grass diminished as they left the village behind. Jacob heard the crunch of Wanderer's hooves on the gravel of the trail. In the light of Alpha Centauri B, he could see evidence of flood damage all along the shore. Alpha Centauri B had set when they reached the mouth of Maranatha Creek. Without a rest they continued rapidly up the now familiar trail. The rush of cataracts and waterfalls broke the stillness.

Jacob began to have doubts. What would they find? What if it proved to be nothing more than a wet cliff face catching the light of the sun? Would Takeo look down on him as a rookie, for making them take these risks for nothing?

They made it to the upper valley with the cave, flag, and cache by five o'clock in the morning. After unloading some of their supplies at the cache and leaving a brief note, they followed the edge of the mesa into the valley beyond. They didn't want to leave their horses here without access to water so they proceeded over the ridge to the small valley with a lake. Jacob saw the torn rags of Joel's tent lying staked and deflated near the water. They piled some fodder on a rock and hobbled the horses. They crossed the ridge again and then used one of the natural stone bridges that spanned the gorge and began their ascent of the mesa. Although the grade here was about thirty meters straight up, there were enough projections and cracks in the rock to make the climb easy—they didn't really need to use ropes and only did so for added safety. When Takeo reached the top, he extended a hand to Jacob and helped him up.

"I'm starved," said Takeo. "Let's have a bite to eat before we explore the mesa."

They sat on a rock in the early morning sunshine and watched the hobbled horses by the lake in the next valley. After completing their short meal, Jacob felt much better. He suggested they skirt the mesa cliff edge since he had a good idea about the location of the reflection.

Jacob led. It was tough going. The top of the mesa was rugged. Weathered rocks projected into the air like broken teeth. Deep, narrow chasms would appear at their feet and force Jacob to travel away from the cliff edge to find a way across. Finally, Jacob spotted the flag and cache below. He looked toward the western end of the mesa where he judged the reflection had originated. Pointing, he said, "It should be about there."

"What's that?" Takeo asked, pointing to a gray-tan blob that pulsated faintly in the wind on the top of a small hill some distance from the edge of the mesa.

"I'm not sure," said Jacob. "Why's it pulsating?"

The longer Jacob looked at the object, the more it looked like a tent or tarp rippling in the wind. But it couldn't be, could it? Jacob's heart began to pound.

"If I didn't know better," said Takeo, "I'd say that's a huge tent. But how could it be?" Fear edged his voice.

They carefully picked their way up to the object, climbing into shallow hollows or wending their way around jutting rocks. Takeo arrived first. When Jacob arrived, they looked at the object and then at each other. It was definitely a camouflage tarp, held down by guy ropes. It covered a bulging structure the size of a small cabin.

Taking a deep breath, Takeo lifted the edge of the tarp and stepped under it. Jacob followed. "Unbelievable!" said Jacob. He was looking at a banged up, gleaming space shuttle that could have come from the Copernicus. On the crumpled bow Jacob could make out the words *Aquinas Cargo Pod 3*.

CHAPTER 37
WE HAVE TO STOP MEETING LIKE THIS

"WE HAVE TO GET OUT OF HERE NOW!" SAID TAKEO. JACOB HEARD THE crunch of boots on gravel behind him outside the tarp.

"Not so fast," said a voice, eerily familiar to Jacob.

Jacob and Takeo ducked under the tarp out into bright sunshine. About a dozen men in khaki uniforms with rifles were climbing out of cover. Jacob noticed a coiled cobra insignia on their shirts. Rousseau, in uniform, and with a sneer on his face, pointed a pistol at them. Next to him, also in uniform, Jacob recognized Rousseau's crony, Litch.

Rousseau laughed. "You should see your face, Kraiser." On cue, Litch joined in the merriment. "Bewildered as usual? Not expecting to meet me four light-years from home? I'm full of surprises. Cuff 'em and bring 'em. I want three men, stationed out of sight on the mesa watching their horses and the cache. A rescue party will be looking for them. Don't make another mistake like the last one that led to this fiasco. I want extra ropes to keep the pod covered until I return. I don't care how bad the storms get. No radio broadcasts. Copernicus could be listening. Keep me informed. Send the third man to the lift and signal the temporary camp using the line-of-sight laser radio."

Their hands cuffed in front of them, Jacob and Takeo were led at gunpoint across the mesa to the side furthest from Maranatha Creek. Here a well-camouflaged metal winch had been rigged up. Jacob and Takeo were ordered to get onto the platform. Four guards joined them. The electric winch motor began to hum and the pulley squeaked as the platform lowered.

At the bottom, Jacob saw four camouflaged, all-terrain vehicles. He and Takeo were put to work loading up the vehicles with equipment. Finally, the others arrived from the top of the mesa. Takeo and Jacob were separated and forced to sit in the back seats of the last two vehicles, each between two burly captors. Rousseau arrived at Jacob's ATV and told the guards to blindfold their captives. Jacob spent the next two hours being jostled and bounced. Once in a while he was cursed and shoved when the rough road bounced him into one of the guards.

When the vehicle finally stopped, Jacob was roughly hauled out of it, his blindfold removed. Looking around, he saw that they were in a steep-sided valley. The huge Aquinas was wedged partway up the valley. She had clearly had a rough landing; the edges of the starship looked like they had been crumpled by the canyon wall. The top of the starship was covered with camouflage netting.

Looking around the open part of the valley in front of the starship, he observed no buildings, but several caves—some of them looked to have been man-made. Unlike the Kinsinger colony, it appeared that no effort had been made here to terraform the surrounding rock. If Rousseau's men were cut off from earth, they would have to rely on whatever plants and supplies had survived the crash inside the Aquinas.

Jacob spotted groups of soldiers relaxing at the cave mouth and under the shelter of the rock walls. Most lounged around rolling dice, smoking, or drinking. But there were also others who looked underfed and poorly dressed in ragged bright orange tee-shirts. Jacob noticed that the lounging soldiers ordered these men about. Indeed, it seemed if one of the workers with an orange tee-shirt finished a task, one of the soldiers immediately commandeered him to get a beer or something to eat.

Rousseau ordered Jacob and Takeo brought into one of the caves, which opened up into a cavern with a small building inside. The two were led into a sparsely furnished room. Rousseau forced them to sit down by a table. He sat on the edge of the table, crossing his arms. He towered over them. Jacob could hear Litch breathing behind him. Rousseau glared at them for a long thirty seconds. Finally he said, "You know, we don't have to be enemies. Just tell me what I want to know and I can make your lives a lot easier for you."

"My name is Takeo Yamamoto. I am a colonist of this planet. I'm a dual citizen of Canada and Coventry. I have nothing further to say"

Takeo set his jaw. Litch punched him in the mouth.

"Not the answer I was looking for," said Rousseau. He turned to Jacob.

"My name is Jacob Kraiser. I am a colonist of this planet. I'm a dual citizen of Canada and Coventry ..." Jacob felt Litch grab his shoulder and braced himself for a punch. Rousseau made a small dismissive motion with his hand. Litch let him go.

"But I can make 'em talk, boss," said Litch.

"I'm sure you can, but they're just going to lie. We can beat them or we can add them to our understaffed labor pool, work their asses off, and wait until they see sense and offer to tell us the truth. I'd rather go the second route."

"So, what happens next?" asked Takeo.

"Oh, this is a wonderfully big, empty planet. We'll be the friendliest of neighbors, don't you think? After all we need each other. If you'd told me what I needed to know, I would have taken you back and made a peace offer. Now I'll have to find another way to convince you we don't have any hostile intentions. Take them away."

Their handcuffs were removed, they were given orange tee-shirts, then put to work with a crew assembling a water pump to transfer water from a nearby creek to a new housing residence that had been constructed inside a large cave to hold more troops.

After they had worked for a couple of hours, Jacob and another worker were sent to glue together polymer pipe for insertion into a ditch to carry water up to the new dormitory. Jacob was tired, thirsty, and felt dizzy from being out in the sun too long. His companion looked around for guards, and then slipped Jacob a small water bottle. Jacob took a couple of big gulps, but felt guilty and gave it back.

"No, go ahead," said the other. "They're punishing you. I've had something to drink."

Jacob began to feel better, even euphoric. *It must be the sun,* he thought.

While working on the pipe, Jacob's companion spoke to him without look-ing up from his work. "Don't let them know we're talking. My name is Thomas Penner. I was crewing the Aquinas when Coventry Africa fell. They enslaved me with the rest of the crew and forced us to work the Aquinas while they learned how to operate the starship. The idiots crashed Aquinas, so they were obviously slow learners."

"Are you by chance related to General Penner?"

"No, I don't think so. Penner is a pretty common Mennonite name."

"How long have you been here?" asked Jacob.

"Only about three months. We took a long detour coming in, sling-shotting around Alpha Centauri B to finalize our approach. Now that we're here though, they're bringing in personnel as fast as they can fit them into the Travel Oaks."

"What about you?" asked Penner.

"My name is Jacob Kraiser. I'm from the colony founded by the Copernicus."

"I'm glad your ship made it. Any problems on the way in?"

"I'm relatively new to Coventry and I don't know much about the history of the Copernicus flight or the crew landing."

"I had a cousin on the Copernicus, Isaiah Tiesen, do you know him? Is he at the colony?"

"Don't know, Thomas. Like I said, I'm new there and I think there are several hundred people there."

Penner looked puzzled. "I would have thought, given the amount of time, that many more people would have arrived at the other colony."

"No, according to my information, they're keeping the numbers low enough that the colony remains self-sustaining through their own agriculture."

"So, they're mostly farmers?"

Jacob was becoming alarmed at the questions and decided to shut down the conversation. "I can't really say."

They worked on for some time, laying additional pipe into the cavern. "One thing still puzzles me," said Thomas, "why did Coventry forget about us?"

"I don't think we ever forgot about you, but it's been seven years since our last contact with you, and your arrival at Alpha Centauri is overdue by at least two years."

Their shift ended and they were taken to the slave's quarters, which consisted of a pit in the back of the cavern, the top of which was surrounded on three sides by a smooth brick wall. The front wall had a locked door. The fourth side appeared to be a cavern wall. The slaves lined up and were given some stale bread before walking through the door. A rope ladder was the only route into the pit. Jacob and Takeo were the last to climb down. Jacob saw the others sitting in groups of five. Many were bowing their heads over their food.

"How can they be thankful for crappy food like this?" asked Jacob.

"I do it because it's better than no food, and it helps me see God for who He is," said Takeo.

One of the groups waved them over. Jacob and Takeo sat cross-legged on the rock floor. "Friend," said a man sitting next to them, "where is the other companion of yours?"

"Other companion?" asked Jacob.

"The fellow who was working with you on the piping for the new dormitory."

"Oh, you mean Thomas Penner. Was he not one of your crew?"

"Nope. Today was the first day we'd seen him, and so we assumed he'd been captured along with you."

"Ohhh ..." said Jacob as realization dawned on him. *I've been such a fool.*

Takeo turned to their friend. "I have a question. Maybe you can answer it. What happened to the Aquinas? How did you manage to get here? How did you land the Aquinas without the Copernicus spotting you?"

"I was part of the crew when the Aquinas was over-run. I saw it happening from on board the Aquinas and I pieced the rest together from what I heard later. The Cobras took the Aquinas by surprise after they over-ran Coventry Africa.

"We had no idea that Coventry Africa had been over-run. Mission Control told us one of our returning personnel had infected our base with a serious viral infection. In all likely hood Aquinas faced a potential viral outbreak. Travel Oak traffic was stopped and Aquinas was placed under quarantine. Who wouldn't listen to Mission Control? We trusted them.

"Mission Control sent a 'medical team' through the Travel Oaks to help with the medical emergency and quarantine. While they were getting ready to act, we received what seemed to us to be genuine, ongoing communications with from Mission Control without letting us know the Cobras had complete control of our home base. They completely fooled us. On board the ship, when they had enough personnel in place, they seized control of the Travel Oaks to Coventry Africa and destroyed the emergency Travel Oaks that connected us to the other ships."

"Once in complete control of the Aquinas, they cranked up the Aquinas' Hoffstetter field generators to their maximum to make Aquinas as impervious as possible to electromagnetic radiation and so rendered us invisible.

"Cobra's spies kept our ship informed of the colonization of Alpha Centauri A-3 by the Copernicus. With that information, the Cobras planned their final approach. They modified our trajectory, swung around Alpha Centauri B and chose a slow approach that kept us roughly in a direct line between A-3 and Alpha Centauri B, or as close as we could manage it. All the B radiation made us very hard to detect. All that subterfuge made our route more circuitous, but I gather you had no idea we were approaching."

"No, we had no idea," said Jacob. We thought your ship had been lost, just like the Faraday."

"I thought so," continued their friend. "Once we came close to Alpha Centauri A, they would periodically open up the Hoffstetter Field to eavesdrop on your ground communication with the Copernicus. They couldn't afford to listen in too often, but knew roughly where you were and picked a landing site close enough for action, but not so close that your colonists might stumble across us."

"Then let me guess," ventured Jacob, "your ship timed her approach so that Copernicus was over the horizon and she landed before they could spot you."

"Right, we entered the atmosphere at the far side, took a long glide path at night, but the Cobra idiots who were in command botched the landing and severely damaged the stern of the ship. Many were killed. Luckily for them but not for you, one of the Travel Oak gardens that linked the ship to Coventry Africa was in the forward part of the ship and the trees weren't damaged."

Neither Jacob nor Takeo said much for a long time. Their friend, exhausted by the conversation, lay back for a nap after a tiring day.

Jacob thought about everything he had been told. He finally decided that thinking about the Aquinas would not make up for his stupidity in speaking to Penner. He had to get word to Kinsinger. Looking around, he saw that the pit they were in was only the front porch of another cave. The back wall formed an overhang, which would be impossible to climb without equipment. He had not seen the cave and overhang until he had descended into this pit.

"Where does that cave go?" Jacob asked his neighbor.

"It goes in a long way. We've only explored enough to see that it doesn't return to the surface nearby. There's no point finding an exit anyway since we can't get very far on a barren planet like this without food. We had better all get some rest. Our days are long and the Cobras don't have any sympathy for fatigue."

CHAPTER 38
WHAT ARE THEY UP TO?

THE NEXT FEW DAYS WERE GRUELING. ROUSSEAU'S MEN WERE PREPARING for the arrival of more soldiers and drove the slaves to ready the camp for the reinforcements. Jacob and the others worked long hours on the new dormitory, but it seemed that a decision had been made to prepare for conflict as rapidly as possible. The buildup, according to the other slaves, had always been rapid, but now it had been raised to a fever pitch. Each day saw the arrival of a Travel-Oak-load of additional soldiers. One day the Travel Oak even brought a small armored personnel carrier. Jacob saw it as it was driven out of the large cargo port of the Aquinas and taken up the road.

Thomas Penner, or whatever his real name was, appeared in uniform and stayed with Rousseau. Jacob was wracked with guilt. He was sure his stupidity in answering the spy's questions had led to this rapid expansion and the preparation for an immediate attack on Kinsinger. In expiation for his sins, Jacob drove himself to explore the cave passages at the back of their nightly prison, hoping to find a way out. Maybe with an abundance of water, he could find his way back to the colony and warn them about the coming attack. The problem for him in his nightly explorations was the lack of light. The cave entrance was illuminated with floodlights mounted on the wall so that guards could periodically check on their status. But once beyond those lights, Jacob soon found himself stumbling around in the dark in danger of getting lost.

Jacob remembered in *The Princess and the Goblin*, how Princess Irene had received a special thread from her Great-Great-Great Grandmother, which led her to her find imprisoned Curdie and then brought them home. The thread had led her unerringly in the utter darkness of the goblin caves.

Jacob wished and even began to pray that he would find the equivalent of the thread. He was learning to work in absolute darkness. He knew the nearby reaches of the back passage by heart and pushed a little further into the darkness every night, straining his eyes to capture a glimmer of light. He felt the tantalizing whisper of fresh air on his face and knew the draft had to come from an opening in the cave ahead.

Finally one day, the passage he was following opened up and he felt the breath of fresh air more strongly than he had before. Up ahead he saw a ray of piercing light. Although faint, it seemed bright in contrast to the stygian darkness of the cave. His goal in sight, his heart swelled with hope and expectation. He moved ahead, but his foot found no rock. He flung his arm back reaching for the passage wall. Too late! His hand slammed into rock twisting his body around. His other foot slipped over the edge. He caught a handhold on the path, and momentarily arrested his fall, but his chest hit the rock hard. Stunned, he slid down a steep incline and fell heavily onto a ledge. His hand was bruised and his shoulder hurt from the wrench he had given it, but nothing seemed broken. Groping around, he realized that the ledge was less than a meter wide. Crawling on all fours in one direction, the ledge narrowed and stopped. It continued on in other direction a short distance, but then also petered out.

Jacob probed over the edge with his hand as far as he could reach, but the wall fell off sharply with no apparent hand or footholds. Standing, he searched the face of the incline with his fingers as far as he could, and found both an indentation and a knob of rock. Placing his foot on the shallow ledge and holding onto the rock projection, he hoisted himself up the wall. He searched for more footholds and handholds. In the darkness, his progress was painstakingly slow and unnerving. Just then, a cloud seemed to lift and a beam of light from Alpha Centauri B showed through the crack on the far side of the chasm, faintly illuminating the cliff wall just over his head. Jacob could see well enough to find what he needed. He reached the passage, just as another cloud obscured the faint second sun.

He was back to the passage and lay panting a silent prayer of thanksgiving for the first time since his childhood.

He limped his way back to the cave entrance at the back of the prison pit to find a nervous Takeo waiting for him.

"Where have you been?" asked Takeo.

"I was exploring and made it further in than I have ever made it before."

"Did you find an opening to the outside?"

"Sort of," said Jacob.

"What do you mean, 'sort of'?"

"I mean I saw light from Alpha B, but I slipped into a deep crevice and had to climb out in the dark."

"You could have been killed!"

"Don't I know it? But never mind Takeo, we have to get out of here. And soon."

CHAPTER 39
A DESPERATE PLAN

"TAKEO, I WENT AS FAR AS I COULD IN THE TUNNEL. BUT WITHOUT A LIGHT, this route is a bust. We need to get out of here some other way and warn Kinsinger about the impending attack."

"Is that why you've been blundering about in the caves behind us? You're convinced that Rousseau is lying to us about trying to get along with Kinsinger—since the planet is big enough for both colonies?"

"Yep, I'm convinced. I knew Rousseau back in Coventry. I saw how he worked to destroy us. He set a trap for me here. Like a fool I told him there were only colonists at Kinsinger—no soldiers. That's when they started to really gear up and bring in as many soldiers as possible. I'm convinced they're preparing for an attack on Kinsinger and we don't have much time."

Takeo looked at Jacob intently, pursing his lips. "I think you're right Jacob. They've decided to surprise-attack Kinsinger and we need to warn our people. But we have three problems. We have no provisions. We don't know where we are; we could choose a route that will miss Kinsinger completely. Finally, we have to get out of this pit because we'll never escape by day."

"I don't think it's as bad as all that, Takeo. For one thing, the Jordan River seems to head roughly southeast from Kinsinger. We never crossed it. So, if we head east, unless the river does something crazy, we should reach it and then simply follow it back to Kinsinger."

"That seems reasonable," said Takeo. "My best guess would be to head northeast. We should see the Storm Mountains and get our bearing from them. If we don't get lost, we should make it back before we starve to death. But that still leaves the third problem of how do we get out of this pit?"

"All the way back from my fall, I've been thinking about that question. Then it hit me. I think we could do it with a human pyramid."

Takeo chewed his lip as he calculated. "Ten meters. Five, maybe six layers of people. The rock rim slopes back slightly. It could work. There are thirty-two of us. Top layer would be the smallest and lightest guy. Second layer, the tallest guy. That leaves thirty bodies to construct four layers: sixteen-eight-four-two. We can try to break out, but what if we don't make it back home in time?" he asked. "I've been thinking about the same problem but along different lines. Did you notice the armored personnel carrier they shipped through their Travel Oaks?"

"What about it?"

"Those beasts need a lot of fuel to operate. They must be shipping fuel like crazy. What if we set the fuel on fire? It would not only distract them, buying us more time to escape, but likely cause the Copernicus to focus their optics on this site. There's nothing on this planet that could give rise to that kind of a fire and smoke. It would have to rouse their suspicion. So even if we don't make it, or are late, we'd have a chance to warn the folks back home by getting the Copernicus to see this camp."

"If there is a fuel dump, it'll be stored in drums. Those drums will be heavy. We won't be able to move them without a forklift."

"Yeah, I know, and they always keep the powered vehicles locked up. This is the problem. I haven't figured out how to get access either to the fuel storage or to the forklifts."

CHAPTER 40
FROM THE FRYING PAN INTO THE FIRE

TAKEO CALLED ALL THE SLAVES TOGETHER. "IT'S PRETTY CLEAR TO ME THAT Rousseau and his cronies are planning an attack on the Coventry colony of Kinsinger. Kinsinger is completely unaware of the danger and unprepared, and Jacob and I want to warn them. Will you help us?"

After making eye contact with the group, one of the oldest slaves named Spengler answered. "We've known for a while that this prison is not especially secure. The guards don't really worry about preventing a breakout. At night they lock themselves into their dormitory, or the Aquinas. If we did escape during the night, where would we go? The land and waterways are barren. Look at us. We're already underfed. In three weeks at the outside we'd either come back here or starve to death."

"Jacob and I want to head to Kinsinger. You don't have to come—only help us get out of here."

"And face the wrath of Rousseau? No thanks," said Spengler. "Do you even know the way to Kinsinger from here?"

Jacob and Takeo looked at each other. "We were blindfolded after capture," said Takeo. "Kinsinger's on a large river. We never crossed it coming here. We guess that Kinsinger is roughly northwest. On our way here, we don't think we traveled past the Kinsinger settlement—too much chance of being spotted. So, our best guess to get back—we travel northwest until we either find a creek we know or see the Storm Mountains—they're an unmistakable landmark because they seem to be constantly covered with cloud and are east of the Jordan River. In either case we follow a creek or bear west of the Storm Mountains to the Jordan River and follow it upstream to the settlement. What do you say?"

"That's a long-winded way of saying you aren't really sure where you are or how to get home," said a surly voice from the back.

"That's about it," said Takeo. "Now will you help us, or not?"

"Give us a chance to talk about it," said Spengler. Takeo and Jacob retreated out of earshot and waited.

Finally, Spengler returned. "We figure this is a death sentence here anyways. We're willing to take a chance. If nothing else, it'll really be fun to think of those yokels having to do all the grunt work they had us doing every day."

Jacob caught himself smiling.

"There's one other thing," said Takeo, "Jacob and I want to create a diversion and light up their fuel dump. You don't have to participate, but anything you know about where it's stored would help."

Spengler took up the conversation. "The fuel dump is in a locked metal building west of here. The building is in a crack in the wall with an overhang. If you ignite the fuel dump in there, you'll immediately trigger the alarm and activate the automatic sprinkler system. Even if the fire started, I'm not sure the Copernicus could see the flames, and the smoke wouldn't be visible by night."

A mechanic named O'Brien chimed in. "In terms of transportation, four vehicles are kept out of sight in the main cavern here. One is currently under repair. So we have three that we could steal. I should be able to bypass the ignition systems. To carry all thirty-two of us, we'd have to hang onto the roof and the fenders. We'd have to stick to the rough roads they've cleared, but that would give us a fair head start and hamper Rousseau's ability to follow us. Just a word of caution," he continued. "Don't count on those three I talked about being the only vehicles Rousseau has. He's smart. I expect he has reserve vehicles inside the Aquinas and another one may be arriving in their Travel Oaks right now."

"We'll need to move some of the barrels into the open and start a fire there. With any luck, we'll set fire to the remaining fuel in storage and set back their invasion. What about the forklifts?" asked Takeo.

"They're stored in a separate area near the entrance of the cavern since they're electric and are charged up by a power cable from the Aquinas. If we can break into the locked storage area, I can bypass their ignition systems as well if you like," said O'Brien.

"One more thing," said Spengler looking at his fellows. "We'd like to be out of here before you set off the fireworks. I think on these rough roads, the vehicles can't carry thirty-two of us. Some of us will have to take our chances walking." He looked at Jacob and Takeo. "I'm saying you two will have to walk out of here since you seem to know where you're going."

"Understood," said Takeo after looking at Jacob. "Now let me explain how we think we can get out of our prison."

Takeo explained the pyramid. Sixteen men quickly formed a rectangle braced against the wall. Another eight climbed on their shoulders, always straddling two fellows below. Next there were four.

"Can you guys get a move on?" groused one of the captives, "for guys on short commons you weigh a ton."

The pyramid complete, the smallest fellow scrambled up the layers and was boosted over the wall. As the men clambered down from the pyramid, they heard the thunk of a heavy beam being removed, and the solid wooden door swing open. The rope ladder was thrown down and everyone climbed out. Two men, on hand signals from Spengler, immediately ran to the exit of the cavern to see if any patrols were about.

The rope ladder was coiled up, the door closed, and the heavy beam replaced. The scouts reported the grounds were deserted. For once, looking over the grounds from the entrance of the cavern, Jacob regretted the twilight caused by Alpha Centauri B. *The light may give us away now, but once we leave the camp, it will be a help to us, even if it makes us visible to anyone who happens to be awake,* he thought.

Spengler went to the garage holding the three vehicles and opened the large door. Next to them was a smaller sealed room. O'Brien forced open the door using a crowbar he took from one of the all-terrain vehicles, then unplugged one of the three forklifts from a thick, black power cable that snaked out of the cavern.

O'Brien went to the back of the forklift and opened a compartment. He took out a screw driver, a wire stripper, and some needle-nosed pliers then set to work. "If you connect these wires," he whispered, "the forklift will operate. Please wait until we're on our way. The fuel dump is down that gully." He pointed across the open space in front of the cavern.

The remaining men drew straws. The six without a ride left immediately on foot, heading north up the rough trail.

O'Brien worked on the three ATVs, until they were all running. One by one the three vehicles, crammed full of men, rumbled out of the cavern and headed north.

Takeo and Jacob waited just outside the cavern in the shadows, afraid that the noise of the ATV engines might have alerted their captors. When nothing happened, they returned to the forklift, started the electronics and rode it down the gully to the fuel depot. The metal building was under an overhang and surrounded by steep rock walls on three sides. The heavy door was locked with a chain and padlock. Jacob, who had worked with forklifts on Venus, maneuvered the machine right up to the door, snagged the chain with the lift and raised the forks until the hydraulics snapped the door handles from the two doors. He backed up the forklift and Takeo opened the door. Next began the process of moving six drums into an open area. Using a wrench from the tool kit, they opened all six drums and tipped one over.

"I don't think we should leave the fuel in the hut untouched," said Takeo. "We need to fire it too. If we can get the fuel dump to go up, even if Copernicus is asleep at the switch and doesn't see the fire, we can set Rousseau and his invasion plans back weeks while he replaces the fuel by Travel Oak."

Jacob agreed. Heading back to the fuel depot, they tipped two drums over onto the floor. The place reeked of diesel fuel. "That should do it," said Takeo. We need to get out of here before the place begins to wake up."

There was almost no wood in the Aquinas camp for torches. They had to improvise. Crafting a couple of makeshift torches from two crowbars wrapped with some rags from the toolkit, they dipped their torches into the diesel fuel and went to the forklift parked halfway between the two spill-sites.

"Lord, help us," said Takeo. Touching the ignition wires together to create a spark, first one and then the other torch flamed to life. Takeo ran to the fuel spill in the open while Jacob, still sore from his fall, limped in the other direction to the fuel depot. Jacob saw a yellow-orange light illuminate the canyon walls, and threw his torch into the fuel dump building. The flame roared up.

In the next instant, several things happened at once: a siren sounded, fire extinguishers in the fuel dump building activated and lights in the dormitory inside the cavern come on.

"No, no, no …" said Jacob as he began to run, forgetting his sore leg.

CHAPTER 41
FROM DANGER INTO DANGER

PANICKING, AND FILLED WITH ADRENALINE, JACOB RAN TOWARD THE forklift. *We should have listened to Spengler. Now we've woken up the whole complex.*

More lights went on in the cavern, and the bay door of the Aquinas opened.

Jacob met Takeo at the forklift.

"Come on," shouted Takeo pointing to the boulder-strewn edge of the valley. "We have to go to ground."

Leaving the forklift, Takeo led them north skirting the steep, western wall of the valley. At the first opportunity, he went to higher ground, and paused to look back at the compound. Men were running everywhere. They had brought another vehicle out of the Aquinas, and were dousing the fire in the middle of the valley.

"They'll have the fires out in a few minutes and then they'll be after us!" said Takeo.

Jacob and Takeo followed the slaves' lead along the road, taking the much slower route on the edge of the valley. The long, steep-sided valley was blocked at one end by the wreck of the Aquinas. Ahead, the steep walls gradually decreased in height. Keeping out of sight of the fire brigade, they headed north in the gloom, flitting from cover to cover.

Jacob glanced back at the fire in the middle of the valley. A team of about twenty soldiers were working feverishly to put out the main blaze. None had started to search for the missing captives yet. Jacob and Takeo crept along the steep edge of the valley until the canyon walls became rounded hills. They could see the well-worn trail of the vehicle tracks. There were high hills ahead and no sign of the Storm Mountains.

"Let's look back to see what's happening," said Takeo. "Maybe we can figure out which way they'll look first once the pursuit begins." Crawling up to a small ridge, they looked back. The burning oil drums were a blaze of light in the middle of the valley. Men were pouring water on the still intact drums to keep them from catching fire. A trench had been dug to capture the burning oil-water mixture as it flowed away. The crew was now using foam on the main fire. Just then an armored personnel carrier exited from the Aquinas and raced up the road. Another group of men split in half and began searching the broken rock on both sides of the valley. They had dogs with them.

"Well, they've started the pursuit much faster than I thought they could," said Jacob.

"Lord, help our poor comrades. Give them God-speed," said Takeo. He thought for a moment. "We'd better head west to get as far from the road as possible."

The two headed over the hills. In the ever-present light of Alpha Centauri B, the country they had entered soon began to look like a collection of broken rock shards, but filled with deep shadow.

When daylight finally came Jacob looked at a bleak landscape of sharp ridges and broken rock. His first thought was to look back in the direction of camp, hoping to see a thick cloud of smoke from one of the fires they had set. There was nothing.

He was thirsty. They wended their way around the house-sized rocks. Others they had to climb. They found no water. Jacob's mouth was dry, his thirst over powering, and he began to wonder if they'd made a mistake.

"Let's take a break," said Takeo. "Are you a praying man?"

Jacob gave Takeo a sharp look remembering his time in the cave on the ledge. "Not really. It seemed the thing to do at Coventry, so I participated to fit in. It's not what I grew up with, and it would've been a cause for severe criticism at the ministry."

"Well," said Takeo, "as a general rule, I figure I can do more than pray after I've prayed, but I can't do more than pray until I've prayed."

Takeo startled Jacob by talking out loud. "Father, you know I've done my best to pick a good route, but it seems to have gone wrong, very wrong. We need water badly. Give me guidance about where to go. We know you manage all things. Going forward, I'll do my best to find our way, trusting that you will honor our prayer. Amen."

"So, did He tell you what to do?" asked Jacob.

"You mean did I hear a voice or receive a clear plan? No, in my experience it doesn't work that way. God expects me to do my best to find the right way forward. The difference is that I'm doing it now acknowledging that He keeps the whole operation going."

"So, let's say we find water, how do you know it wouldn't have worked out even if you hadn't prayed?"

"You're making a false assumption, Jacob, and so you're asking the wrong question. I don't pray to put God to the test, to see if He'll prove himself to me by doing what I ask Him. He's not my puppet or a genie who I have under my thumb. I strengthen my relationship to Him by acknowledging who He is. It's like I'm renewing my vow to Him every time I pray. It's all for my benefit, not His."

Takeo went quiet, intent in thought. Then he began moving a little to their right. "You've been reading George MacDonald's Curdie books, right?"

"Right."

"Do you remember in the second book, *The Princess and the Curdie*, when Curdie is speaking with Princess Irene's magnificent Great-Great-Great Grandmother, and Curdie asks about his mission: 'But where am I to go, ma'am, and what am I to do?' Remember what the Grandmother-Princess said? 'You must not be like a dull servant that needs to be told again and again before he will understand. You have orders enough to start with ...' We've prayed. We know we have to look for water. That's enough for now."

Takeo began walking more briskly. If nothing else, he seemed to have more confidence and appeared more upbeat about their chances.

"I think, I'll climb that rock. Maybe I'll see something that'll help me decide where we should head."

Jacob sat in the shade of an overhang and watched Takeo make his way up the rock. He was still sore from his fall and glad for the rest. Still, he felt guilty. After all, Takeo was doing it as much for him as for himself.

Takeo finally made it back down. "I think we should head that way." He pointed a little more to their right. "Back home, I would've looked for vegetation to indicate water, but here there's nothing, of course. But I saw a mist in the sun. I'm hoping it's a waterfall."

Jacob thought: *I hope his thirst isn't making him hallucinate.* "So, God answered you," said Jacob with a hint of sarcasm in his voice.

"He always answers my petitions," said Takeo smiling, "and sometimes the answer is even 'yes'."

"There's something else. When I was on the top of that rock, I could see the Storm Mountains. I know now where we are and where we have to go."

"But we didn't pray about that," said Jacob.

"That's grace for you. God even answers our prayers when I'm too simpleminded or distracted to remember to ask."

CHAPTER 42
MERCY CREEK

THE NEXT FIVE HUNDRED METERS WERE A ROUGH SCRAMBLE, BUT WELL worth it. They found the small waterfall that Takeo had seen. First, they drank their fill and then they washed and cooled themselves off.

"I guess since we're likely the first to find this creek, we get to name it," said Takeo. "What do you think of 'Mercy Creek'?"

"Works for me," said Jacob.

Mercy Creek headed roughly west, judging by the sun. After two days they reached a broad river. They had come a fair distance out of their way, but it seemed they had found the Jordan River at last. Jacob was weak from hunger and wanted to rest. All he could think of was finding something to eat.

The lack of vegetation aided in the travel along the river bank. At one point they had to hike inland to skirt a deep-sided bank, but they were soon able to follow the river again. They had just crossed a small creek when Takeo pointed to a patch of orange.

"Is this what I think it is?" asked Takeo.

"Yes, I think our friends have passed this way. Remember on our trip to the Aquinas, we heard our vehicles splash through a creek as we forded it? My guess would be that our fellow escapees traveled by vehicle to the ford and followed that creek down here to the Jordan River. This orange rag is a hopeful sign. Maybe they've already warned Kinsinger."

Although they were weak from hunger, the encouragement provided by the fragment of cloth spurred them on. In two hours, they found their friends sprawled in a rough circle by the water's edge. A few jumped up when Jacob and Takeo approached.

Jacob saw two men lying in the shade with red stains on their orange shirts.

"What happened?" asked Takeo.

Spengler answered. "We made it to the ford and then all three of our vehicles stopped working. We should have run for it immediately into the rough ground and followed that creek to the river, but we tried to get them running again. The Cobras roared up in vehicles they weren't supposed to have. We scattered among the rocks, but they shot three of us before we could hide ourselves. Tomkins died almost immediately. They couldn't follow everyone, but they chased us and were shooting at us for about half an hour as we made our way downstream. The terrain was pretty rough and they eventually called off the pursuit. When we found each other the next morning, it was only then that we realized that those two had been wounded." He pointed with his thumb over his shoulder.

"They were able to walk a while, but loss of blood made them so weak that they can't go on. We were just debating what to do when you showed up."

"We need to warn Kinsinger, or all of this will all be for naught," said Takeo. "Our fire wasn't very effective. They put it out before it created much smoke. To stay here is to starve to death. Why not leave four of your most tired men here to look after the wounded? The rest of you come with us. If we reach Maranatha Creek, we'll tell you where to find the cache of food we left there. There's also a med kit. You can carry as much as you need to the others. We'll bring help as soon as we can."

Except for the six left behind, the slaves followed Jacob and Takeo up-stream. They were all so tired and weak from hunger that they were staggering on their feet. Takeo was alarmed. "With all the rocks they're dislodging, they're making an unholy racket. We know Rousseau has a road close to Maranatha Creek. We need to be quiet and careful. We need to hear him before he hears us. If he drives all the way to the mesa and force marches down Maranatha Creek, he could get to the mouth of the creek ahead of us and ambush us. We don't want to walk into a trap. I'm hungry, but still pretty strong. Let me scout ahead. You keep me in sight and let the others follow you. If I signal you like this"—he took off his orange tee-shirt and waved it in the air—"then I want you to hustle back and tell them to go to ground and be still."

They followed the plan the rest of the afternoon. The sun had just gone down, when Jacob saw Takeo rapidly waving his tee-shirt. Quietly, but with speed, Jacob covered the intervening distance to the rest of the party. When they saw him they stopped and hid. Jacob also hid. In about half an hour, Takeo returned.

He sounded worried. "There are about twenty Cobras hiding on this side of Maranatha Creek. I could smell their cigarette smoke before I saw them. I snuck across country and reached the creek a couple of hundred meters upstream. There doesn't seem to be anyone there. I think we can make it to the cache, but the direct way to Kinsinger is blocked."

Takeo led them away from the Jordan and reached Maranatha Creek three hundred meters upstream. Once across, they resumed their formation with Takeo in the lead paralleling the creek. After a strenuous walk, Takeo found the cache without difficulty. They hid themselves from the view of anyone who might be watching from the top of the mesa and stopped to eat. It was remarkable to Jacob the difference a good meal made to him.

Takeo said to the others. "This is now my home turf. Jacob and I will continue on to Kinsinger using a back-country route. You carry supplies back to the others. One way or another, we'll come and look for you. Be careful!"

CHAPTER 48
WHY DOES THIS HAPPEN TO ME?

JACOB SAT ON A ROCK AND WATCHED THE OTHERS, WHO WERE LADEN WITH supplies, head back toward the Jordan River. It was overcast and quite dark. He soon lost sight of them and started to doze off. A rough shaking jolted him awake. It was Takeo. "Jacob, listen to me. We found Rousseau's men at the mouth of this creek. Don't you see what this means?"

"Takeo, I'm so tired, I can't think or even see straight."

Ignoring his answer, Takeo went on. "After we escaped, Rousseau decided to begin the invasion right away. Instead of setting things back, we only managed to speed them up. What if Rousseau marches his band of men to the outskirts of Kinsinger and attacks in the middle of the night? I've got to warn my folks. If you can't walk, stay here and rest. I don't want you lost in the rocks."

Jacob sighed as he struggled to his feet, every muscle aching. "I'll make it, Takeo. You're right. Let's walk."

Takeo headed off cross-country as night began to fall, with Jacob following in his footsteps. The way was rugged, but Takeo was able to pick a path that kept them heading in the right direction. Jacob seemed to get his second wind as they walked in the night air. It rained briefly. It was well after midnight when Takeo whispered to Jacob, "There's a spring of water up ahead that comes out of the cliff behind Kinsinger. Last chance for a drink before we enter the town."

Keeping low, Takeo led the way forward. In the dim light, Jacob saw him suddenly raise his fist. Jacob stopped and crouched beside him. Up ahead, two people with their backs to them were near the spring keeping very still.

"They look vaguely familiar," whispered Takeo.

Just then the young woman and the man turned around. "We know them," said Jacob, recognizing his friends. He stood up and waved to Hanna and Zeke. Hanna's hand went to her mouth, as she stifled a shriek. Zeke came toward him signaling "be quiet."

Takeo also stood up. There were hugs of relief all around.

"What's going on?" asked Jacob.

Hanna said, "After you and Takeo went missing, we were sent back to Venus to report and ask for more cadets. We returned right after speaking with the commandant. We arrived here sometime after midnight when everyone was asleep. We'd just slept in the Travel Oaks and weren't tired so we walked around in the pond park. That's where we were when we saw the lights go on in the main building.

"We were just heading back to the main building when maybe a dozen armed men in uniforms came out and spread through the town in small groups. The invaders went house-to-house and brought everyone back to the main building. We didn't know what to do. We were unarmed and, so we snuck out of town and found this spring. We've no idea what's going on. We're still just trying to figure out what to do. Are these fellows from the Copernicus? Has there been some kind of trouble?"

"You're not going to believe this," said Jacob.

"Try me," said Zeke. "After seeing that surprise attack by humans—on what we thought was a deserted and barren planet—I'm pretty open-minded right now."

"The Aquinas, the sister ship to the Copernicus, was taken over by those uniformed dudes. They finally learned from their captives how to run the ship, took a long detour, glided in undetected and crash-landed during one night, maybe fifty kilometers from here. Now they've brought war and tyranny to Canaan. Rousseau is with them, heading up the operation."

"You're kidding. Our Rousseau?" asked Zeke.

"Yes, *our* Rousseau."

"That's bad, very bad," said Hanna. "He knows us too well. We also know he's going to be ruthless."

"He captured Takeo and me," continued Jacob, "and forced us to work at their camp. We managed to escape with the other slave workers, hoping to warn our colony, but instead we spooked Rousseau into attacking Kinsinger immediately."

"Perhaps we spooked Rousseau into attacking Kinsinger too quickly?" mused Takeo. "They're spread pretty thin, covering two hundred colonists with twenty men. They'll have to keep most of them locked up. Perhaps they'll hold the women and young children hostage and force the men to behave. We have to keep them from getting reinforcements."

"I know we have to do that," said Jacob, "but shouldn't our priority be to communicate with the Copernicus?"

"I think Jacob's right," said Hanna.

"What about food?" asked Zeke.

"You're both right," said Takeo. "First things first. Many of our reserve supplies including food, cellphones, and a few tranquilizer guns are stored in the cavern. I know a back way in. I also know where we can hide a sizeable cache here, so we don't have to go back to the cavern."

Takeo led them to a narrow cleft that opened up to a well-worn passage leading to the back of the cavern. He showed Hanna where to hide near the entrance as lookout, then went to the storage area and, with Jacob and Zeke, began bringing out boxes of supplies. They piled them at the spring. After two hours of work, Hanna and Takeo returned. Takeo opened one of the last boxes and unwrapped a cellphone. He tried to call Copernicus. "No luck, there's no signal," he said. "Rousseau's men must have shut down the communication system."

From the spring Jacob, Zeke, and Takeo climbed up about ten meters to a ledge. At the back of the ledge was a cave completely invisible from below. Deep inside the cave there was a rivulet that disappeared into a crevice, and presumably, became the stream of water that emerged as the spring below.

"As boys," said Takeo' "we camped here overnight, pretending we were explorers. We had a pulley system to haul our supplies up here." Takeo went into the back of the cave and returned with a wooden contraption. He stuck a wooden boom with a pulley into a crevice and lowered the rope. Jacob scrambled back down to the base of the cliff and, with Hanna, loaded supplies into the net attached to the rope. Takeo hauled them up to the cave. In thirty minutes, everything was hidden away.

"Don't you think contacting the Copernicus is still our highest priority, even higher than preventing reinforcements?" asked Hanna.

"How, exactly are we supposed do that," asked Zeke, "lie on the ground forming the letters for 'HELP' and hope Copernicus sees us? Hanna you're the only one bendable enough to make a 'P'."

"It's not funny," said Hanna.

"You know," said Jacob, "the Aquinas pod looked to be in pretty good shape. Those pods are really shuttles on autopilot and have full communications equipment. Maybe we can use that to talk to the Copernicus?"

With backpacks, tranquilizer rifles, and supplies, the four of them headed back to the cache at Maranatha Creek. After an hour they took a rest. The next thing Jacob knew, Hanna was shaking him awake.

CHAPTER 44
MAKING A CALL

IT WAS EARLY MORNING WHEN HANNA WOKE JACOB. "HAVE SOMETHING TO eat, Jacob. Takeo's been up for some time. He and Zeke went off to climb that rock to look around to see if Rousseau has sent any more troops this way." She pointed to a high pile of rocks to the south.

Jacob was just finishing his breakfast when Zeke and Takeo returned.

"Feeling better?" asked Takeo.

"I'm a lot better, thanks," said Jacob between mouthfuls. "Heard you were on recon. See anything?"

"Yeah, we did," said Zeke.

"Not more troops?" asked Jacob, fear gripping his heart.

"Thankfully not," said Takeo, "but I think we saw a spot of orange in the distance."

"Orange?"

"They were too far to make out faces and get a good head count, even with binoculars," said Takeo, "but I think Spengler and the others have moved up here. We should get moving."

Jacob wolfed down the rest of his breakfast, then picked up his pack and tranquilizer rifle. Takeo and Jacob walked ahead while Hanna and Zeke covered behind them in case they were followed.

"Now what do we do?" asked Jacob.

"Somehow we have to warn Copernicus about our trouble down here," said Takeo.

"Won't Copernicus know that something is wrong when Kinsinger goes silent?" asked Jacob.

"Sure, they'll either use the Travel Oak or land with a shuttle and walk right into Rousseau's waiting arms. No one in their wildest nightmare would have imagined that Aquinas made it here undetected under the control of our enemies. Furthermore, I don't even know how many operational shuttles the Copernicus has left. What if Rousseau captures their last one?"

"So, what do you think we should do?" asked Jacob.

"I think we have some time," Takeo responded. "I'm sure the Copernicus will be quite reluctant to break out a shuttle. They'll send someone by Travel Oak first, and if they don't report back they may send a shuttle. I don't think Rousseau would attempt to take the Copernicus like they did the Aquinas. He has too few soldiers here and the command structure is reversed."

"What do you mean?" asked Jacob.

"When the Aquinas was in transit, Coventry Africa was mission control. It was natural for Coventry Africa to send orders to Aquinas and have them obeyed, so they were able to infiltrate the ship. After all, personnel were changed regularly using the Travel Oaks.

"Here, Copernicus is the top of the command structure. We can ask for help, but the Copernicus commander will ask for details and information before he acts. Rousseau would have to take over Copernicus with say, ten men—a very tall order."

After pausing to think for a moment, Takeo continued. "I don't think we have much time. I think we have to do two things at once. We should send one team to the Aquinas Pod to try to contact Copernicus. At the same time, now that we have a couple of tranquilizer guns, and we know most of Rousseau's force have captured Kinsinger, we should try to overwhelm the few guards, if any, that Rousseau left at the mouth of Maranatha Creek."

Jacob and Takeo walked in silence for a while. Then Takeo whispered, "We're pretty close to our friend's camp. Stay here while I scout ahead to make sure this isn't a trap."

Takeo crept ahead, while Jacob signaled to Hanna and Zeke to join him. They waited in silence, until Takeo returned.

"It's all right. Let's go say hello." said Takeo.

Takeo led the way. Walking around a large rock, Jacob saw a man perched up on a pile of rocks looking south. It was O'Brien.

Takeo gestured at Jacob to take the lead. Jacob nodded and whispered, "Psst, O'Brien."

O'Brien picked up a fist-sized rock and swung around. He relaxed when he saw who it was.

"Am I glad to see you," said O'Brien.

Jacob introduced Hanna and Zeke. O'Brien led the four back to camp.

Jacob saw that the escaped slaves had set up camp in a shallow depression with tilted slabs of rock at one end, which apparently served as storage and sleeping quarters. Spengler emerged from there and smiled broadly when he saw Jacob and Takeo. Others appeared as well and soon they were all sitting around a circle.

Jacob recounted their trip. There was murmuring and obvious fear when they realized Rousseau's men had already seized Kinsinger.

"So how come you're here?" asked Jacob.

Spengler spoke for the group. "We all decided to come. Thomas died from his wounds shortly after you left and John was sufficiently recovered to travel. We ate the little food we brought back from the cache and decided to return here. You'd told us there might be guards up on the mesa so last night we moved the supplies here and stayed out of sight. So now what?"

Jacob explained the plan he and Takeo had developed during their walk.

Jacob, Hanna, and six others were to climb up the mesa, and using two tranquilizer rifles to overpower any guards they encountered, they would try to communicate with the Copernicus.

The rest, armed with four tranquilizer rifles were to go with Zeke and Takeo and subdue the guards at the mouth of Maranatha Creek.

CHAPTER 45
WHAT GOES AROUND COMES AROUND

EARLY THE NEXT MORNING, JACOB, HANNA, AND SIX OTHERS, CLIMBED UP
to the mesa. After checking that no vehicles from Rousseau's base camp were
approaching along the back road, they crept up to the crashed Aquinas Cargo
Pod.

There were two guards near the winch, playing poker and smoking. There
were no other guards at the shuttle or watching the cache. Hanna and Jacob
hid in the shadows of a large rock and kept their tranquilizer guns trained on the
two card players, while the other six circled around to subdue them from behind
in case Hanna and Jacob missed. Jacob winced when he heard someone
dislodge a rock, but the card players were so intent on their game that they
did not hear the sound. At a signal when the six were in position, Jacob and
Hanna fired their darts. The two card players looked up in surprise, dropped
their cards and reached for their guns. They slumped over before the others
could reach them.

The eight took pistols, rifles and knives from the guards and tied them up.
Luis Obando, one of the six companions, had been sent along by Spengler
because of his knowledge of communications. With a nod from Jacob, Obando
went directly toward the shuttle and began to warm up the electronics.

After a few minutes, Obando said to Jacob, "All the main communication
systems seem operational. I don't think Rousseau knows this, but these shuttles
are capable of a very tight beam communication. I can spot the Copernicus,

because she's still beaming a '*please answer*' message to Kinsinger. I've set up a tight beam back to her. I suggest you talk to Copernicus and tell them they must keep broadcasting the '*please answer*' message. I'm hoping we can fool Rousseau into thinking Copernicus is still in the dark about what happened. Think about what you're going to say and then I'll patch you through."

"I'm ready," said Jacob. Obando put a finger to his lips, threw a switch, and then gave Jacob the thumbs up.

"This is a tight-beam, urgent communication from Cadet Kraiser for Captain Witt. Critically urgent: keep '*please answer*' script running for Kinsinger. Also critically urgent, respond by tight-beam communication to my location." He repeated the message.

Time passed slowly. Jacob could feel his heart pounding. He had just turned to Obando to tell him something was wrong when the answer came. "Cadet Kraiser, this is communication tech Lancet. Captain notified. Confirm your identity."

Jacob answered. "My ID number is 937064. The Commandant of Torchship Coulson is ...."

"Kraiser, this is Captain Witt. What the hell is going on down there? Why is Kinsinger silent?"

"Sir, Kinsinger has been overrun by enemy combatants from Cobra."

"Say again?"

Jacob repeated the message.

"How can that be?" asked Witt.

"After over running Coventry Africa, Cobra also managed to overrun the Aquinas."

There was silence.

Finally Witt came back on and said in a strained voice, "Report on status."

Jacob told Witt where to look for Aquinas base camp and then recounted how some twenty Cobra soldiers had overrun the town and taken Kinsinger colonists hostage the previous night.

"Now that we know exactly where to look, we can see the road and their base camp. Although it's still hard to see the Aquinas. We see four vehicles being loaded. It looks like they're getting equipment ready to send some reinforcements."

"What should we do sir?" asked Jacob.

There was a brief pause and then Witt answered. "Kraiser, I don't have the manpower to send down a strike force to Kinsinger now. It will take me three days, maybe a week to get enough soldiers and equipment here to set up a perimeter around Kinsinger and begin hostage negotiations. In a week, Cobra will know that we're on to them. Keep me informed and stay out of trouble. Use this channel only in an emergency, but monitor our signal. Over and out."

Obando looked concerned. "Rousseau's getting ready to send reinforcements. Don't you think we need to do something?"

CHAPTER 46
FIGHTING BACK

JACOB AND FIVE OTHERS HID AMONG THE ROCKS LINING BOTH SIDES OF A crudely constructed road that led to the foot of the Pod 3 mesa. A truck and three all-terrain-vehicles crept by. Jacob's crew were armed with two rifles, a pistol, and two tranquilizer guns. Once the vehicles had passed and travelled around a bend in the road, Jacob, Hanna and two others rolled four large stones onto the road and then returned to their hiding places and waited. The others in their group crept up the road and disappeared into the rocks to close the trap.

Twenty minutes later, the four vehicles, having disgorged their soldiers for the march down Maranatha Creek, crept back up the rough road to the stones and stopped. The driver in the lead truck jumped out and looked at the blockade. His face changed to panic and he motioned frantically to the other vehicles to back up.

Jacob pointed his rifle at the driver. "Put your hands up!" he shouted. "We've got guns! You're surrounded! Surrender now!"

The man jumped into his truck and the vehicles all started to back up frantically. The convoy disappeared around the curve in the road. Jacob and the three others raced along the road in pursuit. Rounding the curve, he saw the first truck had run into a boulder. The other vehicles unable to get past it, had also stopped. The four drivers had surrendered.

Jacob and some of the others rolled the stones off the road, and then hid the vehicles in a dry river bed where they removed their ignition wires.

The captors marched the four prisoners to the winch platform at the foot of the mesa and in three trips transported everyone to the top. After securing the prisoners, Jacob rested briefly before heading off again to make contact with Takeo and Zeke. Accompanied by Obando and Hanna, they hiked to the end of the mesa and climbed down to Maranatha Creek. Moving rapidly, they followed the creek. Evening was coming. They had just topped a rise when they saw someone hurrying toward them. Jacob ducked and pulled out his pistol, their only weapon, before recognizing it was Zeke. He looked tired in the dim light.

Jacob and the others stood up and called to Zeke.

Zeke smiled, relief etched on his dust-streaked face. He sat down on a rock. "I have good news and bad news," he said.

CHAPTER 47
GOOD NEWS AND BAD NEWS

ZEKE TOOK A LONG DRINK FROM HIS CANTEEN. "HI HANNA, OBANDO." Turning to Jacob, he asked, "So what do you want first, the good news or the bad news?"

"Give me the good news," said Jacob.

"Well, we captured the guards at the mouth of Maranatha Creek and then we intercepted the reinforcements."

Jacob was really impressed. "Well that's really good." But fear gripped his heart as he wondered who had been killed. "So what's the bad news?"

"Takeo's been wounded."

"Wounded! Is he going to be alright?"

"Probably," said Zeke. "It seems to be a flesh wound. And given that this planet is a pretty antiseptic environment, the first aid consensus is he'll make it. But he can't travel."

"You'd better tell us the whole story," said Jacob.

"Well, said Zeke, "Takeo really knows his stuff. We headed down Maranatha Creek, following some back trails and waited until nightfall. He took us pretty close to the guard's campsite. Although there were only three of them, they seemed pretty sure of themselves—laughing, joking, heating food on their little camp stove. But with only four tranquilizer guns we didn't want to get into a fire fight with them. So we waited."

Zeke took another drink. "Finally, one of the guards got up and walked off to take a leak. After he put down his rifle, we shot a tranquilizer dart into his back. We heard him swear and mutter something about mosquitoes. He tried to swat at the dart, but keeled over before he realized there aren't any mosquitoes on Canaan," said Zeke chuckling.

"Anyway, with two more guns and only two guards left, we shot both guards with darts and rushed them."

"It sounds like it couldn't have gone any better," said Jacob.

"Yeah, that's about right. Like I said, Takeo really knows his stuff. So our next job was to get ready to intercept the reinforcements. After Takeo showed us a place, well off the trail, where we could hold the prisoners—essentially a deep, rock-walled pit—we made ready to ambush the reinforcements we knew must be coming. We also knew we'd be out-gunned, outnumbered and likely they were much better trained than we were. There's a place where the trail to Kinsinger travels along the river edge below a step rocky bank. We set up there. Takeo watched the Maranatha Creek trail and then warned us they were coming. We took our cue from him. He tried to get the lead soldiers to drop their weapons. When they wouldn't, he should have fired, but didn't. He just froze. They opened up on him and he went down. We killed six. Another four jumped into the river. The last we saw of them, they were struggling to stay above the surface as the current swept them down river. The rest threw down their weapons."

Zeke took a deep breath. "Now I come to the part that explains why I've rushed up here. Our best first-aider was binding up Takeo's wounds when he grabbed my shirt and told me I had to do something for him. I had to get a message to you."

"What message?" asked Jacob.

"Takeo said that unless we get the Kinsinger hostages out, many will be killed when the Coventry forces respond."

"Well, how are we going to do that?" asked Jacob.

"Takeo said that when they built the pond system, they flooded an underground entrance to the main building. It leads from the pond closest to the main building—the third pond up from the river—to the back of the pantry in the main kitchen. The cooks still use it to throw scraps to the fish in winter when the ponds are iced over. He wants you to try to get the people out before

Copernicus sends down its shuttles. When Aquinas sees the shuttles landing, they'll know they need the hostages as bargaining chips. Do you know what Takeo means?"

CHAPTER 48
HOLDING MY BREATH

"YOU KNOW WHAT IT MEANS RIGHT?" ASKED ZEKE AGAIN.

"I know which pond he means," Jacob said, "and I know where the kitchen is. I'm going to have to go for a dip and hope I find this underwater passage. I have to find this secret way in. At night. Did I get it right?"

"I think that's what Takeo meant."

"Zeke, are you up to heading over to Kinsinger tonight? I think to act right away is our best chance."

"Yeah, I'm good to go," said Zeke.

"Obando, you need to head up to the mesa and wait by the pod. If I get the colonists out, I'll send up a flare. Please explain to Witt what it means and respectfully request him to send whatever troops he has to Kinsinger to keep us from being recaptured." Obando headed off to the mesa, while Hanna, Zeke, and Jacob walked to Kinsinger.

Zeke was tired but manfully kept up with the rapid pace set by Jacob. It was two o'clock in the morning when they finally reached their destination. After searching the village and park for sentries from The Rock, the three friends crept around the ponds. There were no sentries at the Travel Oaks or anywhere else in the village. All the cottages were dark and looked deserted, but there were lights on in the main building. From time to time, Jacob saw a beret-topped head peering out of one of the upstairs windows.

"I think Takeo read it correctly," whispered Jacob. "They don't have enough soldiers to set up sentries, so they've locked themselves in, and likely have the village people crammed into locked rooms until Rousseau sends more reinforcements."

Jacob made his way to the pond nearest the main building and crouched in the shallow water along the shore where he wouldn't be seen from the windows. He tied a rope he had brought along to a rocky projection and then covered it with dirt. Paying the rope out, he waded into deeper water. Working his way along the rocky fringe of the pond, he kept feeling the perimeter until his toes could no longer feel the steep bank.

This must be it. Here goes nothing.

Taking a deep breath, Jacob dove for the passage. Feeling for the walls of the tunnel in the inky blackness, he payed out the rope as he swam. Seeing nothing, he suddenly felt his whole body shudder as his head collided with something hard. He almost gulped water.

Disorientated and out of breath, he pulled on the rope. He had to get out. He had to breathe.

Use the rope to get out! A part of his mind was shouting at him.

Woozy, he began to pull himself on the rope toward the cave entrance. He broke water coughing and gasping. Returning to his pack on the shore, he tried to calm his pounding heart. No light beams penetrated the night. His loud gasp hadn't been heard No one was searching the grounds. His head throbbed. Feeling it, his hand came away sticky.

He didn't want to try again. He needed a flashlight. Returning to the cache in the cave above the spring, he found a box of military-grade flash-lights. He carried the box back to the edge of the pond.

Taking a deep breath, he took out a flashlight, and went back into the water. He began tracing his path along the steep side of the pond once more. Again he took several deep breaths, dove, and felt his way into the tunnel. After a few strokes, and turned on the light. He saw where he had likely hit his head—a projection on *the* wall as the passage bent slightly to the right. Checking that he still had lots of slack on the rope, he swam with measured strokes down the passage. He was running out of air. *Should I turn back?* he thought, but forced himself to keep going and locked his jaw so he wouldn't gasp for air. After another thirty seconds he broke the surface, involuntarily gasping in several huge lungsful of air. He set his flashlight to the red-light mode and illuminated a small, natural cave that was being used as a storage area. At the far end of the cave he saw a stone wall with a door. At this end, the cave had room for banks of shelves both to the left and to the right. He could hide among them if someone came in.

He untied the rope from his waist and turned off his light. His eyes adjusted to the faint light that leaked around the frame of the door. Walking past storage shelves that reached to the ceiling, he came to an open space with a passage squared into a hallway. Dripping, he sloshed his way up the ramp-like passage to the door. Listening at the door, but hearing nothing, he found the latch, opened the door a crack and peered through. A single dim light was on. Jacob recognized the kitchen. There was no one there.

He had just crept forward and closed the cellar door when he heard a noise coming from beyond the door at the far side of the kitchen. He flattened himself behind a counter. The kitchen door opened. "… enough for twenty men. Sandwiches, beer, cold chicken …" said a man gruffly.

"We don't have any chicken, sir!" said a woman. Her voice sounded familiar, although she sounded frightened.

"Damn, woman! I'm losing my patience. Get some grub together for us and no funny business. Rousseau told me to be nice, but I get angry when I'm hungry. And I'm hungry."

The woman said, "Emily, you and Jen make up a large batch of scrambled eggs. Francis, you begin buttering bread. I'll see if we have any leftovers I can warm.

"We have a bit of beer, but not nearly enough for twenty men. I can give you some wine. We have lots of milk. If you want something hot, I can make a large pot of tea."

"Yeah, get busy," growled the man.

"Pedro, stay near the door and watch 'em. I'm goin' to have a smoke and check the outside."

Jacob could hear the clattering of dishes and the opening of cupboards. Everyone worked quietly. There was none of the banter that normally accompanied kitchen work. One of the women came to the cellar door and opened it. She didn't see Jacob, but Jacob saw that it was Mrs. Yamamoto. In a minute, she came back through the door carrying a clay pot. She saw Jacob, gasped, and dropped the pot with a clatter. Jacob put a finger to his lips.

Bending down to compose herself, she began to pick up the shards. She turned to the guard at the door and said, "Sorry, how clumsy of me."

Disappearing into the cellar again, she came back after a few minutes with another pot, a broom, dustpan, and a pail.

"Emily, please warm this up. I have to clear up the mess I've made."

Mrs. Yamamoto went to work. Once out of sight behind the counter, she shoved a piece of paper into Jacob's hands. Pulling a large sponge out of the bucket, she quickly cleaned up the mess, and returned to help the others.

"These men are hungry." She hurried everyone along,

Several minutes passed before Mrs. Yamamoto spoke again. "We're very tired. If we carry this food up to your men, can we go back to our families? We'll clean up tomorrow."

"Yeah," growled Pedro. "Make sure you bring all the beer or I'll come and get you again."

"I'll get you all of the beer."

Soon everyone trooped off, turning out the main light, and closing the kitchen door behind them.

Alone again, Jacob unfolded the note and read it in the dim red light of his torch.

We're all locked in the main meeting room. We heard distant gunfire and the guards looked worried and locked all the outside doors and windows. Most guards are asleep, but there are patrols watching the windows and some may be outside as well.

He knew the meeting room she meant. It was a small auditorium that also served as a refuge. It had been constructed with a single lockable door and walls designed to survive even a large fire. It was so unusual that Jacob remembered it from his tour of the building. He turned his light to low and crept in the direction that he remembered.

At first he thought he was lost because everything looked so different at night.

He came to a heavy steel door that opened inwards. Someone had welded brackets onto the door, holding two heavy timbers that kept the door from opening. But the lock, which would have allowed the door to be fastened from the inside, was missing, leaving a hole through which he now peered. It was dark and quiet inside. He lifted the timbers and depressed the latch handle. The door swung open quietly and Jacob crept into a large space. With no windows, everything was pitch black, but by the light of his torch he could see people on the floor everywhere.

"Jacob," came a whisper. "We're ready to leave."

The captives began to get up and formed themselves into a line. Five men came first, then women and children. Finally, the rest of the men and older boys stood at the end of the line. Jacob shone the light at his own face and signaled for silence. Takeo's father was at the head of the line.

"Takeo is hurt, but will be fine," said Jacob. "He sent me to get you all out."

"The back door is welded shut and the front door is locked and always guarded. How do we get out?" asked Mr. Yamamoto.

"The same way I got in—the underwater passage to the pond."

"But the children …"

"We'll think of something."

"We'll follow you," said Mr. Yamamoto. "The last man will replace the beams on the door. Hopefully, we'll have some time before they find we're gone."

The rope Jacob had tied into place allowed the adults to pull themselves through the tunnel at a rapid pace. The children were placed in body bags, which had been stored in case of a disease outbreak. Water-tight, they held enough air for the seconds it took to get through the watery passage. They were harnessed to a man who dragged them along the top of the passage as he rapidly hauled himself along the rope. The older children took flashlights inside their bags to keep them from becoming too frightened. The little ones whimpered as they were zipped in. Their cries of fright were muffled by the water.

Once everyone was out, Jacob asked the men to lead everyone to safety away from the town. When they were well away, Jacob climbed up The Rock, fired off a flare, and then quickly followed the others. He sat down where he could keep an eye on the main building. After an hour he saw two bright new stars in the sky. The lights grew brighter. Then Jacob saw the tail jets of the two shuttles from the Copernicus as they landed well away from Kinsinger. The battle had already begun.

CHAPTER 49
US VERSUS THEM

THE NEAREST SHUTTLE LANDED ABOUT TWO HUNDRED METERS FROM THE rough camp that had spontaneously formed as the adults and children huddled and shivered in the night air. Mr. Yamamoto and the mayor had taken charge and posted lookouts in case the Cobras inside the Town Hall discovered their escape.

Jacob, Zeke, and Hanna walked over to the nearest shuttle with their hands up.

"Hold it right there!" said a soldier. "Sit down with your hands on your head."

They sat down. Jacob saw that the side shuttle ramp was already down. Ten soldiers had disembarked and taken up defensive positions amongst the rocks. About fifteen more were hastily hauling out equipment. Within five minutes, the commander waved to the pilot and the shuttle took off.

The commander came over and asked "Who are you?"

"Cadet Jacob Kraiser, Sir!"

"Cadet Hanna Heidel, Sir!"

"Cadet Ezekiel Rempel, Sir!"

The commander checked their voice prints on his tablet and briefly looked at their files. "I'm sorry for the rude reception. Please stand up. Kraiser, you've been here the longest. What's the status on the ground?"

Standing, Jacob answered. "Enemy combatants in the main stone building. Colonists have been extracted. Not sure if their absence has been noted."

"Any casualties?"

"No sir."

"Jenkins collect the scouts and go with Kraiser. Set up a watch around the main building. Krahn, make contact with B Company."

Jenkins and Krahn left immediately on their tasks. "Enns go with Jenkins and Kraiser—I assume you know where the Travel Oaks are located, Kraiser. When Jenkins has the main building secure, follow Kraiser to the Travel Oaks and set up the protective shields around the groves."

Jenkins returned with the scouts and Jacob led them to the Town Hall building. Karl Enns tagged along. After Jacob had pointed out the main building, Jenkins began to position his scouts.

Jacob led Enns to the Travel Oak groves. The latter was a no-nonsense sort of fellow who asked short, pointed questions and wasted no time getting to work.

After speaking on a communicator, he said to Jacob, "My job is to protect the Travel Oaks from damage."

A team of four soldiers and a small robot-controlled wagon, loaded with heavy armored-steel arrived at the Travel Oaks. The soldiers erected a metal frame, cladding it with armored steel beginning with the side facing the Town Hall. The shield had been designed to clip together and went up surprisingly quickly.

"It's the best we could do on short notice," said Enns. "It will stop small arms fire and even light armor-piercing rounds. If they have anything heavier, they'll blow right through it."

The outside of the shield had hand and footholds. When a second robot wagon arrived, carrying more triangular shielding, the geodesic shielding dome was completed. It looked like a dull grey beehive in the night.

Suddenly the lights in the Town Hall came on. As Jacob watched, five armed men emerged from the front door and ran toward the Travel Oak garden. A loud voice ordered the Cobras to halt. Shots rang out from the direction of the Town Hall and Jacob and the others with him dove behind the geodesic dome. Someone called out "We surrender."

Jacob came out of cover and watched the five Cobras marching away into the night. The lights inside the Town Hall went out and Jacob heard the sound of broken glass. The Cobras inside the Town Hall began firing from the windows. Jacob and the soldiers with him scattered and again took cover.

Enns was listening on an ear piece. "They're trying to contact the rest of their forces," said Enns. "It's the first time they've broken radio silence. I guess they realize their hope for secrecy and surprise has been disappointed."

Enns looked at an instrument. "We're jamming their signal now. Still, the Cobras at the Aquinas will guess what's up when they detect the jamming signal."

"What do you think they'll do next?" asked Jacob.

"These guys are surrounded. If they don't surrender, standard tactics would have us bury them inside rather than risk an assault and casualties. But burying them in the rubble isn't our style. We'll likely wait them out."

"What about Rousseau and the others who are out in the open?"

"If they're smart, they'll sneak back to the Aquinas and head home using their Travel Oaks. I'm not sure if they'll be smart."

For several hours, the encircling force fired shots at the windows if anyone showed his head. The gun fire from within the building eventually dwindled and stopped. At dawn the Cobras hung a white flag of truce out of a window and a negotiator came out the front door.

Three inside had been wounded and were sent off to be patched up by Copernicus medics. The rest of the Cobras came out, stacking their weapons near the door and walking forward, their hands in the air. The captured Cobras were made to sit just outside the building while the Coventry soldiers and small robots searched the inside thoroughly for explosives.

"What happens to these prisoners now?" asked Jacob.

"We'll set up a tent camp in the vicinity. We'll keep the location secret to prevent a rescue by the Cobras."

A call came in to Enns on his earphone. "Kraiser, you can tell the town folk they can have their Town Hall and their village back. This part of the operation is over. The Aquinas will be a tougher nut to crack."

CHAPTER 50
HOPING THIS ENDS WELL

"WELL," SAID TAKEO, "NURSING A CUP OF TEA, "THINGS ARE GOING TO BE very different here at Kinsinger now."

"So, what happened at the council?" asked Hanna.

"The Copernicus commander and General Penner decided we'll have to deal with the Cobras and the Aquinas hulk. General Penner's just arrived and she's asked to see you, Jacob. Go figure."

"Oh, yeah," said Jacob, "Suzanne and I go way back." Jacob couldn't stop himself from grinning.

Takeo shook his head and continued. "We're using the Travel Oaks here and on the Copernicus to bring in as many soldiers and as much equipment as possible. We've abandoned the idea of a self-sustaining colony. We're gearing up for war."

At that moment, General Penner and two other generals came into the room guided by Mrs. Yamamoto. Hanna, Zeke, and Jacob jumped to attention and saluted.

"At ease, men," said General Penner. "Mrs. Yamamoto, could I trouble your hospitality further and request a cup of tea or coffee for us? It's been a cramped night in the Travel Oaks. We're bringing in as many men as possible."

Mrs. Yamamoto smiled and soon everyone was feasting on her superb vanilla bran cookies and sipping tea.

General Penner winced at the tea. "I miss my morning coffee."

After another sip of tea she continued. "As you've gathered, we're mobilizing for combat. My plan is to contact Rousseau for a parley and negotiate their withdrawal. The three of you came to Coventry together and were platoon-mates with Rousseau. I need you on my staff. I need to read Rousseau accurately. I've requested you be seconded to me. So, tell me about Rousseau."

Jacob, Zeke, and Hanna exchanged glances. Hanna and Zeke nodded to Jacob to go ahead. "Rousseau is brilliant, ruthless, and can lie without shifting his eyes. It seemed to me from the beginning that he was a trained operative who wanted to subvert Coventry from the inside."

"So, you're saying I can't rely on anything he says or any word of honor he gives me?"

Jacob shook his head. "Absolutely not. He'll tell you anything to gain an advantage, and then backstab you without a qualm. For him, questions of morality, honor, and truth are all irrelevant. All that matters is winning."

"That's my reading of the man, too. Still, I have to try. Copernicus has already used their shuttles to land troops and set up a defensive perimeter in the high ground around the Aquinas base. I'm going to send in one of our prisoners with a proposal for a parley between me and Rousseau."

"If they don't see reason, why not just take them out with high explosives?" asked Jacob. "The Copernicus gives us a huge advantage. Why risk the lives of our men in an assault?"

"Why indeed?" said Penner. "I'm a soldier. The men cowering inside the Aquinas are soldiers. They have mothers and fathers and siblings hoping to see them again. If I can keep Canaan safe and find a way out of this, without having to annihilate them, I want to find it. I owe them that much, soldier-to-soldier. Still, I won't order my men into a killing assault on their well-defended position. But I think I'll get enough volunteers who feel as I do, who will carry the assault out if it comes to that."

The three friends looked at each other. Hanna said, "It would be an honor to serve on your staff, General."

CHAPTER 51
TO TRUST OR NOT TO TRUST

THE FORWARD COMMAND POST WAS ON A HIGH MESA ABOUT A MILE from the Aquinas, which was locked up and sealed. After hailing the ship, Penner and Rousseau agreed to meet in the open, about halfway between the command post and the Aquinas.

That afternoon, the three friends watched as Suzanne Penner and Rousseau walked toward each other, each with a camp chair slung over their backs. When they reached the designated spot, they sat about ten feet apart. A sniper at the command post trained his rifle on Rousseau. They negotiated for about an hour before returning to their respective camps.

General Penner took off her recording device and handed it to one of her staff. "He knows we could blow him off the face of the planet if we chose. He's agreed to relinquish the Aquinas and return to their base on Earth. His only conditions: we return our prisoners to them and that we allow two weeks for everyone to evacuate by Travel Oak. I've agreed to that."

"What's your assessment, General? Will he honor it?" asked the Copernicus commander.

"I think he's lying, but he's also in an impossible position. As I see it, there are three possibilities: one, he'll realize he has no chance to recover this situation, cut his losses, and take his men home. Two, he might think he has a chance because he knows something we don't know. He'll use the two weeks to bring in more troops, then sneak out and attack our positions. Three, none of the above.

"In any case, I want all of our forward observation positions monitored remotely, and I want all our men pulled back to a safe distance, say beyond a reasonable nuclear blast radius.

"I want to hear about any unusual observations. We have a tense two weeks ahead of us. Let's start moving the prisoners now, and then pull back once they're in, just so there's no chance they suspect our withdrawal."

CHAPTER 52
BURIED TREASURE

JACOB, ZEKE, AND HANNA HELPED PENNER'S STAFF SET UP THE NEW observation post eight kilometers from the Aquinas in a shallow valley. The three friends, along with fifteen others, watched the Cobra base through cameras in four-hour shifts.

The prisoners were returned to Rousseau and then Rousseau had the crashed spacecraft sealed up. The two-week deadline for complete evacuation was approaching.

Twenty-four hours before the deadline, General Penner sought out the three friends in the observation room. "We've repeatedly tried to contact the Aquinas to confirm their withdrawal. Each attempt has been met with static. This silent withdrawal has treachery written all over it. I'm sending a new crew to take over your observation duties. Get caught up on your sack time. At tomorrow's deadline, I want the three of you guiding mech-avatars into the Aquinas. We'll be looking for booby traps. We'll also immediately tranquilize the Travel Oaks in the Aquinas so that they can't send us any nasty surprises. I'll have Enns pick you up tomorrow."

When the withdrawal deadline was only hours away, Jacob, Hanna, and Zeke waited outside their sleeping quarters until Enns arrived, driving a small electric van. He drove them down a new road out of the valley to a cavern mouth entering a large rock hill with a tall antenna array on top. Inside, twenty-four new mech-avatar control stations and water tanks had been assembled.

The shipping containers were piled in one corner. A temporary power station had been set up to keep the tank water at body temperature and to power the control equipment. Cables snaked out across the floor and up through the cavern roof to the broadcasting towers on top of the hill.

Jacob introduced himself to his technician, climbed into his empty tank, donned his helmet, tether, mech-gloves, and mech-leggings. When the technician signaled thumbs up that his connection was complete, he returned the gesture to indicate that he was ready for the tank to be filled. He felt the familiar exhilaration of entering a super-video game. His mech-avatar would be engaging in highly dangerous activities, but he would be perfectly safe.

His face plate activated, enabling him to see the shed where his mech-avatar was stored along with the twenty-three others. Since they looked identical, each one had the soldier's name stenciled in front and back of the unit, along with rank signatures on the shoulders. In his briefing, Jacob had been told they were to explore in groups of three for safety. He had been given a temporary rank of Master Corporal. His mech-avatar's shoulders sported two Vees, as they called them, with a single cross on top to designate Coventry Defense Forces.

The major in charge of the operation, gave them the order to move out. The first triad climbed into an equipment truck and drove to the Aquinas. The second triad broke into a trot and was followed by the remaining eighteen, all in groups of three. Jacob's triad, as the least experienced, went last. Their trot, covered ground very quickly. Each mech-avatar had its own processor, which kept the mech from stumbling, or making a misstep on uneven ground. Jacob could concentrate on directing the mech's actions and watching for danger without worrying about keeping it upright.

The Aquinas' main hanger door would not cycle and the side personnel door would not open.

"Open the door," commanded the major.

The first triad moved into position, began unloading the truck and attached a device to the lock mechanism. Then, having cut through a section of the door, they first opened the outer air-lock door and then the inner door.

"Our mech-avatar signal will be cut off by Aquinas' hull. We have to wait until the first triad sets up a relay station inside."

The team set up an outside antenna and then uncoiled a cable through the open airlock doors. After a few minutes they came out and gave the thumbs up.

"Watch your connection signal, everyone," said the major. "If your signal grows weak, stop and report immediately. You'll receive further instructions."

"What happens if we lose connection to our mech?" asked Jacob of his controller.

"Don't let it happen," came the answer. "The mech is programmed to retrace its steps until it either comes back into contact or automatically returns to the storage shed."

"All the way back to the storage shed? When would that be necessary?"

"With all due respect, that might happen accidently-on-purpose if I dropped a heavy wrench on your head because you ask too many unnecessary questions, Cadet Master Corporal."

"All right, all right, we're moving forward."

Jacob heard the major: "We have additional relay stations we can set up if we have to. Everyone begin your assigned tasks."

Jacob's triad was assigned to search the crew quarters. When they entered the airlock, everything seemed wrong. Then it dawned on Jacob that the Aquinas was never meant to lie on its side. Under boost, "down" was toward the engine. During orbital spin, as he was used to in the Coulson, "down" was towards both ends. Now, of course, "down" was toward the side of the ship. Everywhere they were walking on walls. New doors had been cut into the crew's quarters.

They proceeded systematically. Their mission was to search the crew's quarters in the forward half of the ship. Jacob could hear the clop, clop, clop of the mech-avatars' feet on the metal skin of the ship. By design the only parts of the ship that had properly adjusted to the new "down" direction were the huge spheres front and aft that held the gardens. These were on gimbals, which could rotate placing the gardens in a downward position even when the ship was on its side.

"Well designed," said Hanna. "The gimbals even let it level out in a crash landing. I bet the non-essential crew were in here during re-entry. What a surprise for them to leave and find everything on its side in the rest of the ship."

They left the garden and made their way along the skin of the ship to the crew's quarters. Many rooms were inaccessible, but for others they had to climb ladders. Not everything had been taken from inside.

"Anything?" asked Jacob after each had searched a room.

"No," said Zeke.

"A lot of non-essentials, like clothes, are still here. They left in a hurry," said Hanna.

Each room they searched showed similar signs of a hasty departure.

About a third of the way through their search, Hanna called Jacob and Zeke. "Can you guys come in here? There's something funny going on."

"What's up, Hanna?" asked Jacob.

"Check your neutron detector, do you see a slight elevation of neutron flux?"

"Yeah, I do," said Zeke.

Jacob gulped and thought. *Should I call it in now? No, wait for proof.*

"Okay, keep an eye on your neutron detector and let's triangulate in on the source."

Jacob went to the back of the room and found a closet. Like everything else in the forward part of the ship, this closet was detachable from the wall so it could be moved to a new floor when the ship went into spin mode. It now stood upright. As Jacob approached the closet, his detector indicated a slight increase in the neutron flux. Inside the closet he found a large black box with heavy grips. It had no lid, but was a seamless unit. A hole had been cut into the closet wall so that the box, which was clearly too large for one closet alone, could be accommodated by two adjacent closets in rooms along the common wall.

"Major, it's Kraiser."

"What is it Kraiser?"

"Sir, we may have found a nuclear device hidden in one of the forward crew rooms."

"How do you know? Never mind I'll be right there."

Three minutes later, the major and the first triad arrived.

The lieutenant from the triad looked at the box, and then attached an instrument to its side. "I think they're right, Sir. The box is sealed and lead-lined. It may be rigged to blow if we cut into it."

"They moved it here. Perhaps we could move it somewhere else."

"Estimating from the radiation it's giving off and the small size, this is a twenty-kiloton device. We don't want any people near it if it goes off. It will make slag of this whole valley."

"I'd better report in." The major walked out of line of sight so that they would not automatically be included in his conversation with Penner.

The major returned. "Penner says to attempt to deactivate." Turning to Jacob, "Are you three still here? Continue your search."

They had almost completed the rest of the rooms when the major contacted Jacob. "Good work Kraiser. It was a twenty-kiloton-yield plutonium bomb. The triad disabled it."

Jacob and his two friends returned to the garden in the protected sphere at the forward end of the ship. Others had already returned and were gossiping. The mech-avatars automatically opened up communication when unit members were close.

One of them looked at Jacob. "We found another bomb in the mess area in a chest freezer. The first triad just called in that they've disabled it too. It looks like we're home free. I can already taste that celebration beer when we climb out of our tanks."

Jacob saw Zeke and Hanna walking around the garden in a systematic search pattern. He joined them. "What's up?"

"Well," said Hanna, "Zeke had the bright idea that if he were hiding a bomb in a hurry, he'd bury it in the garden. While we're waiting for the major, we thought we'd give the grounds a once-over." Jacob joined the search, beginning from another quadrant.

Hanna and Zeke—or more precisely their mech-avatars—were beginning to dig frantically. Jacob ran over.

"I think we found one," said Zeke.

"Major, I think we found another nuke ..."

Before he could utter another word, Jacob's view screen went white and his emergency light came on. "Full system shutdown" flashed in red letters above his view screen. Jacob felt a tremor, like an earthquake rumble through the facility. He heard a loud crack.

There's no oxygen, I'm going to suffocate!

He fought down his fear and forced himself to remember the safety procedure. Unclasping his tether, he swam to the surface. The glass tank had cracked and the water level had already dropped. Pulling off his helmet, he shed the equipment on his chest, arms, and legs. A technician, who had climbed up the side entry stairs, helped him out of the tank.

"What happened?" asked Jacob.

"Nuclear detonation at the Aquinas. The electromagnetic pulse wiped out the circuit boards in our equipment. Help me get the others out of their tanks."

Jacob and the technician worked feverishly. Most mech operators remembered their training and extricated themselves from their tanks, but a few had panicked when the airflow had shut down. Jacob and another soldier climbed into a tank to lift a thrashing mech-driver above the water so that the operator could disconnect his harness and remove his helmet.

When they assembled for a debriefing, General Penner looked grim. "Well, we tried our best to save the Aquinas. On the bright side, we don't have to worry about any other booby traps. Still, it's a sad commentary on mankind that a nuclear detonation will be remembered as one of the signature events of our arrival on this world.

"Preliminary data suggests that our exposure to radiation from the blast has so far been within acceptable limits. We'll keep an eye on the wind patterns and the fallout. Kinsinger is too far away to have felt much more than a slight tremor, and I've confirmed the Storm Mountains shielded them from any blast effects. The fallout might reach them, but right now the prevailing westerlies are blowing the fallout to the east."

CHAPTER 53
EPILOGUE

HANNA, ZEKE, TAKEO, AND JACOB WERE LINGERING OVER A LATE BREAKFAST of breaded fish, eggs, and hash browns made from recently harvested potatoes when General Penner came in and sat down. She handed a package of coffee to Mrs. Yamamoto.

"Rank hath its privileges," said Penner. When the three cadets started to rise to salute, she said, "At ease. This is a social call. Besides you're back in the space cadets."

She smiled, "You're clearly not army material. You spend too much time thinking and wondering. Bound to cause problems with discipline."

She opened up a small satchel and took out some color prints. "The short-lived isotopes from the blast have decayed. I took in a mech-avatar and took these pictures. This slag bowl is all that's left of the Aquinas and the Cobra's base camp. Even the cavern's collapsed. Still, we're in much better shape than if the Cobras had captured Kinsinger and forced us to grant them a foothold on this world. At least now we have Canaan as a place of refuge."

"So, what happens next, Ma'am?" asked Jacob.

"We'll keep Kinsinger growing. Maybe found a new village a few miles from here, further up the Jordan River. Whatever debate remained about whether or not the threat to Coventry is real has been put to bed. It's patently clear, after this episode, that our enemies know us pretty well. They see us as both a threat and a technological treasure trove. If they can, they'll try to capture us and enslave us for our technology. Failing that, they'll try to destroy us. We don't have much time. We'll prepare for a siege back home, and if possible, accelerate our evacuation plans.

"We'll counter the heightened threat, as we always have, by preparing to move to Venus and gradually to Canaan. I think, one hundred years from now, this will be our home. I hope and pray we'll do better here than back on Earth."

She looked around the room and smiled. "I'm heading back to Venus, and then Coventry. I'm here to say Goodbye."

Jacob saw that Hanna had tears in her eyes. Penner looked at her as well.

Hanna straightened up and said, "I had always thought I would be reunited with my parents. If we evacuate to Venus or Canaan, I'll never see them again."

Jacob, felt a lump forming in his throat. He thought: *I didn't realize until now that Hanna and Zeke may end up separated from parents and family like me.*

Penner said, "I know it's hard to see beyond the tragedy in our own lives. But remember to say a prayer for the people who aren't part of Coventry, but will be left behind to be manipulated by the likes of Rousseau and Cobra. While we were hidden there, we could at least help with our technology in small, inconspicuous ways: maintaining satellite communication, medicines, vaccines, and rural power sources. All that will likely stop. Well, for my part I'm an optimist since I believe God is sovereign and will do what he can for those who look to him for help. That includes those left behind."

Penner rose, shook hands with the Yamamotos, and then saluted the three cadets. They returned her salute and watched as she left.

The End

MAPS

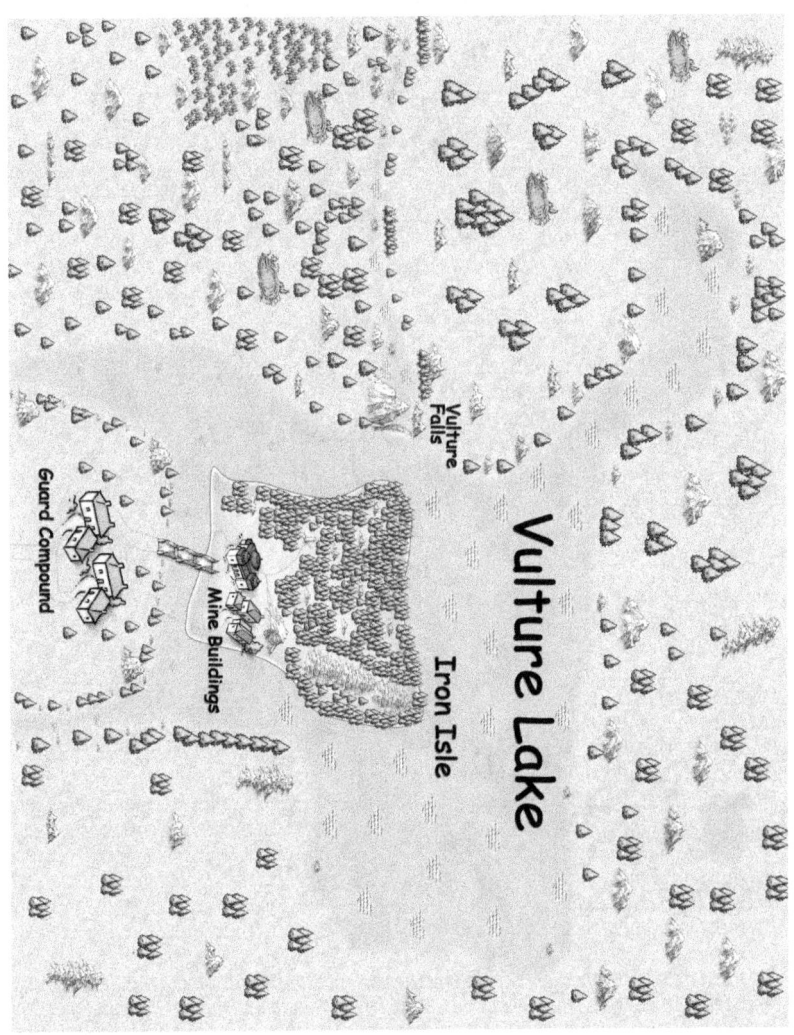

Vulture Lake and Iron Isle, the location of the Coventry Penal Colony

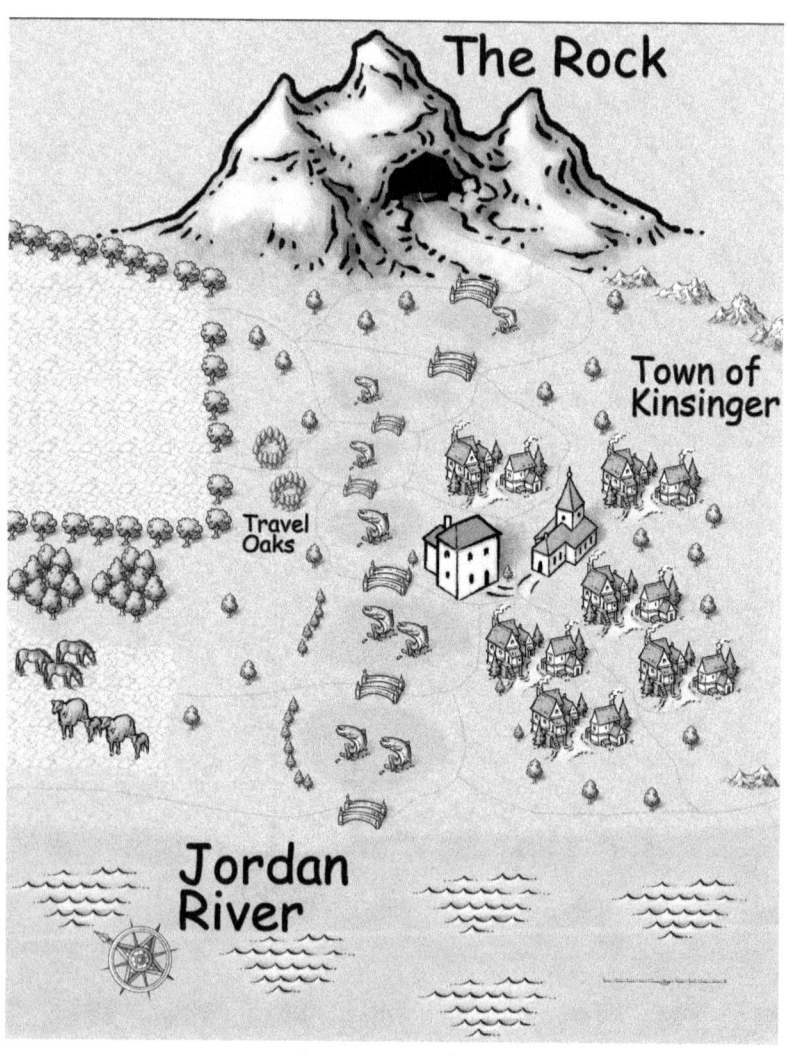

The town of Kinsinger on Alpha Centauri A-3 (the planet also called Canaan)

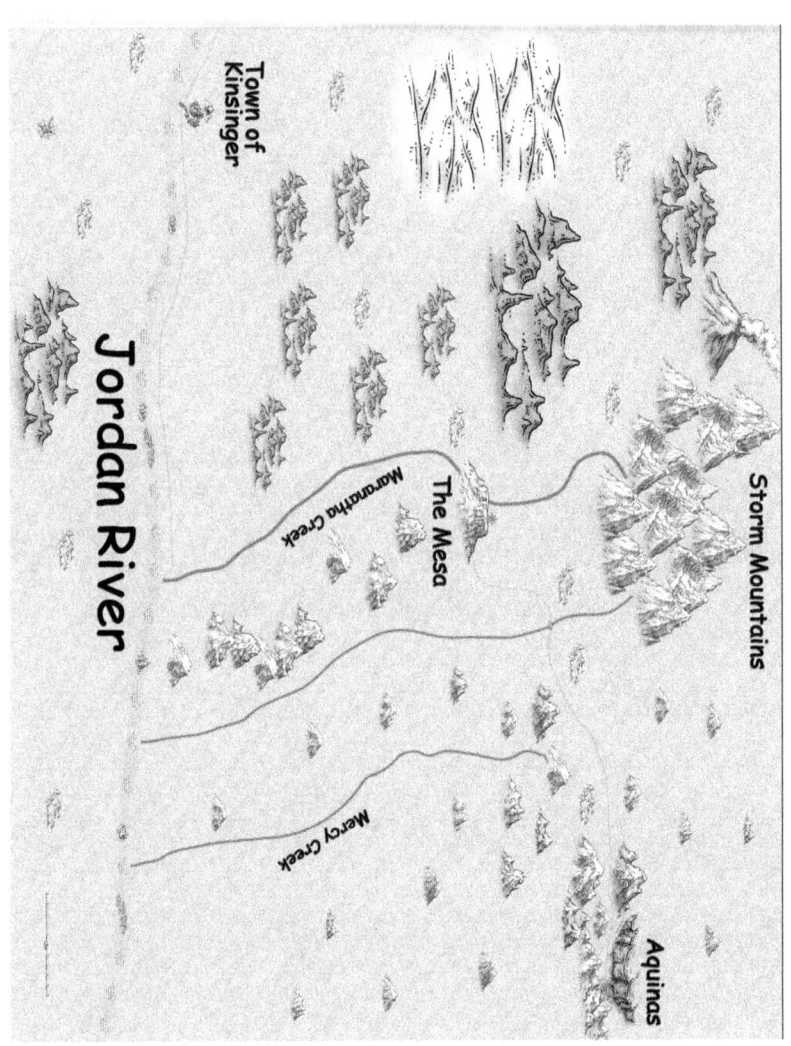

Area around the town of Kinsinger

GLOSSARY

Big Crunch: The name given to the catastrophic population, economic, and technological contraction that began to occur in 2030 AD and continued past 2090 AD. The population decline in the western world accelerated, technological advancement stagnated, and widespread urban unemployment developed. Immigration had largely been stopped because of pandemics, unrest, and single-nuclear-exchanges. In the urban developed world, birthrates continue well below replacement rates.

Black Swamp Oak: Also called Swamp Oak and Black Oak. A kind of fast-growing Travel Oak that grows in swamp. This tree with dark green leaves that appear nearly black forms a pear-shaped profile and can hold one adult for transport to a twin Black Swamp Oak elsewhere. This oak produces one large double acorn which gives rise to the two linked twin oaks when the halves are planted.

Canaan: The name given to the planet Alpha Centauri A-3. Canaan in the Old Testament was the Promised Land. For the Coventry communities, the planet Canaan was their Promised Land, a place of refuge, freedom, and safety.

Christian Mutembe: A historian who wrote *A History of the Coventry Penal Colony*. He was originally from Rwanda.

Christopher Russell: Prime Minister of Canada when the Coventry Penal Colony was founded.

Clive Connaught: Jacob Kraiser's supervisor. A Victimization Index 5 citizen, he arranged Jacob's imprisonment in the Coventry Penal Colony when Jacob refused to transfer a young woman, Cynthia Stapleton, who was working in his own department to Connaught's department after she pleaded against the transfer.

Colin O'Brien: Mechanic and member of the slave labor group at Aquinas base camp.

Coventry Africa: In 2063, through a corporation called Gibeah Mining, Coventry began exploring potential mining sites in Africa and Asia as cities of refuge for persecuted refugees. An abandoned mine about 80 kilometers west of Mount Kenya was chosen in the North African Democratic Republic. To hide Coventry Africa, the shallow shafts of the mine were reopened, and precious metals were extracted from the ore using Coventry technology. In the deeper excavations, colonists founded Coventry Africa. Travel Oaks and Black Swamp Oaks connected Coventry Africa to Coventry Penal Colony in Canada. Coventry Africa began accepting African refugees in 2064. In 2084 all contact with the mining operation and Coventry Africa was suddenly lost. External discreet investigations by Gibeah Mining Corporation into their former African operation, suggested that forces of the Democratic Republic of North Africa had overrun the mining operation and the colony. The status of the Aquinas interstellar craft was unknown. Since communication from the Aquinas to her sister ships ceased about the same time, it was presumed the Aquinas had been destroyed.

Coventry Asia: In 2063 Gibeah Mining Corporation reopened a mine near Lake Baikal in Russia. Colonists from the Coventry Penal Colony prepared the deeper shafts for habitation. Coventry Asia began accepting Asian refugees in 2064. Coventry Asia participated in the Interstellar Project, sending the Faraday spacecraft to Alpha Centauri. When the Copernicus, Aquinas, and Faraday were near maximum velocity, all communication with the Faraday was lost. It was presumed an accident, perhaps a collision at near light speed, destroyed the craft.

Cretins: The pejorative name given to subversives whom the government of Canada held responsible for the disruption caused by the 2051 protest. Subsequently used for anyone sent to Coventry.

Cynthia Stapleton: A young woman on Jacob's staff in Toronto. She asked Jacob to prevent her transfer to Connaught's department. She later accused Jacob of inappropriate behavior after going to work for Connaught as his executive assistant.

Dale Carboneau: Special Envoy to Prime Minister Russell.

Daniel Whitefeather: Jacob's faculty advisor at Klemhofer College.

Edward Mutembe: The son of Christian Mutembe, a history teacher at Coventry and co-author with Christian Mutembe of *The Continuing History of the Coventry Penal Colony*.

Ezekiel (Zeke) Rempel: One of Jacob's two early friends at Coventry.

Fleet Fight: A training game designed to teach flying skills for operations in Venus' atmosphere. Each team consists of a mother ship (pilot and gunner) and four single seat fighters. The computer games master awards a win to the team first to disable the opponent's mother ship using low powered lasers.

Hanna Heidel: One of Jacob's two early friends in Coventry.

Heinrich Schneider: Commandant of Cadets on the construction site on Venus Base Galilee.

Hideo Yamamoto: The father of Takeo Yamamoto.

Jacob Kraiser: Born on a farm near Leslieville, Alberta, the second son in a family of five children. When he was eighteen years old, all the other members of his family were killed in a tragic automobile accident. This tragedy increased his Victimization Index (qv), to such an extent that he was immediately eligible for a well-paying job at the Ministry of Technology in Toronto. Unprepared for city life in the 2090s, Jacob naively fell under the spell of widespread deception. Escalating conflicts with his manipulative and influential boss, Clive Connaught, led to Jacob's eventual banishment to the Coventry Penal Colony.

Jason Kim, Sergeant: Cadet leader on Torchship Coulson.

Jonah Klemhofer: Had doctorate degrees in physics and inorganic chemistry. After his incarceration at Coventry he struck up a life-long friendship with Josiah Kinsinger. Kinsinger gave Klemhofer access to many rare earth metals.

Klemhofer was able to develop several variants of Matrix Fusion Cells that provided clean and nearly limitless power to the colony.

Josiah Kinsinger: A mining engineer specializing in rare earth metal isolation from mine tailings. His small, privately owned company was familiar with the metals available from Iron Isle. After his incarceration he was able to acquire his company's isolation equipment and helped mitigate the starvation at the colony during the Years of Tears.

Karl Enns: A soldier who shielded the Travel Oaks at Kinsinger when the village was recaptured from the Cobras.

Kinsinger: The colony founded by the Copernicus interstellar spacecraft on Alpha Centauri A-3, named after Josiah Kinsinger, the mining engineer who helped bootstrap rare-earth metal extraction from the Iron Isle mine and led the Coventry Penal Colony during the years-of-tears.

Leonard Thompson: Heavy equipment expert in F Company.

Lionel Litch: One of Richard Rousseau's henchmen and bodyguards.

Makoto Yamamoto: Younger brother of Takeo Yamamoto.

Manfred Spengler: Oldest member and *de facto* leader of the slave labor group at Aquinas base camp.

Martin Friesen: Professor and Head of Klemhofer College. His specialty is History.

Montreal Perrot Island Detonation: In 2052, a small nuclear device was detonated on Perrot Island, Montreal, QC. The detonation, directed at an African ethnic community, was likely retaliation for an earlier attack in Africa. However, since several high-ranking officials associated with Cerebretoxin-21 also were caught in the blast zone, the detonation was used by the media to strengthen support for using Coventry Penal Colony to end the unrest of 2051.

Richard Rousseau: A prisoner in Coventry. Using intimidation, he recruited a band of followers.

Rudy Giesbrecht: A pastor, medical doctor, and counsellor at Coventry Penal Colony. At a time Jacob was experiencing frequent nightmares, he met Giesbrecht and they struck up a friendship.

Samuel Witt: Captain of the Copernicus.

Simeon Hodgkins: Welcomed new inmates to Coventry. He was in charge of the Γ Company work group.

Single-Nuclear-Exchanges (SNEs): With the widespread proliferation of small, low-yield nuclear weapons by the mid-twenty-first century, conflicts in the developing world frequently escalated to a mutual nuclear devastation of the warring capital cities. The destruction was so great, that the countries involved degenerated into anarchy. Emigration to Europe and North America was significantly constrained, particularly after the Montreal Perrot Island Detonation in 2052. The reduction in immigration led to a dramatic population decline in the occident, which had a low birthrate. Later, many of the warring factions were overpowered by the increasingly powerful Democratic Republic of North Africa, which further constrained emigration to Europe and North America.

Starship Aquinas: A starship launched by Coventry Africa bound for Alpha Centauri, boosting at 0.66 gravities. Contact with Aquinas was lost when Coventry Africa was overrun by Democratic Republic of North Africa forces. The status of Starship Aquinas was unknown, but the ship was presumed to have been lost.

Starship Copernicus: A starship launched by Coventry Penal Colony bound for Alpha Centauri, boosting at 0.66 gravities. The crew of the Copernicus founded Kinsinger on Alpha Centauri A-3, also called Canaan.

Starship Faraday: A starship launched by Coventry Asia bound for Alpha Centauri, boosting at 0.66 gravities. Faraday was presumed lost when all contact was abruptly lost with the ship mid-voyage.

Suzanne Penner: Brigadier General in the Coventry Defense Forces.

Torchship Coulson: The prototype torchship for the Coventry starships. Torchship Coulson is in orbit around Venus and serves as an emergency evacuation vehicle for Coventry as well as Venus base Hebron.

Torchships: Torchships are constant acceleration ships that could achieve accelerations of 0.66 gravities. Propulsion was accomplished by giant ion accelerators which propelled particles from the ship at almost light speed.

These ships reduce solar transit times to a matter of days and also enable multi-year interstellar travel.

Travel Oaks: A trees that grow in multiple stems that form a ring (or grove) of stems and allows travel to daughter groves made from cuttings from the original tree.

Venus Base Hebron: The inhabited dirigible city floating in the habitable zone of the Venusian atmosphere.

Venus Base Galilee: The partially constructed dirigible floating city in the habitable zone of the Venusian atmosphere.

Victimization Index (VI): A government index, with values from zero to seven, developed to provide government compensation to those deemed most needy. The higher the number, the more victimization one has had to endure and therefore, the more government assistance one is entitled to receive. When Jacob Kraiser's entire family was killed in a car crash, his VI increased from zero to three. The higher VI rating enabled him to receive special training as well as a high paying government job at the Ministry of Technology in Toronto.

Viper: A small spacecraft designed for air and space operation. It was the standard training vessel for space cadets and the workhorse for construction projects such as Venus Base Galilee.

Whorty Dennison: One of Rousseau's henchman and bodyguards. He remained in Coventry after Rousseau and Litch aided the invaders.

ACKNOWLEDGEMENTS

THIS WRITING OF *COVENTRY 2091* WAS HELPED IMMEASURABLY BY A NUMBER of people who contributed their time, their skill, and their enthusiasm to make my work much better than I could have accomplished on my own.

First and foremost, I would like to thank my editor, Patricia Paddey. She tirelessly worked to remove extraneous material, make sure the characters remained consistent, and to correct obscure or wordy passages. Her emendations proved invaluable and measurably improved the book.

I am grateful to my wife Kathryn for her proofreading of the nearly finished manuscript. The polish she provided and the suggestions she made significantly improved the final version.

Darren Kazmaier meticulously read an early draft of *Coventry 2091* and identified obscure passages and readability gaps. His knowledge of rare-earth technology was invaluable in giving this narrative an authentic ring. For his diligence I am deeply grateful.

In writing about the counselling sessions that Jacob had with Dr. Rudy Giesbrecht, I relied heavily on the advice of Iris Armstrong (MEd, MDiv, RP). I am deeply grateful for her input. Although I could not always follow her advice on how an effective counselling session should progress (the dictates of the plot always come first), I believe her help added a bit of authenticity to the sessions. Any deviations from 'best-practice' are the fault of the author.

I owe special thanks to Dr. Andrew Seddon. His insights and comments on an Advanced Readers Copy (ARC) of the manuscript were deeply appreciated.

I am also grateful to the staff at Word Alive for turning the manuscript into a beautifully-crafted book.

I would like to thank the many readers of *The Halcyon Dislocation*, *The Battle for Halcyon*, and *The Dragons of Sheol*. Your encouragement kept me writing.

As a Christ-Follower I claim no special aid or guidance in this work except in the humblest sense. I can see how following the Lord Christ has helped me grow as a person and without His grace and people He was able to use to encourage me, I don't think I would have had the courage to attempt an audacious feat such as writing a novel. Still I readily acknowledge that no work is ever perfect or complete and this story is no exception. The errors, shortcomings, and omissions in this book are my own. Those who have worked with me have helped to make my book better and for that I am deeply grateful.

ABOUT THE AUTHOR

COVENTRY 2091 IS PETER KAZMAIER'S FIFTH BOOK. IN THIS WORK AND IN *The Halcyon Cycle* stories, he has been able to pursue a life-long dream of writing fast-paced novels that explore the intersection between adventure, science, faith and philosophy.

Peter Kazmaier's second book in *The Halcyon Cycle*, *The Battle for Halcyon* received the 2016 Word Award in the Speculative Fiction category.

J. R. R. Tolkien's *Lord of the Rings* , C. S. Lewis' *The Chronicles of the Narnia* , Stephen R. Lawhead's trilogy, *Song of Albion*, and Robert Jordan's series *Wheel of Time*™ are among his favorite and best-loved books. He also very much enjoys science fiction classics such as Robert Heinlein's *Tunnel in the Sky*.

Dr. Kazmaier has spent most of his scientific career as a research scientist in industry and also was appointed as an Adjunct Professor of Chemistry at Queen's University in 1999. He has published more than sixty scientific articles in refereed journals and was awarded the Arthur K. Doolittle award for Best Paper by the American Chemical Society in 1993. Cited as the inventor or co-inventor on more than 175 patents, his strong background in science enables him to bring authentic scientific insight to *The Halcyon Cycle* and to *Coventry 2091*.

Dr. Kazmaier joined the American Chemical Society in 1976, the Chemical Institute of Canada in 1980, and The Word Guild in 2004.

He was married to Kathryn in 1976 and they live in Mississauga near Toronto. They enjoy spending time at their cottage near Seeley's Bay, Ontario on the Rideau Canal.

He blogs at https://PeterKazmaier.com/ and delights in feedback from his readers.

ALSO BY PETER KAZMAIER:

THE HALCYON CYCLE TRILOGY

AFTER A RISKY PHYSICS EXPERIMENT TRANSPORTS THE ISLAND UNIVERSITY of Halcyon to a new world, engineer Dave Schuster and his fellow students struggle to survive in this alien, hostile environment. As tyrannical forces within the University use the catastrophe to strengthen their power and control, Dave encounters an even greater menace which threatens the very existence of their fledgling colony.

Book One:
The Halcyon Dislocation,
ISBN: 978-1-77069-705-8

Book Two:
The Battle for Halcyon,
ISBN: 978-1-4866-0853-9

Book Three:
The Dragons of Sheol,
ISBN: 978-1-4866-1820-0

"Kazmaier does well at quickly getting the plot in motion and describing the new world. The science makes for good reading, too; perhaps no surprise, since Kazmaier is a working and teaching scientist. He makes dimension and time travel seem plausible and comprehensible."

—Lloyd Rang, *Faith Today*

"Throughout the novel [*The Halcyon Dislocation*] there is a keen and vital sense of adventure and discovery with elemental forces at work, both in a material and metaphysical/religious sense. The interest level is sustained throughout."

—*Writer's Digest*

"If you enjoy Tolkien, Lewis, and other good fantasy, this is a book [*The Halcyon Dislocation*] you ought to check out."

—David Hershey, Goodreads Reviewer

"The novel [*The Battle for Halcyon*] has something for everyone with some deft surprises one would expect from any well-crafted, world-building speculative fiction."

—J. R. Baude, author of *The Lazarus Chain*

"I really enjoyed this second book in the Halcyon series, and have to confess that at times it kept me reading long after I should have gone to bed or got on with other work."

—Kevin King, Goodreads Reviewer

"After having finished reading *The Dragons of Sheol*, I can't help but come away feeling as if this is one of the most solid, well-balanced novels within a high fantasy, epic journey setting."

—Tessa Stockton, author of more than fifteen books including the *Brother's Keep* series

"The characters [in *The Dragons of Sheol*] were great, both human and non-human. They were noble and had integrity, even though they all had their struggles. I'm going to miss them. One of my favourites was Hanomer, a badger-like mammal with a hand at the end of his tail."

—Joanne Rolston, author of *The Kingdom: Here Be Dragons, Here be Dreams*

QUESTIONING YOUR WAY TO FAITH

Questioning Your Way to Faith
ISBN: 978-1-77069-964-9